"… all tricksters are 'on the road.' They are the lords of in-between. A trickster does not live near the hearth; he does not live in the halls of justice, the soldier's tent, the shaman's hut, the monastery … He is the spirit of the doorway leading out, and of the crossroad …"

Lewis Hyde,
Trickster Makes This World: Mischief, Myth, and Art

MONSTERS: I BRING THE FIRE PART II

ISBN-13: 978-1500858711
ISBN-10: 1500858714

Monsters:
I Bring the Fire
Part II

C. Gockel

ACKNOWLEDGEMENTS

First and foremost, I want to thank my editor, Kay McSpadden. Kay read and reread this story more times than I can count. I also would like to thank Gretchen Almoughraby. Her suggestions helped me clarify situations and make the action more believable. Also indispensable was Laura Stogdill. She consulted on legal aspects of this story. My brother, Thomas, was great as a myth reference, my dad James Merril Evans lent a hand in editing for content, and my mother and Christina Talbott-Clark helped with editing for grammar (I should note, if you see mistakes they are mine and mine alone). All of my readers weren't afraid to tell me when I screwed up; for that I am eternally grateful. For all their hard work, my editors may pop up in the story from time to time. I wish I could reward them more.

I also want to thank Lewis Hyde, author of *Trickster Makes This World: Mischief, Myth, and Art.* His book was tremendously inspiring and helped in shaping Loki's nature. He also gave me very generous permission to quote him.

Finally, thanks must go to my husband Eric. If he hadn't nagged at me to quit my job and work for him I still might be caught in a nine-to-five grind and the commute time would have eaten up my writing time. And if he hadn't nagged me to stop writing fan fiction and start writing something I can own, this story never would have happened.

CHAPTER 1

Steve Rogers sits at his desk in the FBI's new office for the Chicago Department of Public Liaisons. The small office is on LaSalle Street in Chicago's downtown, the infamous Loop. It's just a few blocks south of city hall, and a little up the street from the Chicago Board of Trade building. Outside, the downtown traffic is a cacophony of engine rumbles, honks, and screeching tires. It's September, but Chicago is experiencing a sweltering Indian summer. The air conditioning in the ancient building hums away, and it's still too hot in the room.

With one hand Steve holds a phone to his ear. In the other, he holds a photo of a little girl. She's wearing a neat navy blue school uniform, her large brown eyes are bright, her hair is pulled back in neat black cornrows, and she's smiling at the camera.

Steve's own skin is very dark. The little girl's skin is cafe au lait like her mother's. Her name is Claire, she's Steve's daughter, and she's eight years old today.

The phone rings once, twice, and three times. Steve closes his eyes, is about to hang up, but then it's answered.

"You missed her. She just stepped out with her grandmother. They're going to go pick up some balloons." The woman's voice on the other line sounds tired and irritated—as usual. She says it's all the anger and irritation she stored up during the eight years of their marriage.

"Awwww ... Dana," Steve says to his ex-wife. "Can you go get them? I just want to wish her a happy birthday."

"They're gone, Steve," Dana says. "Why don't you call after the party, before we go out to dinner with my folks, around three?"

Turning to his computer, Steve pulls up his calendar, "I have a meeting at three today—"

"Busy saving the world," says Dana in a bored voice.

"It's with the mayor," Steve says. Old habits kick in and he goes on the defensive. "I'm actually meeting with the heads of the agencies the city set up after 9/11 to deal with terrorism. I think we'll finally start coordinating."

The FBI's main Chicago office is out west a few miles. The whole reason they opened this satellite branch was so that the Bureau could start leveraging local assets, and to do that they needed agents greasing city hall's wheels. Steve's only been here a few months, but he's managed to charm the mayor and is on a first name basis with most of the aldermen.

Pride creeps into his voice.

He should know better.

"Glad the marriage to your job is still going well. Three o'clock and that's it," says Dana. "Look, I have to go, there's a delivery."

The line goes dead.

Setting the photo down, Steve leans back in his chair and puts a hand through his short cropped hair. He looks at his computer. It's ten o'clock. He swivels in his chair … maybe he should get a coffee?

An enormous shadow alights in Steve's window and he jumps up, hand going to the gun at his hip. "What the … "

Steve swallows. The biggest raven he's ever seen is on the window ledge. Oblivious to Steve, the raven looks down. With a loud "Rawk, rawk," it plunges.

Steve blinks. He served in Kandahar during his stint in Afghanistan as a United States Marine, but something about that big black bird still makes his heart race. He definitely needs a coffee.

Getting up from his desk, he swings on his suit coat to hide his piece. On the way out of his office he nods at the receptionist and at the other agent in the office, Tonya Fitzpatrick.

Older than Steve's 38 by about fifteen years, Tonya is half Irish and half Italian, and that goes a long way in this town. She isn't a natural actor like Steve, though, and that doesn't go over quite as well. When you're dealing with politicians you have to have a high tolerance for bullshit. Steve can tolerate and smile.

Right now Tonya's got her phone pressed to her shoulder and she's scowling, a long lock of curly gray hair falling over her face. Catching his gaze, she rolls her eyes toward the phone and then holds up a hand for Steve to wait a minute.

As Steve watches, she manages to get off the phone with whomever she's talking to and jogs over to him. "Talk to your little girl?" she says.

Steve's stomach sinks and he frowns. When it comes to his divorce and Claire, his acting abilities disappear.

Raising an eyebrow, Tonya says, "Let's get some coffee." She opens her mouth, probably to say something encouraging, but Steve doesn't want to think about his phone call. To change the subject he smiles and says, "You know, you really shouldn't scowl when you talk on the phone. People can hear it in your voice."

Tonya narrows her eyes up at him—she's only 5' 4" or so and Steve towers over her at nearly 6' 5". She maintains her glare and her silence until they reach the ornate but slightly decrepit lobby they share with a bank, a photo shop, and a clothing store. Steve maintains his smile and laughs when her lips quirk up.

They actually get along pretty well together. Steve plays good cop, she plays bad cop, It disorients people when the large black man is seemingly less formidable than the small Irish-Italian mom-grandmother type.

Together they step out of the building. They take their first breaths of the Chicago heat. Tonya scowls. Steve does, too. Steve spent his early childhood in rural Alabama. Chicago heat is worse than Alabama heat. It's just as humid, maybe more, the sound of traffic is grating, and Steve's sure he can taste the pollution on his tongue. They're just about to cross over Jackson to the wide open plaza in front of the Chicago Board of Trade when a loud "Rawk! Rawk!" sounds above the din of traffic.

Next to him Tonya says, "Those are the two biggest crows I've ever seen."

Steve scowls at the sky. Ravens aren't city birds ... and these two are enormous, their feathers so black, they're nearly blue. "Those aren't crows, they're ravens," he says.

"How do you know?" Tonya asks.

Before he can answer, both of their phones go off. Meeting each other's gaze, they pick up. "Agent Rogers," he says, as Tonya says her name nearly in unison.

The voice on the other end is eerily calm. "We have a stray kitten reported in the tunnels beneath the Chicago Board of Trade. Containment teams are on their way. Civilian personnel laying fiber optic lines in the LaSalle tunnel just north of Jackson need to be evacuated. All available agents are requested to assist."

"Stray kitten" is code for suitcase nuke, and it is currently right under the building just a few yards in front of Steve and Tonya.

Their eyes meet, and Steve doesn't have to ask if she received the same call.

"Better to take the entrance to the tunnels in the basement of our building," says Tonya, and Steve can hear her forcing herself to stay calm.

Turning back the way they came, Steve nods. "Do you think that the local law enforcement has caught wind of this?"

From a few blocks up LaSalle Street comes the screech of police sirens. "I think so," says Tonya.

"I'll go talk to the fellas repairing the fiber optic line," says Steve. He smiles broadly. Anyone passing by will think they're having a normal conversation. Tilting his head toward the cop cars ensnared a few blocks up in the Chicago traffic, he says, "You handle them."

Tonya nods and Steve darts back into their building. He's at the far end of the lobby when he hears a woman scream behind him and a loud, "Rawk, rawk!" Turning, he sees the ravens swoop past a cowering woman at the door and then rise to circle the lobby.

Steve's mouth falls open, but he doesn't have time to deal with it; he heads to the staircase that will lead him to the tunnels. Entering the stairway, he takes the steps down, two at a time. When he reaches the basement level there are two doors. One goes to the basement proper and another leads even further below, to Chicago's underground tunnel system. The tunnel system is behind several security doors, but Steve has keys and authorization for emergencies just like this. He's putting his key into the lock of the first door when he hears a door open and shut above. He freezes. "Tonya?" he calls.

For a moment he swears he hears the flap of wings, the clack of claws on metal, and then there is nothing else but the sound of his own breathing.

Shaking his head, he turns the key and carefully opens the door. A blast of cold air hits him and the door swings wide, banging against the wall. Steve has a strange sensation, like someone just pushed past him. He looks back. No one. He looks in front of him. He's alone. There is just a dark, narrow alcove with ancient concrete walls and a fire door with a deadbolt. Beside the fire door is a touch pad for scanning fingerprints and a keypad for entering his personal access code.

Taking a breath, Steve goes forward and forces himself to stay calm. But the hairs on the back of his neck rise, and he finds himself shivering. He tells himself it's the sudden change of temperature. Down here by the tunnels, it's only about 55 degrees. He swallows. Still ... the pressure in the room doesn't feel right. He feels as though someone is in here with him.

With another deep breath, he touches his thumb to the fingerprint scanner. A green light goes on and he enters his code. There is a sound of two bolts unlocking, and then all that's left is one more key activated deadbolt.

He has the key in the lock and is almost about to turn it when there is a loud click beneath his fingers, and this door swings wide, too. There is another strong gust of cold air. He feels pressure on his chest and finds himself pressed against the door as though by an invisible hand. Something sweeps by him into the darkness, and just as quickly as it came, the pressure on his chest is gone.

Steve doesn't panic as a general rule, and he's not panicked now. Could there be something in the air making him hallucinate? He picks up his cell, says, "Tonya," and gets the no-service message. He should have expected that, even if he wasn't at basement level. There is a nuke threat; the FBI is going to block all cell phone signals in a wide radius to keep the nuke from being triggered remotely.

Steve looks ahead. There is a poorly-lit stairwell with dark crumbling brick walls and stairs that are just bare metal mesh. The stairs lead down to the tunnel level. Steve goes forward and down, the metal mesh ringing under his feet.

The tunnels were built in Chicago in 1903. They were originally designed for laying telephone lines but by 1914 were being used to haul coal and freight to downtown office buildings along miles of crisscrossing underground rail tracks. By the mid 1950's, they were no longer being used for freight anymore and were mostly derelict until the silicon era when firms started using some of the tunnels for communication lines.

The wire mesh stairway gives way to a concrete platform once used for receiving coal. This area actually belongs to the building he works in and is lit by emergency lighting.

There's a low drop of about 2 feet to the tunnel proper and nearly complete darkness. Steve doesn't notice any fiber optic junction boxes, or more importantly, any technicians. He is about to hop down when he notices a long feather, so black it's almost blue, on the floor. Picking it up he looks around nervously. Slipping it in his pocket, he pulls out his keychain with attached maglight. He is about to turn it on when he glances south where the LaSalle tunnel intersects with the Jackson street tunnel. Where he stands the tunnel is only about 7.5 feet high by 6 feet wide, but beneath the Board of Trade is a "station," a wide open space where many freight cars could park and men could gather to receive coal and load used ash. That is where a containment perimeter should be established. He sees light there and what looks like the shapes of men in hazmat suits, but they move so little they seem frozen in place.

Steve looks quickly up the tunnel to the north. He sees no sign of fiber optic technicians—he should look for them, but … He puts his maglight away, pulls his gun from his holster and goes as quickly and silently as he can southward, toward the light.

Walking along the wall, he carefully avoids stepping on the metal tracks in the middle of the tunnel. The sound of his feet don't betray him, but as he gets closer to the "station" below the Board of Trade, he thinks the loud beating of his heart might.

There are men in hazmat suits on the station platform. And a bomb robot, too. They are all as still and silent as statues. In the middle of the Board of Trade platform is what looks like an exploded duffel bag and an exposed metal casing of some kind. In the casing is a sphere, about two hands wide, alternately pulsing with light and darkness. Pacing around the pulsating sphere is a Caucasian male, about 50 years old with a gray beard and an eyepatch. He's dressed in armor that looks like renaissance fair meets SWAT. Circling around him are the two ravens.

Oh. Shit.

Steve finds himself frozen, too, not sure if he's hallucinating. From just a few feet behind him he hears the sound of footfalls. Cursing himself for not paying attention, he turns, gun upraised. And then he lets his arm fall.

Two men are in the tunnel he just came down, one older, one younger. The old guy is holding up his Bureau badge, but Steve doesn't need to see it to know they're on the same team. The old guy oozes FBI, and he's probably ex-military, too. He's got the classic high and tight haircut, and a black suit on. The younger man has a mop of unruly brown hair, a rumpled suit and he looks like he just rolled out of bed. He's carrying a large cylindrical case over his shoulder and something that looks almost like a Geiger counter.

"Agent Rogers," says the old guy. "I'm Assistant Director James Merryl and this is Agent Ericson," he tilts his head at the young guy. The young guy nods and swallows. Putting his badge away, Merryl says, "We're from the FBI Department of Anomalous Devices of Unknown Origin, also known as ADUO."

"What?" says Steve. He's never heard of ADUO before in his life.

From the platform comes the raucous rawk of the ravens, the beat of wings, and Steve spins again, gun at the ready, to find the ravens flapping just a few meters in front of him. He looks past the birds, the motionless men in their hazmat suits, and the silent robot—the old guy by the sphere is paying Steve and his companions absolutely no attention.

One of the ravens looks at Steve, follows his gaze to the old man, and then turning back to Steve starts to shriek. "What? What? You thought that Odin needed the staff Gungir to stop time, human? Well, you are wrong! Wrong! Wrong! Wrong! Gungir only concentrates and strengthens his powers! He doesn't *need* it! It's like Hoenir's hut! Or Loki's—"

"Muninn, shut up!" squawks the other raven, landing on the ground.

Beside him, Steve hears Ericson whisper. "Yep, this is definitely our department."

The raven on the ground rises into the air. "You think you can contain Odin, All Father, Agent Miles Ericson?" It cackles maniacally.

Beside him, Steve hears Ericson swallow.

"You tell him, Huginn," cackles the other raven. "The World Seed will be his! His!"

Steve looks past the ravens to the old man they call Odin, still hovering around the sphere. As Steve watches, Odin bends down and tries to lift the sphere. There is a bright flash of light, and then the space around the sphere goes absolutely pitch black and the man disappears. Steve's ears pop, and he feels air rush from behind him. The two birds flap their wings, squawk and struggle not to be sucked backwards.

Beside him he hears Ericson shout, "My readings are through the roof!"

There is another bright flash of light, and Odin is standing there in front of the sphere again—but only for an instant. The sphere pulses, there is an electric sounding crackle, and then Odin is flying backwards through the air. With a loud thud he hits the far wall.

The ravens shriek. The sphere hovers in the air about a foot off the ground. The robot inches forward, and the guys in the hazmat suits begin to move.

"Go check on Odin, Agent Rogers," says Merryl. "Ericson, you're with me!"

Gun still out, Steve walks over to the old man in armor, now lying on the floor. The ravens dart around him, gibbering and rawking. It's not English, but sounds eerily human. Behind him he hears the robot whirring. He picks up snatches of conversation from the guys in hazmat suits. "No radiation readings or biohazard signs … How did those guys get in here? What happened?"

Steve prods the old man with a shoe. Odin, if that is his name, doesn't move; his eyelids don't even flutter. But his armor swirls with light.

From behind him he hears someone say, "What are those guys doing?"

Steve turns to see Ericson and Merryl erect a strange silvery wire fence woven in hexagonal patterns around the sphere. As they close the seam of the fence, it seems to melt and coalesce over and under the sphere, forming a sphere of its own about four feet in diameter. The glowing sphere thing hovers in midair in the center.

"What the hell?" says a guy in a hazmat suit.

Taking out his badge and holding it up, Merryl says, "Department of ADUO."

"I thought those guys were a joke," someone else says.

Next to Merryl, Miles bends over his Geiger counter thing, seemingly oblivious to everything. Shaking his head he says, "Readings are still off the charts."

Within the new mesh sphere, the first small sphere begins

to pulse again with light and dark. Suddenly, prongs of a dark material shoot outward from the glowing sphere like spokes and twist around the hexagonal netting.

"What the hell?" says someone.

And then the outer shell begins to grow, the hexagonal pattern stretching and throbbing, black material from the glowing sphere's spokes crawling and curling around the mesh.

Miles and Merryl turn. "It's never done that before!" Miles shouts as Merryl pulls him back.

From beside Steve a deep male voice roars. "What have you done?"

And then everything stops again. All the guys in hazmat suits are immobilized, as are Merryl and Ericson. The only things moving are the mesh sphere, pulsing outward, the silvery wire transforming to thick bars of black and silver, and for some reason, Steve and the robot, rolling towards the sphere. The robot is just a small three-by-three foot black metal body on tread wheels, with one long groping steel arm. As the arm hits the outer sphere, now composed of dark bars, sparks fly around the machine. There is blackness within the outer sphere. There is the rush of air again—this time it is so brusque some of the immobilized people by the sphere actually fall over, including Ericson and Merryl. Steve's ears pop again, and then the robot just isn't there.

The darkness fades, and through the bars he sees the pulsing blue light of the sphere.

"You will tell me where you got the technology for the outer sphere!"

Steve turns. The old man with one eye, Odin, is standing beside him, his armor pulsing with the same blue light as the sphere. Steve hears the ravens' wings, and far off a subway.

Before he can process what is happening, Odin's hand shoots to Steve's neck. Steve tries to move—but he can't. Below his neck his whole body feels numb.

He doesn't have the foggiest idea where the technology came from, or even really what the Department of ADUO is, but no way in hell will he tell this guy.

Odin blinks. His one eye widens and then he smiles, and it does not make Steve happy.

Still, with a smile of his own, Steve says, "Agent Steve Rogers, Identification number—"

"You don't know, but perhaps the Department of ADUO does," the man hisses. "I hear you in my head, Agent Rogers."

Steve's mouth drops open.

One of the ravens lands on the man's armor and whispers something in his ear.

Leaning forward Odin whispers. "Steve Rogers, people I hear tend to be destined for greatness, the gallows, or both." He pulls back. "Things will want the World Seed. Very bad things. Very bad people. You must keep it safe."

The other raven lands on Odin's opposite side and says, "Claire! Claire!"

Steve's eyes go wide. He spits and hits the damn bird squarely between the eyes. With a squawk it rises into the air.

Odin's smile becomes almost grandfatherly. "Keep her safe, Steven."

The hand releases. Steve blinks and Odin and the birds are gone.

From behind him he hears movement. He turns, and over the heads of Merryl, Ericson and some of the guys in hazmat suits he sees the sphere … the outer shell is nearly 8 feet by

8 feet now.

Someone says, "What the hell happened?"

Ericson, looking at his Geiger counter ... or whatever it is, says, "It's still growing, but it seems to have stabilized. Magic levels have dropped."

"Where's the bomb bot?" someone says.

"Shit," says someone else.

That would be Steve's assessment, too.

A cell phone goes off. Dusting himself off and standing up, Merryl pulls his phone out of his jacket mumbling about a secure channel. And then he turns to his partner Ericson and says, "Just got a report of an eight-legged horse on the corner of Jackson and LaSalle." He takes a breath, phone still at his ear. "And now it's gone."

Saying something under his breath that sounds suspiciously like a curse, Merryl looks around the room. "Did anyone see what happened when we were immobilized?"

"Immobilized?" says someone else.

Stepping forward, Steve lifts a hand.

With a nod, Merryl says, "Agent Rogers, you're coming with us."

Amy Lewis stands across the desk from Agent Steve Rogers in the new downtown office of the Department of ADUO. The department used to be located in the main FBI office way out on west Roosevelt in kind of a sketchy neighborhood, but a few days ago they suddenly moved to a new office right across from the Board of Trade.

She plays receptionist for ADUO. "Plays" is the operative word. All the calls that come in seem to be classified and bypass her completely. It gives her lots of time to read, though, and that gives her a chance to keep up with her studies and apply for financial aid for next year and reapply for her scholarship. Also, the pay is good, the hours regular.

Steve is standing between piles of files in cardboard boxes, looking out the window, a huge black shadow in silhouette.

"You called me in, Sir?" she says, wringing her hands. Steve hates her. She's not exactly sure why.

"Why were you an hour and a half late today?" Steve says turning around. His face is flat and unreadable.

"Well, I was coming in at my usual time, and as I was walking down the alley a pigeon with a broken wing came running toward me … because obviously it couldn't fly … and well, I tried to ignore it, because you know, there are feral cats in the neighborhood and they deserve to eat, too, but it climbed up onto my shoe, I think it imprinted on me, and you know once something thinks you're its mother, you can't abandon it."

Agent Rogers' mouth opens slightly.

Amy looks at the desk, "Which doesn't exactly explain why I'm late. I'm late because I took it to the clinic. I left a message on Assistant Director Merryl's voice mail—"

"Assistant Director Merryl has been reassigned," says Rogers. "I'm Acting Assistant Director for now."

Amy bites her lip. Oh. Shit.

"Miss Lewis," says Steve, "I haven't gotten to your file yet," he waves a hand at the desk, and Amy sees a stack of old-fashioned manila and red folders. "But I have to wonder, what are you doing here?"

Amy's mouth opens; but she's uncertain what he means, and no sound comes out.

"I mean, what are you doing at this job," says Steve.

Oh. Well then. "I'm here because Agent Merryl offered me a job after he interviewed me," she says. Right after she found out Loki stole all her money, and her grandmother broke her hip and then had a stroke, Agent Merryl had shown up at the hospital. He interviewed her extensively about Loki's time with her—and confiscated her and Beatrice's Alfheim clothes, and their Subaru. All Amy's got left of the trip is a hadrosaur feather and a few glowing hairpins Beatrice misplaced in the garage by her gardening tools.

"Uh-huh," says Steve. "I never see you actually answering the phone, Amy, or doing any typing or filing."

Amy blinks. "Well, no one ever really gives me anything to—"

"Do you realize how deep in debt our country is?" Steve says, sitting down and scowling up at her.

That's got to be a trick question. Amy tilts her head. "Doesn't it change minute to minute with compounded interest?"

Steve is quiet for a moment. And then he gives her a hard glare and says, "I love my country and I hate to see anyone taking advantage of it ... even in small ways."

"Yes, Sir," says Amy.

"There is no *I* in the word *team*, Amy, and no deadweight either. Find work to do, or find another job."

Amy swallows. She can find a new job, but one that pays as well, and one she won't have to relocate for, or force her to buy a car? Not in the months before she goes back to school. She's promised the university one year off and nothing more.

She's found a great place to live, the upstairs is owned by a fellow vet tech and her doctor fiancé. And Amy gets to work at the vet clinic on nights and weekends and keep her skills up. She actually got to take part in a surgery last weekend. She *can't* lose this job.

"Um, Sir?" she says.

"Yes, Miss Lewis?" says Steve looking down at a manilla folder with a bright red post-it attached on his desk.

"Do you have anything you'd like me to do?" she asks.

Steve looks up at her like he wishes she would spontaneously combust.

And then he spins in his chair, gets up, grabs a large box of files marked, "Purchase Orders - Non-Classified" and nearly throws it at her. "Take this and organize them in reverse chronological order. Make sure anything on the same date is alphabetized, too."

Stumbling back a little bit under the weight of the box, Amy says, "Okay, yes, Sir," and leaves the office with Steve already bent over one of the folders.

Amy takes the box back to her desk and tries not to cry. Why did Agent Merryl have to leave? It turned out ADUO had been watching her house ever since she met Loki. Merryl was the same old guy with too square jaw she'd seen buying ice cream one day—and the Mexican ice cream guy? ADUO, too, Agent Hernandez. She likes Agent Merryl. He is steadying, calm, and kind.

Now she is stuck with some patriotic hard-ass.

Opening the box, she rifles through a few folders—this assignment makes her want to cry even more than Rogers yelling at her. The files already look like they are in order ... which means she's just verifying they are in order, which is

worse than ordering them to begin with. There is a special
room in Hell for file organization quality control. Swallowing
back her tears she rifles through the files. She blinks. There is
a red folder wedged beneath the purchase orders.

Red almost always means classified.

She should pick it up and take it to Rogers right now. She
digs out the folder and is going to take it to the office, really,
when she notices the words "Agent Steve Rogers" on the tab.

Hum.

She shouldn't.

She really shouldn't. She looks at the red folder in her
hands. She looks back at the box of filing. Her heart falls; just
looking at the box bores her nearly to tears. She looks at the
red folder again in her hands. This might be interesting. And
she'll just take a tiny peek. What harm can it do? And he's got
her file, and also her Alfheim dresses, and the Subaru so ... .

She starts flipping through the folder. At first it is just
his history. How he was born in rural Alabama to poor parents, and then moved up to Chicago when he was eight or
so—where he remained poor. She'd kind of have sympathy
except, he just yelled at her. There's his stint with the Marines,
a bachelor's from Yale on the GI bill, and a master's degree
in public policy from the University of Chicago. She tilts her
head. So he's an impressive ass; those are the worst type. She
flips through a few more pages; his hobbies include Kumdo,
whatever that is. And then she reads his recent history—marriage, birth of his daughter, promotion to Public Liaison for
the FBI's Chicago branch, divorce, and then ...

Uh-oh.

Amy's hands start to shake but she can't put the folder
down until she's done reading.

She swallows. Okay, she'll just take it to him and pretend she just found it. No problem. Easy. Hopefully, he won't notice her trembling.

Taking a deep breath, Amy walks down the hall. It's pretty empty in the building. Most of the agents seem to be elsewhere most of the time since they moved here. It's a lot different from a few days ago when they were in the office on Roosevelt and all the ADUO agents seemed bored.

The door to Steve 's office is closed. She's about to turn back when she hears a muffled, yet extremely familiar voice. Her eyes go wide and she's suddenly too angry to even be afraid of Steve. Bursting into the room, she sees Agent Rogers behind his desk which is now on fire, aiming a gun at Loki.

"You really should tell me where you got the technology," Loki says quietly.

There is the sound of the gun firing twice. Amy screams. There are two dull thuds in the wall next to her and Loki turns to her apparently unharmed.

Loki's wearing a light gray suit, or at least he's pretending to wear a suit. No tie though. And he looks like he has lost a lot of weight. His hair is black now, which is weird.

He blinks. "Amy," he says. He blinks again. "I tried to wire you money, but apparently your bank account is no longer open?"

Her nostrils flare up, she goes hot—and it has nothing to do with the blaze in the room. There's a fire extinguisher on the floor. Picking it up, Amy pulls the pin and aims it at Steve's desk and yells at Loki. "You steal all my money and then you come here. Are you trying to make me lose my job, too?" She's finally got a new plan, and things are going to work out, and he's going to ruin everything all over again.

"You know him?" says Steve.

Loki's face goes livid. "I stole nothing! You offered it to me! You said to take as much as I needed."

"I didn't mean to take it from my bank account!" Amy shouts. She can feel the veins in her neck popping.

Raising his arms, Loki says, "What did you mean, then, pray tell?" His eyes widen. "You can't have meant just the money in your change belt? How was that supposed to buy me an airline ticket to Europe?"

"Ticket to Europe?" says Steve.

"You gave me your oath you wouldn't steal!" says Amy, throwing the spent fire extinguisher at Loki. Of course it just goes right through him. She rips off the heavy sweater she's wearing—it's Chicago and the temperature fell 40 degrees literally overnight. Dropping it on a flame that's not quite out on the floor, she steps on it with her shoe since Steve seems to be in some sort of shock.

"How did the fire extinguisher just pass right through him?" says Steve. "And why didn't my bullets work?"

Ignoring Steve, she narrows her eyes at Loki. "You walked into my bank as *me* and withdrew all my money! That's stealing and probably a felony."

What is obviously an astral projection of Loki takes a step closer. Bending so his face is next to hers, he points a finger at her chest and says, "You told me I could take as much as I wanted. I thought your law was higher than any nation's law!"

Amy stands, breathing heavily. Loki looks down at her chest and smiles. Amy follows his gaze. The shirt she was wearing underneath the now ruined sweater isn't really meant to be seen without an upper layer.

She crosses her arms over her chest and gives him a dirty

look. And then she closes her eyes. A tear falls out; she swallows and puts her hands to her face.

"Oh, damn it," she mutters. The thing is, she can totally see how this happened. She did say to take as much as he needed, and he had seen her bank account info, and he just doesn't understand rules and morality the way humans do.

For a moment there is no sound in the office but the click of the air conditioning that really should have been shut off when the heat wave ended. And then it's like a dam that's been building up for months finally breaks. Amy takes a heavy breath—and sobs. "After you left everything went to Hell! Beatrice broke her hip and had a stroke, I forfeited my scholarship because I didn't have any money to pay for extras and because I was maybe in shock, and to take care of her, but then it didn't matter because my mom came back and got durable power of attorney because I didn't have a good lawyer, and she brought her creepy boyfriend, too, and I lost my home."

She wipes her face. And despite it all she was kind of worried about Loki, angry, hurt and confused—but worried, too. She'd desperately hoped that his draining her bank account was some horrible misunderstanding, that she wasn't *that* stupid, that she hadn't been so misled by him of the inappropriate comments yet surprising heroism. And now she knows it was a misunderstanding, and she's relieved ... and more worried than ever. He's too skinny, he's unshaven and, "Why is your hair black? Is that just your astral image or is it real?" she asks. It makes his pale skin look absolutely sickly.

Loki's just staring at her, his mouth slack. At her words he nervously runs his hands over his head. In the trail of his fingers the ginger color returns. "Oh, that—"

"That's a very sad story," says Steve, outside of Amy's line of vision.

Loki gives him an angry look and then turns to Amy. "What is a stroke?"

"Blockage in the brain," says Amy with a sniff.

Loki looks horrified. "Is it curable?" he whispers.

Shaking her head, Amy wipes her nose. "She's really old; her brain isn't as plastic. She doesn't remember me anymore or anything really."

"Why isn't my phone working?" she hears Steve say, pacing around the room. "Or the fire alarms?"

Loki's eyes flit briefly to Steve and then he looks back to Amy. "I'm sorry. I would offer to try and help. But I really am hopeless when it comes to fixing things. I'm better at—"

"Setting things on fire?" says Steve.

Both Loki and Amy turn to Steve.

"You pointed a gun at me," Loki says.

"But it wouldn't have hurt you," Amy says, brow furrowing. "You are in your astral form."

"You set my desk on fire," says Steve, in the same sort of calm voice you might use to comment on the weather.

Loki winces and turns to her. "You know how it is. Lately, when I'm excited ... " He raises his hands. "Poof."

"Like the candles in the living room and the kitchen?" says Amy, remembering him setting them alight.

"Yes," says Loki, nodding earnestly. He looks down. "And those pictures in Malson's portfolio."

"Oh," says Amy, going cold. She couldn't fault him for that. If she could burn the images from that psychopath's collection from her brain she would. Amy glances at Steve, his eyes are narrowed, and he's looking between the two of them, but he's quiet.

"It does happen when he's upset," says Amy.

"Hmmmm … ." says Steve. He doesn't even look mad anymore. Or frightened. Which is creepy. Granted, he's had a little experience with Norse so-called-god types himself, so maybe that's why he's so put together … although it seems unfair that he seems to have pulled himself together a lot faster than she did.

Leaning in closer Loki says, "There is something in the basement of the building down the street, Amy. Something very dangerous. Something very dangerous things will want."

Amy shivers and Loki looks at Steve. "It would be for the best if you let me help you get rid of it. But to get rid of it, I first have to break through that nasty outer containment field."

"The Promethean Sphere around the World Seed!" says Amy. She knows because it was mentioned in Steve's file. Steve's eyes flash to hers.

Uh-oh.

Loki smiles gently. "Is that what they're calling the containment sphere around Cera? Do you know where they got the technology, Amy? It looks vaguely Vanir, but mutated. I need to understand it if I'm to … fix it."

The Promethean Sphere was just a side note in the file. Shaking her head vigorously, she looks at Steve.

Narrowing his eyes at Loki he says, "You know, you could be one of those very bad things."

"He's not really bad," says Amy. "You should have met Thor. He was a creep. And Loki didn't try to strangle you … " She stops herself just before she says, "like Odin."

Both Loki and Steve's eyes slide to her. Steve looks angry.

Loki looks bemused. "Your own intelligence says I'm the good guy," says Loki, eyes sliding back to Steve.

Steve's brow furrows. "I don't know anything about that."

Giving a twisted smile, Loki tilts his head. And then he looks back at Amy. "I never renege on my oaths, Amy." He winks. And then he's gone. No poof, or pop, or anything.

Amy looks back at Steve and wrings her hands.

"How did you know about the Promethean Sphere?" he says quietly.

Amy looks at the red file she dropped on the ground. Steve follows her eyes. And then he looks back at his desk, covered under fire extinguisher foam. For the first time Amy notices the smell of burnt plastic in the air.

She looks at Steve and swallows. Prepared for, "You're fired, or you're going to jail," she nearly jumps when Steve says, "Do you have a jacket or anything at your desk?"

"Uh ... no," says Amy. His eyes flit to her chest and the tight lacey undershirt she's wearing. She crosses her arms again.

Steve turns around, goes to a duffel and pulls out a large gray sweatshirt that says Marines in black letters. "You can wear this," he says, carefully keeping his eyes on hers. She pulls it over her head. It smells like Tide and duffel bag vinyl. Walking past her, he says, "Let's go find an office that isn't filled with poisonous fumes."

Sitting in a conference room, Steve opens a laptop, turns it on, and checks the Promethean counter next to him. The beige device has a circular head the size of a petri dish attached to a handle. The head of the device has a flat circular screen. Right now the screen is slate gray. In the presence of dark energy, or as some of the tech guys around here scientifically call it, 'magic,' it glows blue. Steve had one at his desk. It had begun to glow just before the apparition calling itself Loki popped into the room.

Across from him is Amy Lewis, the receptionist he had flagged as a classic example of government waste. She may have just saved his life. Though she seems to think Loki's setting his desk on fire was an accident, Steve knows better. Loki started the fire on purpose. But Steve doesn't disabuse her of the notion of his innocence. Something is tickling at the back of Steve's mind, and he doesn't want to give up any cards just yet.

He glances up at Lewis, now wearing his sweatshirt. It is a very weird ending to a very weird day and a truly bizarre week.

Merryl had drawn Steve into ADUO just days after the incident under CBOE. Merryl said someone with Steve's military experience and 'people skills' would be a great asset to a department that was largely techies and lawyers that the Bureau couldn't place anywhere else.

Steve has ambitions of leaving the Bureau and getting into politics someday; joining an obscure department like ADUO diverts those plans for a while, but he does have priorities. Seeing that the country's third largest metropolis doesn't blow up is at the top of the list. He may not know exactly what the World Seed thing is, but he knows it isn't good.

And now there are the events in Wyoming.

This morning Steve received a call at 0400 from Assistant

Director James Merryl. The first words out of Merryl's lips over the phone were, "Steve, there is an outbreak of trolls in Wyoming. I have to be out of the office this week. I'd like you to take over."

It was a bad idea. Steve's not up to speed yet on anything. He's been too busy helping to secure the perimeter around the World Seed and keeping the damn thing's presence quiet. He's barely familiar with the department staff. And he only knows a bit about the Promethean devices — the magic detectors and containment fields. The technology was given to ADUO by an operative code-named Prometheus. No one seems to know who he is or where he came from. Or if they do they're not telling Steve.

But considering it was 4 in the morning, it's understandable that the first words out of Steve's mouth weren't something logical and coherent like, "Do you think that's wise when I'm so new to the department," or even, "Yes, Sir, thank you, sir." Instead Steve said, "Trolls...on the internet?"

Merryl's response was, "No, Steve, more like the Incredible Hulk. You'll be fine." There was yelling in the background and then Merryl said, "The damn thing isn't dead. I have to go."

So here he is playing catch up after nearly getting himself toasted by an entity that may or may not be a Norse god.

Shaking his head, Steve hits a button on the laptop on the conference room table. Amy Lewis' file opens. A few days ago Steve asked Merryl about Lewis and Merryl had said, "Read her file." Steve assumes that meant the pretty receptionist without any security clearance reading a magazine during his tour wasn't important enough to discuss.

He skims through the few pages and puts his hand to

his jaw. What was the adage? Never assume. It makes an ass of you and me. He sighs. He does feel like an ass. Merryl brought Amy into ADUO because having her work for him in the office meant he didn't have to have a security detail stalking her 24/7. Steve's boss had figured, correctly, Loki might come to call on her again.

More than that, although Steve had taken the girl for an unambitious leech on the government payroll, she actually looks like a good kid from rough beginnings. Her dad, now in jail for fraud, split when she was little, and her mom has been married five times. Miss Lewis left home as soon as she was eighteen and moved in with her grandparents. She got her GED in Chicago, went to community college, earned straight A's, and then went to the University of Illinois on scholarship where she earned a degree in biochemistry. She got a full ride to vet school from there.

And then she met Loki during a run in with serial killer Ed Malson on a highway late at night. He taps a finger on the desk and scowls. "So this Loki character saved your life?" By beating Malson to death with a small log.

She jumps in her chair and then says, "Yes. He heard me somehow — I think like Odin heard you."

She stops.

Steve shrugs. "You were filing, you saw the red folder, you were so shocked when you pulled it out of the box it fell out of your hands, you couldn't help but see certain details."

Lewis's eyes go wide.

Steve restrains a sigh. He gently prompts her. "Because that's how it happened. Right?"

"Okay," says Lewis slowly, as though unsure.

Steve nods. "What do you know about this 'hearing'?"

Because he's pretty damn curious. Having his mind read is one of the most frustrating things he's ever experienced.

Lewis looks away again. "From what Loki told me they — Asgardians, and I guess Frost Giants — they hear people in their heads if it relates to their higher purpose somehow."

Steve leans back as much as he can in the conference room chair and taps his hand on the desk. "And what is that purpose, do you think?"

Shrugging, Lewis still doesn't look at him. "Odin is the king or chief of the gods. Loki is the trickster and god of mischief and lies. Loki brings about the end of the world — supposedly, in the myths."

"And you brought him home," says Steve, rubbing his eyes. Just like an injured bird.

Lewis looks sharply at him. "It wasn't the brightest idea, I know. But he had nowhere to go, or I thought he didn't, and he really isn't that bad. And I don't think he realized the consequences of his actions when he took all of my money, really. And he has set things on fire...accidentally."

Steve should put her in witness protection, right now. But...

There is a large pulsing thing under the streets of Chicago that sucks anything that touches its shell, the Promethean Sphere, into never-never land. In a matter of weeks the top of the thing's shell will come into contact with the bottom of the foundation of Chicago's Board of Trade and no one knows what will happen. In Lewis's little interaction with Loki, Steve's picked up something that hasn't been mentioned by anyone when the subject of the Promethean devices has come up.

He taps his hand on the conference table. "So when he

said that the technology looked Vanir...do you have any idea what that meant?"

Looking up, she purses her lips. "The Vanir are one of the races of the Nine Realms. Not much is known about them, really. They had some big war with the Aesir —"

"The Aesir?" says Steve.

"Yes. Odin's people."

"And Loki's?" says Steve.

She shakes her head. "No, he's a Frost Giant." She holds up her hands, as though she's afraid Steve will react in some undesirable way. "But he knows it, not like in the movies where he goes crazy when he learns that he is actually not an Aesir."

Steve stares at her blankly. He seems to remember a movie a while back with Loki as the bad guy, some superhero flick. Steve hasn't been interested in superhero flicks since he was a kid, though.

She swallows. "But he does turn blue...like the movies, but he says Frost Giants aren't blue...." Brow furrowing she whispers, "And when he turns blue he gets really self-conscious about it and grumpy."

"Uh-huh," says Steve, wondering if this is relevant. He tilts his head. "You said higher purpose...and gods...do you think they're gods?"

Lewis makes a face like she's just eaten something distasteful. "No. A god wouldn't be so interested in my boobs."

Steve laughs, because it's funny, but also because he's relieved. She's not that naive.

Bowing her head, Lewis laughs, too. After a moment, she says, "So you aren't going to fire me?"

There is no way Steve is going to lose his connection to

these...whatevers. He gives her his most calculated, charming smile. "Nope."

She scowls a tiny bit as though she's studying him. Her lips purse. "May I go?"

Steve looks back to the computer and all the material he has to read — he hates reading on the screen and silently curses Loki for charring his paper copies.

"You can, for now," he says. "I'll call you in if I have any questions."

Amy gets up and practically scrambles to the door. But then she stops. "Also, you probably know this already ... but Cera means power in Russian."

Steve stares blankly at her for a moment. Lewis ducks her chin. "Cera is what he called the World Seed ... I think."

"I didn't know that," Steve says. And it is giving him goosebumps for some reason. "Thank you," he says. "You may go."

Without even a nod she scampers out the door.

Steve turns back to the computer. He remains there long after Lewis goes home. He's not just reading her file, but there is something in her file that keeps drawing him back.

When Loki, under the aliases Thor Odinson, was released from police custody after slaying Ed Malson, it was due to the interference of ADUO. The department had intelligence that tagged Loki as "the good guy." More specifically, that intelligence had come in the form of a phone call to ADUO's directors in Washington.

The phone call had come from Prometheus..

CHAPTER 2

Loki walks down a tree lined street in one of Chicago's residential neighborhoods. Beyond the red mist that is Cera's presence are brownstones he'd guess to be no more than a hundred years old. He's wearing his armor, but to any observer it would look like he's wearing a pair of faded black jeans that sit a little too low, a gray tee that is too loose, and a fedora. He looks like a wandering minstrel of this age, which fits with the very real guitar case he's carrying.

He has a headache, as he has nearly constantly since he left Amy and Beatrice to track Cera down. His headache is not helped by the fact that Cera is whining again, in Russian. Cera only speaks Russian. "I'm trapped! I'm trapped! Have you forsaken me?"

Scowling, Loki clenches his teeth. Not for the first time, he wishes the Promethean Sphere was strong enough to contain *all* of Cera, instead of just doing a bang up job of keeping him out.

In Russian he says, "I will release you as soon as I figure out how to get through the Promethean Sphere." As though chasing her literally across the globe only to lose her in a port in Karachi doesn't prove his dedication.

"I don't see how going to see the human helps," says Cera, swirling around him in agitation.

Loki scowls. Demanding, insolent, stupid creature. She is so locked in the rules of the quantum world she can't even grasp the concept of *relative* position and couldn't, until recently, even give him her exact location..

"I am in her debt," he mutters. "And she is my one link to the inner workings of ADUO. I need to get back in her good graces."

Not that Loki wouldn't pay her back anyway.

He stops in front of a slightly sunken, crumbling three story building he's identified as Amy's new address. Set back from the road, the building has sunk to nearly six feet below street level in Chicago's soft soil. The ground in front of it has been dug out to form a little yard area. Steps lead down from the sidewalk to a brick walkway that crosses the yard. There is a unit at ground level with rusting bars on the windows, and a staircase, newer and better maintained, leading up to a unit above it.

Loki hops down the first steps and saunters over to the door of the lower unit. He knocks. There is no answer.

Closing his eyes, he sends an astral projection of himself into the dwelling. Amy's new home is one small open room divided by a low bookshelf into a living area by the door and a bedroom further in. Past the bedroom is a bathroom, closet, and a kitchen with a counter against the far wall. In the kitchen is a door that leads out to another yard. It is humble by North American standards, but absolutely palatial compared to some of the dwellings he saw and frequented during his search for Cera.

He sees no sign of Fenrir. Amy is bent over something on the kitchen counter Loki can't see. There is a pot boiling on the stove.

He knocks again.

She doesn't even look over her shoulder.

Loki turns around and surveys the street. He sees an unmarked car with a gentleman sitting in it drinking a coffee.

"They see us. They know we're here! Leave!" Cera cries. Loki rolls his eyes. Only since he's known Cera has she developed the ability to 'see.' For a while she could merely sense magic. It took her a long time to understand that the patterns in the photons bouncing in her direction meant something. Now that she does see she thinks she understands.

Instead of following Cera's advice, Loki raises his hand, smiles and waves at the agent. The ADUO agent puts his coffee down on his lap and picks up his phone but makes no move to leave the car.

Loki turns back to the door. Tired of waiting, he considers using one of the many lock picks he keeps in the cuff of his armor to open it—just to keep his non-magic lock-picking skills up to snuff. But thinking better of it, he takes a half step back, waggles his fingers dramatically in the air, and produces a useless flair of green light.

The lock barely even clicks as it disengages, and Amy is too caught up in whatever she is doing to notice when he enters. Schooling the scowl off his face, Loki says brightly, "Amy, so good to see you again!"

Amy jumps and turns her head, eyes wide. There is a flapping noise, and she turns back to the counter and leans over quickly. Something scoots under her arm and there is a thud. Loki blinks. There is a pigeon on the floor holding its wing at an awkward angle.

Turning around and diving for the bird, Amy says angrily, "You scared Fred!"

Loki blinks. He looks at the pot on the stove. "Are you butchering it? I can help; I love squab, and I'm famished."

Amy's face contorts into a look of horror. "I am not going to eat him. I was changing the dressing on his wing!"

Loki's eyes go to the side. Belatedly he notices a large bird cage in the living room. Oops.

From the back door comes Fenrir's yelping.

Amy closes her eyes. "Could you please distract Fenrir while I finish?"

He stares at her. How many times has he heard Mimir say something similar? Loki, would you distract the butterfly snake while Hoenir reanimates the spider mouse? He is hit by a wave of desolation that is so intense for a moment he is motionless.

And then, almost automatically he says, "Of course." He goes to the door, but the dog cowers, whimpers, and backs away from him. It takes Loki a moment to realize that the beast is afraid of Cera. In Russian he whispers, "Back off."

"I don't see how this helps," Cera says bitterly. But the red mist withdraws until only a wisp of pink is left in the air.

Fenrir wiggles over to Loki. He scoops the beast up into his arms and rubs its head absentmindedly. Distracting butterfly snakes was about the greatest boon Loki ever granted Hoenir. And yet Hoenir did so much for him.

To save Anganboða from Baldur, the first step is saving her from her brother. Even if Loki hadn't made an oath to protect Anganboða, it's a task he would have relished anyway. It's a game of wits, really—of playing up to passions and prejudices, and the prize will humble the crown prince. What was not to love?

He goes to Freyja, the would-be Goddess of Love and Beauty, his sometime bedmate and leader of the Valkyries. This morning she has ebony skin and long black braids of hair, like a dark vision from an Egyptian hieroglyph. But her ears are pointed like an elf's and her eyes are deep green. Loki wonders idly what man's fantasy she's enacting. Freyja's appearance is never the same twice. She waxes and wanes between lean and voluptuous. Her skin, hair and eyes have taken on every hue—even rare colors like lavender. The only thing that remains the same is her magic. It is always pink and very feminine. The problem with Freyja's many guises is that beneath it all she is still Freyja, primarily concerned with herself and her position among the Valkyries.

But her predictableness is helpful. He feeds Freyja a sob story of a young maiden whose family wants to sell her to a vile lord to increase their social standing. He leaves out the part about the lord in question being the crown prince and plays up Anganboða's intellectual talents and desire to be a tutor.

After such a story, were Freyja not to aid Anganboða she would face scorn among her Valkyrie sisters. As expected, Freyja immediately suggests a position tutoring the Valkyrie Göndul's daughters and offers to recommend Anganboða immediately. But she wouldn't be Freyja if she didn't see ulterior motives in Loki's interference. Smiling slyly she says, "A little tidbit you want for yourself, Loki?"

Loki rolls his eyes and sighs. "Actually, I'm under oath to observe her honor."

Freyja lifts an eyebrow.

Waving a hand and looking to the ceiling, Loki says, "Hoenir extracted it from me. I think he fancies her." He's never known Hoenir to fancy anyone—woman, man, child or beast, but Freyja would never believe Loki made such an oath willingly. He barely believes it himself.

Freyja's smile vanishes. "The last woman Hoenir fancied was Lopt."

Loki straightens. Sometimes he forgets that Freyja is older than he, just as Hoenir and Odin are. And they all had lives before him. "Lopt was female?"

Eyes completely cold, Freyja says, "Lopt was a bitch. She was the one who suggested wagering my hand to the beastly giant who completed Asgard's wall." A feral smile stretches across Freyja's lips. "She paid dearly for it."

Restraining a shudder, Loki turns to the window. "This lady is so uncalculating it is dangerous to her own safety."

Freyja's voice softens. "I will help, of course."

By midafternoon, Anganboða is installed in the hall of the Valkyrie Göndul. Her brother dares not approach her.

Baldur is another matter.

A week after Anganboða's escape, Loki goes to Göndul's hall to pay a visit. It is Anganboða's one afternoon off. Göndul turns him away saying, "She is being swept away by the charms of the crown prince, Trickster. I think he fancies her as a mistress. I shall be sad to lose her, but it is good that such a fortunate ending could come to such an unfortunate girl."

Loki feels himself go hot. For a moment he actually believes Anganboða is being swept away by Baldur, just like everyone else. He makes his exit, but sick fascination compels him to astrally project himself through Göndul's home. He finds Anganboða and Baldur on a bench in the garden. Anganboða sits ramrod straight, face downcast, body like stone.

She looks so miserable. Loki lets the astral projection dissipate. Picking the gate of the garden he is soon approaching the couple from behind, passing curious gardeners and servants as he does.

"I beg thee, Lady. If I have offended, forgive me," Baldur is saying. "I was overwhelmed by my passion for you. Take this small token as a gesture of my good faith." He pulls from his cloak an elaborate wooden box. He opens it and Loki sees an exquisite necklace of Grecian design. "From the House of Thebes, my lady," says Baldur.

"Please keep it," says Anganboða, back rigid. A servant gasps somewhere.

They are dangerous words to a prince. Not for the first time Loki finds himself thinking Anganboða might be slightly touched. He also finds himself smirking.

Baldur stiffens. His upper lip trembles. For a moment Loki thinks the prince might strike her.

Before such a confrontation can occur, Loki says, "Excuse me, your highness. I have a parcel for Lady Anganboða that it is most urgent for me to deliver."

Though taken in by Odin, Loki is technically only a retainer. Baldur is the crown prince. It would be customary to be announced first, but Loki's relationship with Baldur's father is ... special. When Baldur stands and turns to Loki, his face is furious, but he does not admonish him.

By contrast, Anganboða's face is radiant. "Loki!"

Bowing low, Loki does his best to stifle a smile, but it is creeping around the edges of his lips when he straightens. From his cloak he presents her with the parcel he intended to give her. It is a book, ragged, worn, and smelling slightly of mildew, even in the bright sunlight.

Baldur snorts and draws back. "Ah, the Trickster is obviously bestowing a trick on you".

Ignoring him, Loki says, "It is 'The Book of Three,' from Wales, m'lady. I believe you expressed an interest."

Anganboða actually bounces on her feet in delight.

Forgetting himself, Loki smiles. He's won this game.

But for that smile he winds up summoned before Odin in the king's private study not one day later.

Pacing the room, Odin does not meet his eyes. "The crown is a heavy burden, Loki. Monarchs deserve some compensation."

Loki's stomach rumbles, and he puts a hand to it. He isn't quite sure where this is leading, or why he was called away from his breakfast. He looks out the window and restrains a sigh.

"I would ask you to leave the woman Anganboða alone," Odin says.

Loki straightens; his eyes focus on Odin. Odin is not "asking" anything; he is commanding.

Before he can even ask why, Odin says, "You publicly humiliated my son yesterday, Loki—over a trifling dalliance, a passing fancy."

Loki smiles bitterly. "Are you referring to your son's intentions toward the lady, or my own?" He bows to keep from lunging, but his eyes are glued on the other man. "Because if you think my intentions toward her are anything but honorable, you are mistaken." Damnable oath.

Odin stops his pacing. Turning to Loki, he scowls. For a moment his eye is bright, but then he lifts his hand to his forehead and massages his temple. When his hand drops his gaze has a far off dreamy quality, as though he doesn't quite know where he is or what he is doing. It's a gaze Loki often sees when the subject is Baldur.

"Don't be so selfish. It would give him comfort … " Odin says. "That he deserves … the weight of the crown … "

"He doesn't wear the crown yet!" Loki says, his voice a low snarl.

For a moment Loki's words seem to reach Odin. The fog leaves his eye and something calculating replaces it. Walking forward until they are just a pace apart, the older man says, "You are that interested in this woman, Loki? Do you intend to marry her? Give her children? Will you let yourself be bound so?"

Taken off guard, Loki's mouth falls a little. And then shrugging as nonchalantly as he can, he says, "If she will have me." It is surprising how much he means it. Whether it's because he wants her, or because he can't bear the thought of her with anyone else, he isn't really sure.

"You're right," says Odin. "She probably is just a passing dalliance for Baldur."

A weight drops from Loki's shoulders, but almost instantly the fog drops in front of Odin's eye again.

Turning from Loki, he walks toward the bookshelf. "If you still want her when Baldur is done, I will not stand in your way."

"What!" Loki steps forward, a small throwing knife from his sleeve falling into his hand, the air between him and the All Father starting to shimmer.

Odin spins toward him, eyes alight and Loki feels himself go heavy.

"*I said, let him go!*"

Loki blinks. It's Frigga's voice, coming from behind. Odin is no longer in front of him. A beam of sunlight that wasn't on the bookshelf before is illuminating the volumes. How did the sun move so quickly?

Loki turns slowly, feeling heavy and disoriented. Odin is standing just a pace behind him. How did he get there without Loki seeing him move?

In the doorway is Odin's wife, Frigga. Next to her is Hoenir, Mimir mounted on a staff at his side.

Loki was raised by nurses and maids, but when he was a very small child Frigga used to come to him sometimes. She would play with him and read him stories, not so much a mother figure as a beloved aunt. She was very powerful in magic, and cunning, too. She was one of the few who would occasionally outwit Odin—and one of the few whom Odin would permit to do so. The humans called her the goddess of marriage and said Frigga spun the clouds and could see the future. Once when he was nine years old or so, Loki had asked her about this. Smiling, she had said, "Clouds are formed by water vapor. I do spin threads like the Norns though, on occasion."

Loki remembered his heart beating at the mention of the women who supposedly spun fates. "You do see the future!" he had said.

Tilting her head, Frigga had smiled softly. "There is no future, Loki. Only possibilities that become probabilities and probabilities that become realities. The threads help me see the many possibilities. As realities take shape, I trim the threads to see how the probabilities have changed in this reality."

"There is more than one reality?" Loki said.

Frigga laughed "No one knows. Perhaps there are just missed possibilities." She'd rubbed his head affectionately and smiled at him.

It was a very happy memory. Her words had filled Loki with wonder and made his mind pleasantly dizzy with the implications of many realities, and many Lokis.

Now he blinks. When had those pleasant moments with the Queen come to an end? When she was pregnant with Baldur? Certainly by the time her little prince was born.

Even now she is not looking at him. She is scowling at her husband. "Hoenir and Mimir have told me of Loki's affections for the young woman. Do not order them apart." Her voice shakes. "In fact, tell Baldur to stay away from her."

Loki's jaw drops. He cannot see Odin's face, but the older man straightens and murmurs something to Frigga.

Frigga snaps. "The trollop is beneath our son! You are his father and king. Order him to stay away from her."

Odin turns. "You are free to do as you please, Loki."

Loki bows to Odin. As he takes his leave, he bows even lower to Frigga. "Your Highness, I ... "

Frigga's voice is a low hiss. "Stay away from my son, Loki."

Loki lifts his gaze, shocked. Frigga doesn't meet his eyes, only walks toward Odin. Loki looks to Hoenir instead and mouths the words, "Thank you." Looking sad, Hoenir pats him on the shoulder and turns away.

At the time Loki believed that Frigga's interference in Baldur's "courtship" of Aggie was due to her respect for the institution of marriage. Now he wonders if it was more to buy

Baldur time.

"Loki?"

He turns to find Amy wiping her hands on her hips, the bird, Fred, in the cage. She's lost weight since she moved out of her grandmother's house.

"Hi," the girl says. Brow furrowed, she whispers. "I think you should probably know that the house is under surveillance."

Loki blinks and raises an eyebrow. "And I think you're not supposed to tell me that." Nonetheless, he is touched.

She looks away. "No … .but … " She shrugs. And then her phone rings. Pulling it out of her pocket, she says, "That's Steve. I can try to cover for you … "

"Don't," says Loki. "You're a terrible liar."

She visibly relaxes. "Okay. I'm going to answer this then." She puts the phone to her ear. "Hi, Steve."

Fenrir on his arm, Loki walks over behind her and with a smirk says, "Hi, Steve."

"Um, he's here," says Amy. "No, I'm fine. I don't know … " She looks over at Loki. "Why are you here?"

Loki smiles, feeling the weight of his oath almost lifted. "To repay you, of course!"

Amy scowls, just a little bit. Loki hears Steve's voice but can't distinguish the words.

Nodding, Amy says, "Okay, I will. No, I think I will be fine." She hangs up the phone and says, "I'm supposed to ask you how you know the Promethean Sphere is Vanir."

Loki tilts his head, a little surprised that they aren't talking about her payment. "The design," he says. "But it looks … malformed … "

Amy leans in and whispers. "I think that was an accident."

Loki is very curious as to what she knows. And fairly certain she shouldn't be talking about it.

Shaking his head, he puts a finger to her lips. She doesn't withdraw. The trips through Afghanistan and Pakistan's tribal regions were not uneventful. It has been, he suddenly realizes, a rather long while since he has touched anyone in anyway that was not calculated to bring pain or death. The moment feels heavy, her lips extremely soft. He lifts his gaze to her eyes; they've followed the motion of his finger and are now very crossed.

Seductress she is not. He almost snorts. The headache he'd felt earlier begins to rise behind his eyes—when had it gone away?

He takes a breath and then wrinkles his nose. "Is something burning?"

Steve climbs out of his car on the quiet street Amy Lewis lives on. He immediately looks up into the trees. Sure enough the ravens are there. He grits his teeth. This is the third time this week they've shown up.

Bobbing up and down, one of the ravens says, "Think you can escape our sight by driving?"

Hopping on a branch, the other says, "Not in Chicago's traffic, Roger's son!"

Steve wants very, very, very badly to whip out his piece and shoot them, but he doesn't. Instead, he locks his door and walks down the block to another familiar car.

As he does, one of the ravens swoops over his head and

says something to the other in a strange Slavic-sounding tongue. Steve is sure he hears the word Loki. Both rise up into the air and disappear. He glares at the retreating shadows. After some debate it's been decided that ravens don't benefit from the Bill of Rights, even if they do talk. They've tried to bring them down with tranqs, but somehow Steve's feathery shades always escape. He shakes his head and grits his teeth.

A few minutes later he approaches the car Agent Bryant McDowell sits in across the street from Amy's apartment. McDowell and his brother, Brett, were primarily ADUO's tech guys until recently. This is one of Bryant's first field assignments. McDowell is of medium height and build. His hair is a nondescript brown. He isn't ugly or particularly handsome either. You wouldn't look twice at him, which makes him, by appearances at least, the perfect spy.

Bryant is also a comic book aficionado. The first time he met Steve he said, "Captain Steve Rogers, just like in the comic books!"

Steve Rogers was the given name of a popular comic hero. Steve had sighed. He'd heard it before. "Yes, that's right, Agent. If that Captain was a large black man and a *Marine*, not a soldier, I would be him."

As usual, it had earned Steve a laugh, and as expected gotten him in ADUO's tech department's good graces.

Slipping into the seat next to Bryant, Steve asks, "How's she doing?"

Nodding at the radio, Bryant speaks with his slight West Virginia twang. "Listen for yourself, Sir."

Lewis's voice fills the car. *"Like you can cook better?"*

Raising an eyebrow, McDowell looks at Steve. "She burnt the bulgar and tofu."

Steve grimaces.

Loki's voice comes over the speaker. *"You know I could if you had anything in your house that wasn't rabbit food!"* There is a sound like a refrigerator closing.

"It's only a little burned," says Lewis.

There is a snort. *"I'm starving and you couldn't get me to eat that. We should cook Fred. Here birdie, birdie!"*

There is a whack and Loki yells. *"Ow!"* But there is a very audible smirk in his voice. *"You're right, he's too small. Fenrir, come here. Ow! Ow! Ow! Stop hitting me!"*

"This guy is dangerous?" says McDowell. Steve just shakes his head. This is why the guy is dangerous—pretending to be harmless is just a game to him. He can set things on fire or kill a man with a stick, and then dance with your granny, and make jokes in your kitchen.

There is a feminine huff. *"Did you come here just to insult my cooking?"*

"I came to repay you."

Lewis huffs again. *"You do realize that anything you give me ADUO will probably confiscate?"*

Steve blinks. That's true. A lot of people want to know where Loki is from, where he's living, how he's living. Anything Loki gives Lewis will be taken as evidence. The only reason there isn't a warrant for Loki's arrest is the word from Prometheus, and quite frankly because if there was a warrant no one's really sure how they'd catch him. Prometheus' word or no, ADUO's Director Stuart Jameson would like to get Loki behind bars. But Steve's convinced him that trying to arrest Loki will only piss him off. For now, they think their best option is to study him, try to figure out the extent of what he can do, and how much he knows about the thing under

Chicago's streets—the thing that is still growing.

"Someone's not happy," says McDowell. Steve looks at the speaker. The silence at the other end is ominous.

Loki's voice crackles. *"And I suppose you'd be hopeless at lying to them."*

There is a moment of silence and then Loki says, *"Get dressed, we're going out to eat."*

"Where?"

There are some rummaging sounds and then Loki's voice again. *"Somewhere you can wear this."*

"I'm not wearing the heels."

Steve blinks, looks at the speaker and has a small epiphany. You can *hear* a man roll his eyes.

"Very well," says Loki.

A few minutes later Lewis says, *"What about your guitar?"*

"Leave it."

Then there is silence.

Pulling a pair of binoculars from his eyes, McDowell scowls at the small garden apartment. "They disappeared—*literally*. Should we go in?"

Steve nods.

McDowell has a key to Lewis's place, and the door opens easily. But the dog thing Fenrir is barking loud enough to wake the dead. As soon as they enter, the dog lunges for Steve's ankles. His natural instinct is to kick it, but McDowell scoops it up, catches it in a practiced hold, and throws it in the bathroom. The damn thing does not let up. Steve can hear it throwing itself at the door.

Upstairs the neighbors shuffle. "We better make this fast," says Steve slipping his phone from his pocket. He dials Lewis's number and curses when he hears her phone ring on the kitchen counter.

"Uh, Agent Rogers ... " says McDowell. Steve looks over. McDowell has on plastic gloves; the guitar case is opened in front of him. It's filled with neatly stacked 1, 10, 20, 50 and 100 dollar bills.

Steve looks at the top of the case and sees traces of white powder. He has a bad feeling about this.

"I think we should bring this in." says McDowell.

Rubbing his temple, Steve sighs. "Yeah."

They're in the car, heading back to headquarters with the guitar case in tow a few minutes later when Steve's phone begins to vibrate with a text. The number isn't familiar, but he picks up anyway.

Hey, it's Amy. Forgot my cell. Am ok. In a cab.

Steve answers as fast as his large fingers can on the tiny keys. *Where?*

He stares at the three little dots on his screen telling him Amy's texting back. Instead of an answer he gets. *Hi Steve! It's Loki. I am not telling. I am throwing this phone out the window now. Bye ;-)*

Steve scowls. The so-called-God-of-Mischief uses emoticons. It disturbs him almost as much as the white powder in the guitar case.

"Wow, this is a really nice restaurant," says Amy.

Loki looks around. "According to Google," he says. The main dining room is in subdued blues and grays. The ceiling is as high as the prison cell in the tower. Servers in black suits move around them with the precision of dancers. It's been a long time since he's had a really good meal. Cera is bouncing around the room grumbling about ostentatiousness and petty bourgeois, but Loki craves calories that actually taste good. He's so hungry lately—and eating is becoming such a chore.

"Can you pay for this?" Amy whispers as the maitre de leads them to their table.

Scowling at her, Loki whispers back. "Of course."

Amy's eyes narrow. "And you promise the money is real and not stolen?"

Loki smiles. During his journey he dug up some gold he had buried by a wall in Moscow for emergencies just like this one. He has some more in various capitals around the world—but may not need to touch them.

Since he's been back in the states he's discovered derivative trading. He does it just to soothe his mind when he isn't sending out astral projections to spy on ADUO, or trying his hand at hacking.

He will not, however, be using any legitimate funds for this meal. ADUO would trace it. He will be paying with the cash he stole from the same source as Amy's repayment in the guitar case.

Biting back a gleeful smile, he adopts an air of seriousness. "You have my oath that I now have a source of revenue that is completely legal." All true! Just a slight bit of misdirection.

… That Amy immediately falls for. Eyes widening, Amy says, "You have a job?"

Loki scowls at her again. "Don't insult me. I won't be a wage slave like you."

"Down with the proletariat!" Cera screeches, her magical voice unheard to everyone else in the room. Loki shoots the mist a warning glance as they sit down. His head throbs suddenly and he can barely pay attention to the waiter. "We'll take three of the nine course prixe fixe and two wine pairings," he says—he had read the menu on Google.

The waiter shifts on his feet. "Are you expecting a third person?"

"No," says Loki massaging his temple. "I'll eat two."

"Sir," says the waiter. "I don't think that is wise."

Loki is about to snap, but Amy pipes up. "He can manage. Trust me."

Loki relaxes infinitesimally, but still isn't fit to really listen as Amy says something more about eating fish but nothing with hooves or feathers.

"This is a waste of time," says Cera. "She's not going to just tell you."

"I need to eat," Loki mumbles in Russian.

"So steal a few pounds of butter," Cera says.

Loki's stomach drops; he's had to resort to that of late. Feeling a bead of sweat on his brow, he tries to smile as benevolently as he can. Leaning toward Amy, he whispers conspiratorially. "So you think it was an accident that the Promethean Sphere grew?"

Amy leans forward. "Yes. From what I read in Steve's file … I think ADUO is actually really afraid … It wasn't supposed to grow."

"Oh," Cera whispers. "She is going to tell you."

Loki's headache melts away.

He does not roll his eyes at the red mist in the air. Instead, he leans closer to Amy. The new position gives him a glorious view of her breasts. He does his best to keep his eyes on her face.

By the third course he's drawn out everything she knows about Steve and Cera's run in with Odin. He doesn't even have to work hard at it—which, actually, is a little disappointing.

Loki knew most of the story from Cera. As soon as Odin had touched the World Seed, Cera had read the All Father's mind, realized he was the Tsar of Asgard, and panicked. Cera tried to suck Odin into the In-Between—the emptiness beyond the World Tree. Odin was strong enough to resist, unlike the religious fanatics who dumped Cera beneath the Board of Trade building, and ADUO's little robot.

" ... and then Steve spit on the raven," Amy says.

Loki almost chokes on the caviar he is putting in his mouth. Cera hadn't told him that.

He snorts happily. "You mortals are just getting so impudent!" And hadn't she called Thor the God of Blunder? He sighs happily. "I like you more and more."

Amy's cheeks turn red. She thinks he means her and not humankind in general. Ah, well, let her think he's enamored. He smiles. "How did you get Steve's file?"

Amy's blush spreads to her neck. She looks to the side. "I wasn't really supposed to see it; it is classified ... "

"You stole it!" he says, feeling a sudden wave of admiration.

Her eyes shoot back to him. "No!"

Loki blinks.

"I found it ... " she says slowly.

Chuckling, Loki raises an eyebrow. "And then you read the entire thing?"

"He gave me a really boring filing job to do!" Studying a spot on the tablecloth, she says, "His file was more interesting."

Loki swirls the wine in his glass. Loki's not particularly good at following rules, but he respects them in principle.

He'd been a retainer of Odin for a very, very, long time. Looking over his glass, he says, "Naughty, Amy, very naughty … ."
And then telling him about it, too.

As if reading that thought, she says, "They shouldn't be keeping this information from you. They should be working with you. There is something that may be very dangerous to everyone and you might be the only person who can help."

Putting his glass down, Loki puts his elbows on the table and leans toward her. "Has it occurred to you I may be the bad guy?"

He's not sure why he says it; he shouldn't plant that idea in her head. Maybe he said it just to tease, or maybe, as Sigyn says, he just has to make things difficult. He frowns, and takes a sip of his wine. It turns bitter on his mouth, as Sigyn used to say.

"You're not," she says without even looking at him. "Oooh, here comes the next course … " She looks sideways at him. "I don't think I've ever had a meal this good in my entire life."

The little kernel of doubt he planted has been completely dismissed. Worse yet, he feels something uncoiling in his stomach, something he hasn't felt since Cronus and the peasants, and Hothur and Nanna. It's faith and it's heady like a drug.

He can't decide if he loves it or hates it.

CHAPTER 3

" ... and then he ate most of the chocolates on the after dinner chocolate cart thingy," Miss Lewis says. "I'm fairly certain that even in humans it would have been enough to cause theobromine poisoning. It would have put an English mastiff in the emergency room."

It's the kind of off-the-wall comment that Miss Lewis has occasionally made during her debriefing that reminds Steve there is a very clever mind buried beneath her youth and naivete.

"Theobromine?" says Steve.

"It's an alkaloid found in chocolates." Glancing up at the ceiling Amy says, "The wire mesh is on the ceiling, too. Why?"

"That, Miss Lewis, isn't important." Actually, it is the same wire mesh used for Promethean Spheres, and it's very important. Steve's tech guys have covered the ceiling, floor and walls of the conference room with it, hoping to keep apparitions of Loki out. In some places they've stretched the mesh tightly; in other places it hangs awkwardly. They ran out of staples toward the end and used duct tape. The tech guys think it's great. Steve thinks it looks like he's wandered into the den of a mad spider. He suggested he wear a tinfoil hat, too—no one seemed to find that funny.

He looks at the screen of the magic detector by his side. The mad spider Promethean web seems to be working. No sign of Loki in here, and they were reasonably sure he'd sent one of his 'apparitions' into the building with Miss Lewis this morning.

"Why don't you tell us about the rest of the evening?" Steve says.

Lewis looks back down at them. "He took me home. I asked him in the cab if he really got Thor to dress up as a woman to get his hammer back from the giant, and he said it was true! Loki even managed to convince Thor his magic wasn't enough on its own to disguise them, so Thor put on a real dress and makeup!"

She grins.

Steve and Bryant stare at her.

Looking embarrassed, she says, "It's funnier if you've seen Thor." Looking down at the table she adds, "He's big and has a beard."

"Uh - huh," says Bryant.

"Did he get the hammer back?" says Steve, smiling and trying to look interested in this part.

"Yes," she says. "And then the cab dropped us off at home. He noticed you guys took his guitar."

Bryant and Steve look at one another.

"Had to," says Steve. "Evidence."

"Did he seem upset?" Bryant asks.

"No," says Lewis looking between the two of them. "Are you going to give it back? I mean, it's just a guitar, right?"

"We won't give it back," Bryant and Steve say in unison.

"Geez," says Lewis.

"You're dismissed," says Steve.

A few minutes later Bryant and Steve are walking down the hall.

"She belongs in a witness protection program," Bryant says. "She's obviously infatuated with him."

Steve squeezes the styrofoam cup in his hand and it cracks with a pop. "I'll give her that option," says Steve.

"Don't give her the option. Make her take that option," says Bryant.

Steve's jaw tenses. "I've got a conference call with Merryl," is all he says. Stepping into his office, he nearly collides with two agents who are starting to put up Promethean wire.

"You guys can hold off on that for now," Steve says.

Nodding at him, they exit the room, closing the door and leaving a rolled up bundle of wire. As they exit, Steve notices that the "magic detector" next to him has started to glow. He sits down at his desk and pretends to be absorbed in some paperwork.

He's barely raised his pen when a familiar voice says, "You stole my guitar case and the money I owed Miss Lewis, Steven. I am very disappointed."

Steve doesn't even look up, just clicks the pen and starts signing some papers on his desk. "Yep."

"Are you going to give it back to her?" says Loki, or the apparition of Loki, leaning over Steve's desk.

"Nope," says Steve.

"Tsk, tsk, and I thought one of the loveliest things about this country was its respect for property rights."

Steve pushes back in his chair. Loki is wearing a dark gray suit with a mint green shirt. His hair is ginger again, and too long. He's got an obnoxious smirk on his face.

Meeting the apparition's gaze, Steve says, "I don't think Miss Lewis would accept the repayment if she discovered you stole it from a drug lord and ignited a turf war." They identified the white powder on the guitar case. It came from a den on the west side where over $100,000 in cash had disappeared—only a few grand of it actually had been in the case, so Loki's got a wad hidden somewhere. The gang in charge of the den blames a rival gang, of course.

Loki smiles. "Brilliant, wasn't it? I repay my debts and help rid your city of its criminals all at once."

"Yes, it's brilliant," says Steve. "Two children have already been hit in the crossfire." And this is why Steve really should insist that Amy Lewis go on the witness protection program. Anyone who incites this kind of chaos is bound to bring pain to everyone in their orbit.

The apparition lifts his head. For a moment his eyes go completely black, and he stares down at Steve with an emotion Steve can't place.

"But I guess that wouldn't bother you," says Steve, looking back down at his papers.

His papers are suddenly rising up to his nose, and he hears carpet tear. Looking up he sees Loki tip the other side of the desk upwards. Steve tries to move, but the edge of his desk already has him trapped in his chair, and he's flipping over, chair, desk and all. His head hits the thin carpeting on the floor and bounces, and the edge of the desk knocks the wind from him. He's pinned. Loki springs over the tipped desk, a dark shadow silhouetted by fluorescent lights.

A hand, solid and real, grabs Steve's collar. "I am not like *your friend* Odin!" Loki screams, so close Steve catches a whiff of peppermint and soap.

Steve's hands go to Loki's. But he's already gone. Disappeared ... Steve turns his head. The little magic detector is on the floor beside him and it is glowing brightly and beeping like mad. Grabbing the device, he pushes the desk off him and climbs unsteadily to his feet. The machine's beeping slows and the light dims. He hears running footsteps outside his office. He feels a gust of air, like his door has just opened, but he doesn't see it move.

And then all of a sudden Bryant bursts in. "What happened?"

"Block all the exits," Steve says, knowing it's too late. But he also feels better about not putting Miss Lewis on the witness protection program.

He's following Bryant out of his office when he notices that the roll of Promethean wire mesh that had been sitting by his door is gone.

Love is a tease. When you first fall in love with a woman you think you will never be able to get enough of her, that your passion will never be sated. That is how Loki felt through the first early years of his marriage to Aggie. But of course, eventually the passion in their relationship did wane. It wasn't as though Loki hadn't been warned. Odin always said, "Show me the most beautiful woman in the nine realms and I will show you a man tired of fucking her."

But the true inconvenience of love, Loki decides, is that even as passion wanes, love is still there. If anything, his love for Anganboða grows stronger over the years. Maybe it is from sharing books, and making jokes at Baldur's expense. Or maybe it was her forgiveness when he wagered their house on a 'sure thing' and lost—though he promptly won their home back on a long shot. Afterwards he put their small hall in her name so that their short experience of homelessness didn't happen again.

And even if the sex most of the time is by rote, there are times when after a lull the fires are stoked again, and it is better than anything Loki has experienced with anyone else.

Loki knows that tonight will be one of those times. He is standing on the boat Skidbladnir afloat on the seas of Asgard with Odin, Frigga, Baldur and Thor. With them is Frey, leader of the Vanir, his sister Freyja, guards, and ladies of the court of Vanaheim.

Anganboða is also there, playing maid to Frigga. Anganboða is no maid, but one of Frigga's ladies was sick. Though Anganboða is married to Loki, she isn't considered truly a woman; she has borne no children—and not by lack of trying. The court blames Aggie—it is always the woman's fault. But Loki knows it is him, that's why Odin doesn't like him mucking about with Hoenir isn't it? Loki makes life go wrong.

Right now Loki is not at fault though, even though people on the boat are screaming. The ladies are to one side, being 'guarded' by Baldur and a few other cowards. Thor, Odin, Freyja and Frey stand at the other side with Loki and Aggie. Freyja has her sword ready, Thor has Mjolnir in his hands. But Odin only looks bemused; Loki knows there is nothing to fear.

Typically, lost in her own world, Anganboða did not hear the cry from Baldur for all the ladies to retreat to his side of the boat. Or maybe she did and chose to ignore him. Either way, her calm, the wonder on her face, her heedlessness to the crown prince; they are all making Loki remember what he first saw in her.

The water next to the boat swirls and a serpentine body, nearly as wide as the boat itself, with dark green scales rises up, a blue fish-like-fin at its top.

"It rises again," says Freyja, as the body and the fin disappear beneath the waves.

"It is Jörmungandr, the world serpent," says Aggie breathlessly, and Loki recognizes the fins and the scales from a book they borrowed from Hoenir just recently.

Not looking at her, Odin says, "Yes. We are in no danger." If there was a slight bit of tension between Loki's shoulders, it disappears instantly. Jörmungandr patrols the seas around Asgard, and is a servant of Odin as much as he; but neither Freyja nor Thor put down their weapons.

The fin and body disappear and there is a collective sigh from the boat, but then out of the water shoots an enormous head, as wide as the boat, as tall as a man. The boat rocks and people scream. The serpent has a huge maw, with glistening sharp teeth. But what is truly startling to look upon is its forehead. It is high and flat, directly above its jaws—almost hominid. Its eyes are to the side and small, where its gaze falls is difficult to tell. Magic hangs in the air around it, thick and as green as the dark seaweed in its teeth.

From its mouth comes a voice like the roll of thunder. "All Father," it says. "And I see you, Thor ... is that the lovely Freyja ... and Loki?"

"Begone, beast!" shouts Thor.

Jörmungandr huffs. "So rude is your son, Odin. But who have we here?"

The beast lowers its head so that its bottom jaw is level with Aggie's face, long whiskers that sprout from its chin coiling at her feet. Loki's heart stops. But he is not so foolish as to show anger or fear. "My wife

Anganboða, Sea Thread."

"Pleased to meet you," says Aggie, holding up a hand as though to touch its face but catching herself.

The boat creaks and rises a little, and then Jörmungander rubs his mighty whiskered chin against Aggie's hand. There are intakes of breath from across the ship. To Loki's immense bemusement, Aggie just laughs with delight even as Baldur shouts, "Leave her alone, foul serpent!"

Loki is sure to aim a self-satisfied smile in Baldur's direction and lay a possessive hand on Aggie's hip.

"Pleased to meet you, little mother," says Jörmungander. Mother is something one would call any wife in Asgard. Of course Aggie isn't a mother. But Jörmungander's words are heard by all present, and before Aggie has borne a child, she becomes 'Mother of Monsters.'

After several decades, Aggie does, eventually get pregnant. Loki is frantic and wonders if he should go on some sort of quest with Thor for the duration to be on the safe side. But times are distressingly calm, and he remains in Asgard.

Aggie goes into labor on a day when Loki is helping Odin craft new terms for World Gate access for the dwarves. The dwarves have 'kindly' acquiesced to withdraw from Midgard—under threat of war. Odin's never fully explained to Loki why the withdrawal was decreed, only that it was so that 'Midgard be for humans.' Now it is done, and Odin is seeking to soothe short trading partners.

Loki doesn't leave Odin's side when he hears news that labor has begun. It just isn't done by men. He sends apparitions of himself to wait outside the delivery room. He doesn't go into the room, even in astral form. It just isn't done. Beside the door also waits Fenrir, a giant wolf that followed Loki home from Jotunheim one day—Aggie took a fancy to the beast. In the court they whisper Fenrir is another one of Aggie's 'children.'

Loki has been dismissed by Odin and is walking home very quickly when Aggie begins to scream. He breaks into a jog. Before he even reaches his home, Aggie has quieted, and there is the wail of a babe and Loki is running. He is just entering the front door when Aggie begins to scream again. This time there are words. "What are you doing? Give me my baby! Let me see! Let me see!" and then frantically, "Loki!"

By the door to the bedroom, Fenrir starts to whimper. A midwife passes through Loki's apparition shaking her head, a wailing bundle covered in a sheet. She runs into the real Loki and drops the bundle with a scream.

Catching the wailing, writhing, tiny form flailing against the cloth, Loki shouts, "What are you doing?"

"It's for the best," says the midwife. "I'll take care of it for you … "

"Take care of it?" says Loki, yelling to be heard above the wailing. But as the words spill from his mouth, he knows. The midwife means to kill the child, his child, the one whose lungs are exploding with ear-splitting effect. The one she's already draped in a funeral shroud.

"Get out!" Loki screams. Beside him Fenrir begins to growl. The woman's face goes white and she runs.

Frantically, Loki casts the sheet aside and looks down. The wailing ceases as though by enchantment, and the babe no longer struggles, just gasps air hard and fast. It … she … has limbs that seem bent at erratic angles, too thin, too spindly, and he knows somehow they are wrong. But he can hardly look at that, because what he sees first and foremost is his baby's skin. On one side she is pale, jotunn, with a gray eye like Loki's. On the other side she is blue, like the horizon of the Midgard sky on a cloudless day, and her eye on that side is completely black, like he is staring at the infinity of the void. Though she is only a few minutes old, the air around her is thick with magic of the same blue. Her magic is so strong where Loki's skin touches her, his own fingers turn that same color.

He does not know how a creature like himself could be part of a creation so beautiful.

Valli and Nari weren't as magical as Helen. But Loki loved them, too. And he lost them all. There is something about losing a child; it seems to tear against the order of the universe. Maybe that's why it keeps happening to him.

His apparition, standing across the street from the dilapidated house where he stole the drug money, grits his teeth. There are men coming and going, and women he'd recognize as whores in any realm.

He feels sick to his stomach and he wants to set the whole building on fire. Maybe that will end the 'turf war' he's started. He looks down. Or make it worse. Nothing he plans works out quite the way he intends.

He hears gunfire in the dilapidated house and lets his projection fade.

He blinks and his physical form takes a sip of coffee in the small cafe near Amy's apartment. Since the neighborhood is Little Italy, he's taken the disguise of an elderly Italian grandmother type for the occasion—though beneath the disguise he wears his armor and his sword Lævatein is at his hip.

Amy was right. ADUO will confiscate anything he gives to her. Nor, he suspects, would she want the money if she knew where it came from.

Red mist curls around his feet.

"Why must you repay her?" Cera says. Loki just scowls. Because he knows the danger of lies, how one can lose track of what is truth ... that is why he always, always, keeps his oaths. But he says to Cera, "She gives me access to ADUO, and to you."

"You are wise!" says Cera, and she slips into the air and away.

Loki lifts his head. Where is Miss Lewis? He sends an apparition to her home, just a few blocks away.

It is dusk, and the TV at the front of Amy's apartment is on, but Amy is in the kitchen by the back door. She is dressed in black. Giving a hasty pat on the head to Fenrir, the girl takes a deep breath and then darts outside. She runs through the tiny backyard and slips quietly through a back gate, looking quickly from side to side as she does so—as though she's trying to run away from someone.

Loki tilts his head. She is running away from someone, the agents who are charged with observing her. How curious. Ignoring the stares he stands a little too quickly for an old woman, walks to a nearby alley, and then down another, and lets himself fade into invisibility.

In his invisible form he slips behind Amy just as she pokes her head around the corner of a house.

"Coast is clear," she mutters.

"Actually," says Loki, not bothering to make himself visible, "there is an agent in that car just to the right, though you can't see him at the moment."

Amy jumps around with a yelp and narrows her eyes in not-quite Loki's direction.

"Oh, there he is," says Loki as the agent's head pops up into view. "He must have dropped something."

Putting her hands on her hips, she says, "Well?"

He tilts his head. Have they told her about the money and its source? It would be the sort of thing she'd upbraid him for. And she might take Bryant up on the 'witness relocation program' offer Loki's apparitions have heard about.

She's staring at a point just below his collarbone, which is disconcerting. He lets himself become visible again. "Well, what?" he snaps, prepared for the worst.

Bouncing a little on her feet she says, "Are you going to help?"

She doesn't know about the drug money. He actually feels relieved.

Waving an arm, she snaps him from his reverie. "Make me invisible!"

And suddenly, everything is a fun game. He smiles and taps his chin. "Why should I help you escape from your masters? Were you another girl I would suspect a tryst with a lover you wished to keep hidden, but since it's you—"

She holds up a small beige device that has a faintly glowing face at the end of a handle. "So I can get to the micro lab at UIC's med school in the next ten minutes and put the glowy-organic looking stuff inside this thing under a scope."

Loki draws back. He's seen these devices at ADUO but he hadn't divined their purpose. "Humans can't detect magic," he says.

Scowling a little, Amy says, "Really?" She pushes it closer to Loki and it glows brighter. She smiles. "I think we can."

Loki stares at the glow. They're using Vanir technology to restrain magic—he's investigated the wire mesh they used to attempt to contain Cera, and it is definitely Vanir in origin. In attempting to escape from it, Cera had panicked and fused part of herself with the mesh, ironically, making it physically stronger and more difficult to get her out.

Of course, to contain magic you have to know it's there.

Loki is suddenly very curious about this little device. Smiling, he puts a hand on her arm and lets invisibility fall over them like a shroud. "Let's go," he says.

The stairway of the main building of the University of Illinois Chicago's Medical School is dark and too hot. A heater is clicking. It smells like burnt dust.

Loki's arm is on hers. He held her arm the same way last time he made her invisible, when they slipped by the ADUO agents to get to the restaurant.

Amy's grateful for his arm. You don't realize how much you see of yourself until you can't see yourself. Glimpses of hands and feet, breasts, and the tip of her nose are little signals to her brain that she exists. Without them, it is disorientating.

Amy bites her lip. "I think you can make us visible now."

She doesn't feel anything, but she blinks and the tip of her nose comes into focus—or unfocus, rather. She sighs with relief.

"Come on," she says, pulling Loki toward an elevator bank. They pass some med students on the way. They don't even glance at Loki and Amy. Amy swallows. She misses veterinary school. She knows her job with ADUO is only for a year, but sometimes she feels like everything she learned is slipping away. That her brain is turning to mush. She is so bored, except for present company. She squeezes Loki's arm.

She catches herself as they step into the elevator. Dropping his arm, she smiles up at him apologetically. Loki is focused on the numbers above the door and doesn't seem to notice.

He was 'wearing' a suit when he first popped up behind her this evening, but now he's wearing jeans, a gray V-neck tee shirt, and sneakers. She blinks—exactly what one of the med students had been wearing. As if aware of her gaze, he turns to her and smirks.

She rolls her eyes.

The elevator stops at the Microbiology Department and they step out. There is a long white hallway with locked lab doors on either side. Loki peeks into the windows of one of the doors.

"Microscopes!" he says. Looking pleased, he turns to her. "Your people put a lot of effort into educating your healers."

Amy peers into the little window and sees lab tables lined with scopes. Nothing special. "I guess."

"Hoenir had the only microscope in Asgard. You have dozens here!"

"Yeah, ummm … .and we have them in some elementary schools, most junior highs and almost every high school, too," says Amy.

Loki turns his head to her, his eyes wide. "So much general access to the magics of your world," he says.

It takes a moment for Amy to process that. School was always an escape for her, a place away from her mother and her revolving door of husbands and boyfriends. Someplace where there was stability and order. Math and science were her favorite subjects because they were so much less subjective than history and literature. In particular she loved biology because of its connection with living things. Her veterinary school education had taken her deeper into microbiology and histology, and she found she loved those subjects, too—even though the critters didn't come with cute furry tails and whiskers. Life, on whatever scale, is fascinating to her.

She stares at Loki. "I have a feeling I'd hate Asgard."

Loki draws up and tilts his head, a thoughtful expression on his face.

At that moment a familiar voice booms from down the hall. "Amy! It's great to see you!"

Amy turns and smiles. It's her friend James from her undergrad days. Amy has been called an "over achiever" in her life, but James puts her to shame. Just a few years older than her, he's just finished his Ph.D. in microbiology and has a bachelor's in computer science. He's healthy, tall, handsome … and married. Her eye catches at the flash of his ring. In typical perfectionist fashion, he's managed to find a wife who is a beautiful, brilliant neuroscientist.

Laughing, James slaps a hand on her shoulder, nearly knocking her over. "Great to see you here. Katherine and I were so sorry you couldn't make the wedding."

"Yes, well … " she says.

He turns his eyes to Loki. "And who have we here?"

Before Amy can answer, Loki holds out his hand and smiles. "Loki." There's something a little bit challenging in his tone.

If there is a challenge there, James doesn't see it. He takes Loki's hand and pumps vigorously. "Ha, ha, ha! Your parents are mythology buffs! Mine are literature buffs! I was a coin toss away from being named Rudyard after Kipling. Are you studying veterinary medicine, too?"

Loki tilts his head. "No, my area of interest is … physics."

Amy winces. Oh, no, he's going to talk about physics with James.

Dropping his hand, James beams and gives a covert wink

at Amy. "Really, my brother is a physicist working for NASA. Where did you go to school? What is your specialty?"

"I went to Oxford," Loki says, chin high, and sounding far too pleased with himself. Amy winces again. Of all the schools …

"I went to Oxford on a Rhodes scholarship," says James, happily leading them down the hall to his lab. "Who did you do your thesis with?"

Amy bites her lip, but Loki is saved from having to answer by a young man walking up to James, book in hand. "Dr. Swanson, I really don't know why I need to know what bacteria survives in space to become a surgeon!"

For the first time, James' smile drops. Amy hears him mutter, "Med students." Turning back to Amy and Loki, he says, "I have to get to my lecture. Amy, you know where to go."

Amy and Loki watch as he starts back the way they came, the med student next to him, saying something Amy can't make out.

"You know, Amy," Loki says quietly, "I never thought I'd see the disadvantage in the ease of modern Midgardian air travel."

At that moment James turns around and calls down the hall. "Remember, in return for this favor, you're going to tell me where you got that feather!"

Loki looks sideways at Amy, a glint in his eye.

With a gulp, Amy runs into James' lab and hustles over to a counter with a microscope hooked up to a television monitor.

Loki follows and shuts the door behind them. With a too knowing grin on his face, he says, "Feather?"

Putting the 'magic detector' on the lab counter, Amy doesn't meet his eyes. "I may have sent James a picture of a hadrosaur feather. He might have a slight interest in dinosaurs, a slight familiarity with comparative anatomy and avian and reptilian histology, and a general burning curiosity … and might have recognized it as being not quite feather like, but definitely not scale like."

She swallows. She was on strict orders from ADUO not to talk of her trip to Alfheim, or about Loki, to anyone. Technically she didn't talk about anything, though. She just sent a picture.

"Mmmmm-hmmm," says Loki, walking over to join her, the magic detector glowing brighter as he does. She takes a nail file out of her purse. There is a seam in the plastic that runs along the side of the detection device. If she runs the nail file through it, she can loosen the outer casing and open it. She's already done it once at her desk when she was being ignored … as usual. Swallowing again, she looks up at Loki.

Biting her lip nervously she says, "Ummm … so I'm really not supposed to be doing this. This little thing is supposedly worth 30 grand and it doesn't even have the fancy gadgets and meters on it. It's one of the prototypes."

Bending close, Loki whispers, "I won't tell."

Amy lets out a breath and relaxes a little—but not too much. Loki is really close, leaning over her shoulder and making her nervous … or something. Running the file along the seam she says, "Bryant just gave it to me because he said I had a right to know if you were spying on me while I was in the shower or dressing."

Pulling the nail file out of the seam she blushes. "Of course, I know you'd never do that."

Loki says nothing, but he draws back a step. Amy hazards a glance at him.

One eyebrow cocked, Loki purses his lips. "You know, Amy, sometimes I think you're very clever."

Smiling, she turns back to the gadget in her hands.

"Other times," says Loki, "I think that you are just a child with breasts."

Amy scowls, then shakes her head. "Ha, ha, ha. Very funny."

He sighs, but she's not really paying attention. The device is coming apart. Other detectors may have fancy electronics and gizmos inside, but this one is surprisingly low tech. There are just two glass plates in the top above the handle; sandwiched between them is what looks like agar. On it is a light blue substance covering the plates in an irregular pattern. Well, it is light blue most of the time. Now with Loki around it's glowing and almost white.

Loki steps close again.

Holding the plates up to the light she says. "See that, it looks organic. Now to grab a sample … "

As she preps a slide, Loki leans in so close his nose is inches away from the mystery substance. The plate flashes brightly, and he pulls back.

Amy grabs a Q Tip, swipes a bit of the mystery substance off a plate, dips the Q Tip onto the slide she's prepped, and puts on the cover. Slipping the slide beneath the scope, Amy peers into the lenses and focuses. And then she backs away from the slide and puts her hand to her mouth.

Loki looks over to her, his eyes slightly wide. "What is it?"

Shaking her head, Amy stares at the long thin bacteria on the screen. They look like blades of pale blue-colored grass with striations crossing them horizontally. "I thought it would be something exotic—that's why I wanted the monitor, so I could take pictures ... "

She thought she might have to spend hours trying to find a near relative.

She bites her lip. "But this is so obviously Cyanobacteria. What species I have no idea, but definitely Cyanobacteria."

"Cyanobacteria," says Loki slowly. "Does it have another common name?"

"It's most commonly known as algae ... blue green algae," Amy says.

Loki blinks. "Little organisms that float on water?"

"Yes," says Amy. "They feed on sunlight."

"These don't feed on sunlight," says Loki looking down at the glass plate. "They feed on magic. Light is their waste product."

Amy's eyes go wide. "Like midichlorians! Like in *Star Wars*! "

Loki turns to her and blinks. "What are midichlorians? And what do these little organisms have to do with your country's space defense system?"

She didn't make him watch *Star Wars*! She'll have to remedy that later. But now she's bouncing on the balls of her feet, incredibly excited. "You've got little organelles in your body that feed on magic and they allow you to convert it into energy!"

Loki scowls. Then he snickers. "A fine hypothesis, but no. Not right. Trust me, I don't shit light." He snickers. "Or fart rainbows."

At that he doubles over laughing and has to sit down on a chair. "Though my wives would have preferred it if I did!"

Amy stares at him. What is with men and potty humor?

Getting annoyed, Amy puts her hands on her hips. "So how do you use magic? And why can't I?"

Loki straightens and wipes his eyes. "Oh, because you lack the proper neural tissue in adequate quantities. It's called ... it's called ... "

He looks away. "Well, you don't have a name for it ... I suppose that makes sense. You might not have discovered it since you have so little of it." Turning, he gives her a look that is almost sympathetic. "Your species is retarded."

Deciding to let that insult drop in the interest of science, Amy takes a step closer to him. "Where is it? In the frontal cortex? In the brainstem? Maybe in the subventricular zone?"

Loki stares at her. "In my species it is everywhere there is neural tissue."

"Is it part of white matter?" says Amy. "Gray matter?"

His mouth drops a little, and then he shrugs. "I don't really know. Biology isn't my thing." The side of his mouth quirks up. "I never did get into the soft sciences."

Amy's eyes go wide. She wants to say something biting about maybe if he knew a little more about biology he might be able to heal things instead of just blowing things up. But something tells her that would go badly. Instead, she just stands glaring at him, nearly blind with rage.

Seemingly oblivious to the violence in her glare, Loki wanders over to the plate again. "But these little critters—they do eat magic. They're from Vanaheim. I've heard of them, though I've never actually seen them ... "

There is a flash of light from the plate, and Loki takes a deep, strangled breath. Amy looks over with alarm. He's trembling.

"Loki?" she says, moving quickly to his side. He starts to fall backwards and Amy whips a lab stool around for him to sit on.

He falls onto it, his weight pushing it back and its feet scraping the floor.

"Loki?" Amy says again. But he's staring into space seemingly oblivious. And then his pupils blow out wide until there is no color at all in his irises. The skin around his eyes and his fingers starts to turn blue—and then the blue spreads across his face, and up his arms, like a wave rolling over sand. Where the blue meets his hairline, his hair begins to turn black; where it meets his clothing, the t-shirt and jeans turn to his armor. He's actually wearing his sword. Some pieces of the plating on his left arm seem to be missing and she can see his limbs are turning blue, too.

He stares ahead. Perfectly still. And Amy catches her breath. He just looks so … magical.

He is with a man and a woman, young, familiar and unfamiliar. They are by a river, beneath the stars; and from the constellations Loki knows they are in Vanaheim. The man turns to Loki and says, "No ale shall pour, unless it is brought to us both." They have no torches, and no fire, but it doesn't matter because the slow water of the river is glowing.

And it would be mesmerizing if the woman weren't more so. She is, he supposes, beautiful. But there is more to it than that. The softness of her form is an oasis Loki wants to dive into. Her eyes are soft, too, as soft as her magic, pale and gold—but abundant, full, and generous. As generous as her lips that are spilling into a smile. She turns, goes to the river, and brings back three crystal goblets full of the shining water. In her hands the water in the goblets swirls as bright as the sun. She passes one cup to Loki and one to the other man. "In lieu of ale," the water fetcher says.

He is almost afraid to take the goblet for fear the light will dissipate. But the light only grows brighter as he tilts it to his lips ... almost bright enough to burn through the dark velvet magic that swirls around the other man, his eyes piercing, his face smiling, his own goblet a star in a dark night.

A hand touches his cheek. The woman with the pale gold magic ...

"Loki?"

Loki blinks, and Amy pulls her hand away as though she's been burned.

"What happened?" she whispers, her brows drawn together.

His jaw tenses. He's hallucinating now? As the Midgardians say, *oh fuck.*

He rubs his face with his hands. "I think I'm just hungry." Although he actually doesn't feel particularly hungry. He doesn't have that horrible gnawing feeling in his stomach at the moment. And his head is clear.

He meets Amy's eyes and smiles.

Her brow relaxes, her lips turn up, and her chest heaves as she takes a breath. "You should have said something! We're right by Little Italy. We can find a place where you can eat enough for an army."

She's wearing the most atrocious heavy black sweater that makes her look boxy and fat. But still, his memory can supply the details of the outline of her breasts, the narrow curve of her waist, the gentle slope on her side as her belly flows to her hips. He feels a buzz underneath his skin and his body goes hot; it's almost a shock. He's felt so dead for so long, and now, suddenly for no reason he can quite account for, he is, in the local vernacular, extremely turned on.

He stares at Amy and remembers her blushing at the restaurant when she thought he was praising her. It would be so terribly easy ...

"Loki," she says, holding out a hand toward his face.

Catching it in his own hand, he kisses her palm.

She gasps and takes a heavy breath. He looks up at her. Her lips are wet and parted, and she brings her other hand up toward his temple but doesn't touch him. The look in her eyes is as though she is under some sort of spell. It's been too long since anyone has looked at him like that.

With a gentle exhale of breath, she puts her hand to his temple and whispers almost reverently, "You're blue."

Loki goes cold. For the first time, he notices the hand holding hers. Why didn't he see it from the first? He is as blue as ... as ... Helen. But he isn't blue; why is this happening?

Dropping her hand he closes his eyes, concentrates, and lets his skin wash back to its normal color. He makes the Midgardian clothing reappear, too.

"Better?" he whispers.

Tilting her head, Amy, says, "You know, if you're naturally blue, because you know, you're an alien—it's okay. I don't mind, it's kind of—"

Wrapping his hand around the hilt of Lævatein he

clenches his teeth. "I'm not blue!"

She jumps back.

Closing his eyes, he says, "I'm sorry. I'm … I'm just hungry." And it's true now.

"Okay," she says. "I'll just clean up. I mean, you can go if you want … "

He takes a deep breath and tries to look benign. "Actually, I would prefer your company. I get rather bored eating alone all the time." And that is also true.

"Oh, okay," she says. "Just a minute."

He smiles as kindly as he can and walks to the corner of the lab and stares at the window. It's dark now, and he sees little beyond his own reflection. His ginger hair is back, his eyes are light blue.

Cera swirls around him. "What happened? I thought you'd left … Did you learn anything?"

"Dah," he mutters under his breath.

Humans have access to Vanir magical devices and have adapted Vanir species to their own technology. But how?

He narrows his eyes at the mist. The Vanir are after the World Seed.

CHAPTER 4

The night is cooler when they leave the restaurant in Little Italy. Loki's hunger is sated, but he feels a growing prickle of worry. The Vanir are coming. They have to be ... and he can do nothing about it.

Thankfully, Amy has been asking interesting questions that have kept Loki at least partially distracted. Questions like why Loki hasn't managed to bring hundreds of exotic germs to Earth and wiped out half the population by now; and why Earth germs haven't affected him. The answer to both, is, of course—magic! Magical creatures predominantly get magical diseases, that humans are immune to, and vice versa.

Now, as Amy wraps her arms around her she says, "When we create virtual images with computers, it takes a lot of computing power. I can kind of imagine how you turn magical energy into light to create illusions ... But how can you maintain the illusion without focusing on it?"

Pleased with the question, he says, "Well, there you're wandering from science into philosophy."

"No, no, I think we crossed that line long ago," says Amy.

He raises an eyebrow. "Fair enough." They are talking about something she can't see, hear or touch. Still, it's nice to talk about science and magic without being accused of being deviant and argr, unmanly.

Holding out a hand, he lets an illusion of flame shoot up. "At first you need concentration, but at a certain point, magic itself takes over." He pretends to catch the imaginary flame, gives it the shape of an owl, and sets it upon Amy's shoulder.

"Oh," she says, eyes widening, but she doesn't shriek or shirk away.

Loki scratches the imaginary fire owl behind its illusory ear and begins to walk again, letting the owl remain on Amy's shoulder. She grins at it, her eyes alight with undisguised wonder.

He looks down the dark street. "The belief held by Hell-bendi, the most prominent of the magical scholars, is that magic wants to be used, that in using it, we give it access to a larger consciousness it wishes to be part of. We give it purpose, an outlet, and in return, it keeps our imagination in motion."

"That sounds like a whole lot of conjecture that can't be tested," says Amy, scowling a little.

"You humans haven't figured out how gravity works, but you know that it does," Loki counters.

Amy perks up; her eyes widen. "Do you know how it works?"

Loki blinks. "No. Most of our science is wrapped up in the workings of magic. In some ways we are even further behind your species in understanding the basic mechanics of the unive—"

He feels a buzz of electricity beneath his skin and stops. The fire owl, figment of his imagination that it is, hops to his shoulder.

"Is something wrong?" asks Amy.

Loki looks to their right. Across the street there is a park with a large black statue of a man in Renaissance-esque attire standing atop a fountain. Around the statue are three large embankments of concrete, filled with plants and trees.

Loki's eyes narrow. He feels the bend and curl of magic. His eyes dart to the red mist of Cera snaking through the trees. She feels it, too.

The magic feels tethered to a consciousness; it is the same sort of energy he feels near a World Gate, but shifting and flickering. His eyes widen. Is someone creating a new branch of the World Tree? It's something he's only seen Hoenir do; Loki can't manage it himself.

He looks at the terrain. The embankments form a fence of sorts between the statue and the parkland beyond. And between them are openings that function as gates. World Tree branches are drawn to human gateways …

There is also a fence about 100 paces away beyond a small copse of trees. It surrounds a field. There are two openings in the fence that he can see from here. He closes his eyes and sends his consciousness around the park. There are three more gates about another 600 paces to the northeast, east and southeast.

He scowls. Fantastic. Loki can only destroy a branch with his physical form, he can only destroy a branch after it materializes, and there are 6 places where the branch is likely to emerge.

Someone is coming. His jaw tenses. The Vanir. They won't want Earth—they were the first to believe in non-interference with mortals. But they will want Cera, and then Asgard, back.

He puts his hand on Lævatein's pommel. They can't have Cera, and only he is allowed to take Asgard.

Loki's mouth falls open as he has a sudden realization. He does have a small army at his beck and call.

"Call Steve, Amy," Loki says, eyes still on the forest.

"I didn't bring my phone," she says. "They can track it."

Loki scowls and hands her the temporary phone he picked up downtown.

She stares at it. "Uh, no, you know, they can worry about me for a little while. I don't like thinking about my boss unless I'm getting overtime pay."

"Overtime pay?" says Loki, looking quickly to the gathering magic and then back to her.

"You know, work that's above and beyond 40 hours a week … The FBI gives it to its hourly workers; they give danger pay, too."

Loki stares at her, and then turns his head to the magic. He has a few minutes …

Struck by inspiration he smiles. He can quash the Vanir or anything else that comes through this gate and repay his debt to Amy.

Thrusting the phone in her face he says, "Dial Steve!"

It's close to 9:30 p.m. on a Wednesday, and the

brownstone-lined street of the residential section of Little Italy is very quiet. Steve checks the sky. Not a raven in sight.

Aside from Steve, Bryant and his brother Brett, the street outside of Amy Lewis' apartment is empty. Generally, the FBI does not tolerate cronyism, and having a pair of brothers in the same department would never fly. But ADUO is special. Not in a good way. In Brett's words it's special in a "hold the place together with spit, bubble gum and duct tape" kind of way. Steve's working on fixing that, but he's dealing with layers of bureaucracy, and getting to the surface will take time—even with a slowly growing ball of something nasty under Chicago's Board of Trade.

"She just disappeared again," Bryant is saying.

"Yep," says Brett. Steve has never heard Brett say more than Yep or Nope, but when it comes to making tech work with spit, bubble gum and duct tape, he and Bryant are both masters. Brett came out here to test a more sensitive magic detector.

Bryant shakes his head. "We kept up with her until she cut through the neighbor's lot there. Couldn't quite see her behind the building, tried to move into position. And then—"

"Poof." Brett says in a dry voice. Drawling in the same West Virginia twang as Bryant, he adds, "I don't think this detector is as sensitive as Ericson makes it out to be." He holds up something that looks more like a radar gun. "Maybe I can reread the manual and make some special modifications myself."

Steve blinks. Those are as many words as he's ever heard Brett say.

"Witness protection program," says Bryant. "Really, you have to convince her."

Bryant, on the other hand, never shuts up. Steve is spared the rest of Bryant's commentary by his phone ringing.

He glances down at the unfamiliar number. He picks up. "Agent Steve Rogers here."

Loki's voice rings in his ear. "Steve, so lovely to hear your voice."

"Where is she, Loki?" Steve says. Bryant and Brett move closer.

"Where are you?" Loki's voice says. And then from behind him he hears more clearly. "Oh, look, I found you."

Steve turns. Brett and Bryant immediately draw their weapons.

Loki just rolls his eyes. He is in a suit, as seems to be the usual. Narrowing his eyes, he steps toward them. "I've had a lovely time with Ms. Lewis tonight, and I think she'll have lots of interesting things to tell you." He smiles tightly. "And she should be compensated for such."

Steve tilts his head. "Why?"

Loki gives him a tight smile. "Because your organization offers danger pay. And I think we can all agree, I am dangerous." He raises an eyebrow.

"That's true," Bryant mutters.

Loki lifts an eyebrow at him and then turns his eyes to Steve. "Also, you're about to have visitors from another realm. I'm guessing Vanaheim. Most likely hostile. If you move quickly we'll be able to intercept them."

"What? Where?" says Steve.

"Danger pay," says Loki, face expressionless. "For every moment I am with Miss Lewis henceforth."

"Fine!" says Steve.

Leveling his eyes at Steve, Loki says, "Call back up."

"Bryant," says Steve.

"On it."

Loki closes his eyes. "It's emerging ... Amy says the name of the place is Arrigo Park. The north-west corner, near the statue of Christopher Columbus."

Loki disappears.

Bryant is barking into a phone.

Brett tilts his head to the east. "That's a block away but there's a dead end between us and the park. We're better off running."

"Let's go," says Steve, pulling his gun and hoping the entity known for mischief is playing a bad joke.

Nodding, Brett sets off up the street and Steve follows, Bryant still on the phone behind them.

He's not even out of breath when Loki and Amy come into view, standing in front of a large statue of Columbus. On Loki's shoulder is an owl ... made of fire. Amy is dressed all in black and looking slightly guilty.

"What's going on?" she asks.

"Nothing at all," says Loki with a cheerful smile. Fixing a death glare on Steve he says, "Agent Rogers is just going to see that you get safely home."

Steve tilts his head at the implicit command; not that he is going to disagree. Hearing Bryant's footsteps behind him and the sound of cars screeching to a halt and doors slamming, he says, "Bryant, get Miss Lewis out of here."

"Right," says Bryant.

"Loki?" says Amy. He doesn't answer, but the owl hops to Amy's shoulder.

What is evidently only an illusion of Loki walks right through her and nods at Steve. "Follow me." And then the illusion seemingly runs around the statue, past a concrete embankment filled with trees, and heads into a forested area, his suit shimmering and turning into body armor that looks a lot more high tech than anything Steve ever got to wear as a marine; it blends into the trees, and the lawn beyond, lit by streetlights and moonlight. Only Loki's chin is barely visible beneath a shimmering eye piece—and a long glinting sword at his side.

Steve tilts his head. If Loki is only an illusion, why does he need armor?

He checks the street as Amy and Bryant get into a car. Steve doesn't see any civilians walking about. Hoping this isn't a trap, Steve raises his gun, nods to the four agents beside him and sets off past the statue and into the trees.

Just ahead there's an opening in a black metal fence. Standing on either side of it is a crowd of Lokis, dressed all the same, all with a sword upraised. There's a bright flash of light, and a shadow begins to swirl in the gap in the fence. It's nearly as big as an elephant, but hominid.

"Oh, fuck," the Lokis say in unison. Steve mentally echoes the sentiment.

The form solidifies. It's green, gargantuan, and dressed in animal skins. Steve's about 5 meters away but he can already smell the stench of rotting flesh.

"It's the Goddamn Incredible Hulk!" says one of the agents.

"It's a troll," says Steve grimly. He's seen them in Merryl's reports.

"Aim for the eyes," shouts Loki.

"You heard him!" Steve says. Gunfire goes off around him, and the Lokis are pulling out what looks like knives.

The troll swings at the Lokis. Encountering only empty air, it roars in frustration and begins lunging through the trees toward Steve and his men. Steve and his guys are all excellent shots, but it is very dark beneath the trees, and low hanging branches block their shots. Someone's bullet hits the troll in the cheek; it pauses for a moment, roars, and then holds an arm up to its eyes.

The agent next to him says, "Sir, I have a shotgun in my car."

"Get it, and call for more backup!" Steve shouts as he and the other agents fire uselessly at the creature's raised arm.

Flashes of light halo the troll's head. And for a moment it drops its arm and begins pulling wicked looking knives from its neck. Nearby there is the sound of a woman screaming. Ripping out the knives the troll looks in her direction.

Steve opens up his Glock; the troll turns its head and snarls as though annoyed by insects. Forgetting about the woman, the troll throws up its arm to protect its eyes again and lunges at Steve.

Seeing civilians at the corner of his vision, Steve dances backwards. "That's right! Come and get me!"

The troll takes the bait and comes forward, trapping Steve against the embankment wall. Steve's guys are now at its side, and they won't be able to get a clear shot at its eyes.

There is the sound of a shotgun firing, the creature lets out a blood curdling snarl. A liquid, thick and tar-like, bubbles from the troll's shoulder, but it doesn't turn from Steve. There's nowhere to run. Steve keeps his gun upraised, hoping he'll get a clear shot when the thing inevitably grabs him.

There's a shimmer of silver on the pavement, the sound of steel on rock, and suddenly at Steve's feet there is a sword.

"Use it!" screams Loki. Holstering his gun, Steve scrambles to pick it up. It's lighter in his hands than the Kumdo swords he's used to, and the way it catches the light—it's almost like a light saber.

A huge meaty fist is coming toward Steve's face. Reflexes born of years of practice kick in and Steve brings the sword down on the troll's wrist.

There should be the shock of steel impacting against bone. But the blade slices through the troll's wrist—bone, muscle, tendons, and armor-like skin—as easily as butter. The hand lands on the pavement in front of Steve with a soft thud.

Leaning back, the monster howls. And then there is a shimmer of something from behind it. Steve blinks. Loki is on the troll's shoulders, over 12 feet above the ground. The troll reaches with its one hand to pull him off but before it does Loki brings two knives into the beast's eyes; and then Loki slips off, or falls, Steve really can't see. There is the sound of two nearly simultaneous explosions and two flashes of light and half of the troll's head is suddenly gone.

In the distance Steve can hear sirens wailing and people screaming.

Panting, blade still upraised, Steve watches the troll fall to the ground. Destroying their brains is just about the only way to kill trolls, the damn things have redundant hearts, and apparently can reattach their limbs.

Steve swallows. Loki killed it. But why?

There are a few Lokis walking around the fallen creature. One of his agents comes forward, presumably to intercept Loki—one of them is real, but Steve holds up a hand and nods in the direction of a crowd of people forming just beyond the park. "Form a perimeter," he says.

The agents nod and back away, but Brett holds up a phone and raises an eyebrow. A little red light is flashing. He's begun recording this. Steve nods at him and Brett doesn't follow the other guys.

The Lokis continue to pace. One of them turns to Steve and says, "This THING should not be here, Steven. Trolls are magical but barely self-aware! It could never create a world gate on its own." Walking toward Steve, Loki shouts. "What is it doing here?"

"I wish I knew," says Steve calmly.

The apparition of Loki looks away. "Cera. Fuck. Fuck. Fuck. Cera." And then he begins saying something in a language that sounds familiar but Steve can't place. He looks over to Brett. His agent nods and lifts the phone. Thankfully, this is going on record.

A Loki closer to the troll aims a foot at what remains of its head. There is a wet thud and the sound of bone cracking. "I. Hate. These. Fucking. Things!" Loki says, kicking it over and over.

With a snarl he begins walking toward Steve. "I know about agent Merryl's adventures in Wyoming, Steven." He hisses. "You're going to have a lot more visitors everywhere your precious little prisoner beneath the Board of Trade has been."

Steve tilts his head, not dropping Loki's sword. Prisoner? Wait. What? Feeling himself shiver, Steve takes a breath. "Go on."

Loki rolls his eyes. "And since you still keep her here, Chicago is going to become the grand central station of the worlds." He smiles. "Luckily you have me. The good guy."

"Uh-huh," says Steve as Loki closes the distance between

them. With one quick motion Steve could pierce Loki's heart with his own sword.

Loki looks at the gleaming blade. "Nice work, by the way. What was that ... Kumdo?"

Steve blinks. And then suddenly there is an incredibly strong pressure on his wrist and the blade goes hot in his hands. He drops it and it falls to the ground with a clang. Steve feels a gust of wind and then the sword is gone. He looks up and the Loki he was speaking to is still standing there, smirking, of course. "I've been known to lend out Laevithin upon occasion," Loki says. "But I always take her back."

Scowling, Steve walks through him. "Care to tell me a little more about trolls so next time I run into one we're better prepared?"

"Maybe later," says Loki, and even though Steve can't see him, he can still hear the smirk. All the Lokis suddenly disappear.

"Got it all," says Brett.

"Good man," says Steve.

He hears the voice of a woman in the distance. Looking up, Steve sees his agents keeping a small group of neighborhood residents at bay.

"What was that?" the woman says.

Behind him he hears the slam of car doors and someone shouts, "Chicago Police!"

Steve sighs. Plastering on his happiest smile he says, "Just a little horror movie shoot, people!" Pretty close to the excuse of an amateur fantasy film shoot that the FBI had used to explain the eight-legged horse on LaSalle a few weeks back.

"Where are the cameras?" someone shouts.

"What stinks?" says another.

Brett holds up his phone. "It's an indie film—we're going for the hyper realism look."

One of the officers shouts, "We never got no permit for no film shoot."

Steve sighs again. It's going to be a long night.

CHAPTER 5

It's 8:30 a.m., the morning after the troll landed in Chicago. A little later than Steve normally starts a day at the office. But then, he never went home last night. Steve, Brett, Bryant, and Laura Stodgill are in ADUO's conference room, seated at a long table. There are two large monitors on the wall. Merryl is in one monitor, the shadow of a gray beard on his square jaw, dark circles under his eyes. Behind him are trees. In the other monitor is Director Jameson. Although he's known informally as Director Jameson within ADUO, his full title is Executive Assistant Director of ADUO, and he's just one step below the FBI's Associate Director. Jameson's narrow face is magically smooth, his blue eyes bright and rested. He's even wearing a suit. Behind him is the emblem of the bald eagle.

Glaring at Jameson, Steve stands from his seat. "We need to let Chicago's other anti-terrorist agencies and police know what is going on, Sir." And they need to prepare the Chicago Board of Trade to pack up and move out before the sphere gets too much larger. But he and Merryl have been saying that for weeks now.

Straightening, Jameson tilts his head. "That is not a decision for you to make."

"I agree with Agent Rogers," says Merryl. "If Loki says that there will be other portals opening, Chicago needs to be prepared."

Steve relaxes minutely but keeps his eyes glued on Jameson.

"Loki is an unreliable witness," says Jameson.

Steve fights the urge to curse. Instead he smiles. "He has reasons to want to work with us on this—"

"—to distract us from paying attention to him! Where are you on finding out where he lives, on getting him into custody?" says Jameson.

Steve takes a breath. Nowhere. Keeping his face neutral he says, "Where are you in getting me access to the ballistics report on the Subaru that went to Alfheim?"

Jameson sits back in his chair. His lips tremble but he meets Steve gaze. "There was no ballistics to report," he says. "The girl is also an unreliable witness."

Keeping his eyes locked on Steve, Jameson smiles just a touch. He's lying but thinks he's getting away with it. Steve doesn't roll his eyes, but it's hard, really hard, even for him.

It's then that Steve notices Jameson's hand tapping nervously at the desk. He is scared. Steve feels himself wilt inside a little. Jameson's background is law with an undergrad in public policy from an expensive but unimpressive private school on the east coast. He has no military or law enforcement background. He has a father who is a senator, and he's had the job as ADUO's director for a long time—since ADUO was essentially a joke.

Now he may hold the fate of the city of Chicago, hell the fate of the country, in his hands.

Jameson's mouth tightens. "I will let you know when other agencies are allowed to become involved. That will be all."

The screen goes black. Steve sits back in his chair and frowns. By limiting the city's response options, Jameson is forcing him to rely on Loki. Like Hell, Steve will try to have him arrested.

His phone beeps with a text. Glancing down at it and seeing Lewis's name on the ID, he opens it. *R u sure Loki is okay? The fire owl disappeared after I came home!*

He runs a hand over his face and then looks down at his phone just in time to see another text pop-in.

He's here! Loki ... not the owl.

Steve sighs and starts typing furiously with his thumbs. *Ask him to breakfast.*

A few seconds later another note pops in.

But I'll be late ???

Steve looks at the guys around him. "You're dismissed," he says curtly.

As they file out, Steve types back. *Is ok. Have questions for you to ask him. Discreetly.*

He taps all the questions out, and then shaking his head, hits send.

He is going to have to rely on Amy Lewis, too.

It's a dreary gray afternoon, about a week after the troll in the park and breakfast with Loki.

Amy looks out the window of Chicago's Redline 'L' train. There must be an event of some kind because even though it's Sunday, the train is packed.

Amy's on her way home after visiting Beatrice. She should visit Beatrice more often, but it's an hour and a half away by public transit, and Beatrice shows no sign of recognizing her—or anyone. It's ... discouraging.

Amy looks down at her hands. Her mother has put Beatrice on the waiting list for a cheaper nursing home outside of Chicago. When Beatrice gets in, it will be even more difficult to visit. That is both saddening and a horrible relief.

Amy closes her eyes and leans her head against the cold glass of the window. Her stomach growls, she hasn't eaten anything since breakfast. "Next stop Belmont," the train conductor says. Amy lifts her head, suddenly struck by inspiration. As the train shudders to a halt, she jumps from her seat and barely makes it through the crowd in time. A few minutes later she's walking along Clark Street.

"My, aren't you far afield?"

Amy stops, feeling a spark at the base of her spine she tells herself is magic. She turns and smiles.

Loki isn't in any sort of disguise, besides the blue jeans and leather jacket she's pretty sure aren't real. When they went out for breakfast he'd made himself look like a younger incarnation of Bob Marley.

Her brow furrows and she looks around for the agents she knows are following her.

Lifting an eyebrow, he says, "You lost your tail on the train."

She turns back to him. "Are you hungry?"

Loki tilts his head. "Does a cockatrice shit on stones?"

Amy blinks.

He looks heavenward. "Maybe the Midgardian expression is 'Does a dragon shit in a cave … '? No, no, that can't be right."

She bites back a laugh. Grabbing his arm and telling herself she absolutely does not go warm at the touch, she pulls him along. "Come on, I know a place that serves all you can eat Indian."

"Please, Sir," the manager of the Indian restaurant says to Loki. "Please—we have no more."

Loki looks hard at the man. "You're lying."

"Loki—" says Amy, looking sideways at the empty buffet. This perhaps wasn't the best idea she's ever had.

Bowing, the little man says, "The food I have left in the kitchen is for dinner service—please. I beg you. No more! "

Loki stares at him. "Oh, very well. But my companion and I desire tea."

"Yes, sir! Yes, sir! Coming right up," says the manager, stepping quickly away.

"Now, where were we?" says Loki, tearing off a piece of naan bread still at the table. "Oh, yes, nanotechnology with bacteriophage delivery systems." He smiles. "If your kind doesn't destroy yourselves, you're going to make the nine realms so much more exciting."

Amy wants to answer with something she read in Science,

but she suddenly notices how late it's getting. Fumbling in her pocket she pulls out a folded sheet of paper. "I should probably ask you Steve's questions."

Something wicked flashes through his eyes. "I wouldn't let you forget."

"Right, well … " Amy clears her throat. "First off, they still want to know if Cera is conscious or not."

"And my answer is still, I'm not telling."

Nodding, Amy says, "Right."

Pulling out a pencil she jots that down.

Loki snorts. "I believe you're supposed to work these questions into the conversation and keep mental notes."

Amy glances up. "That's what Merryl and Steve say, but I'm supposed to earn your trust. How can I get that by pretending I'm not spying?"

Loki chuckles. "You're funny."

Amy looks down. "Next question: you said beyond fully sentient creatures we can expect more trolls, wyrms, kappas, and possibly unicorns … " She blinks at her notes, "And unicorns are very dangerous."

"Probably not to you," says Loki. He smiles at her. Amy bites her lip. Flushing, she says, "You know I'm not really a … "

His eyebrows rise above wide eyes. Leaning closer he says, "A what?"

Face hot, Amy looks down. "Never mind. Okay, the guys in the office want clarification on what a wyrm is."

Loki scowls, and looks up as though searching for a word. "It's a dragon—without legs or wings," says Loki. "How can they not know that?"

Amy shakes her head. "That's what I thought! No one

listens to me."

"Hmmm ... you might want to look out for the occasional Al-mi'raj," says Loki.

Amy looks up at him. "Ferocious, predatory, horned rabbit," Loki says as the tea arrives.

After the waiter departs Loki steeples his fingers and says, "What of the surveillance I suggested around those places in Europe and Asia? Has that been put into place?"

Amy looks at her notes. "Steve says he's working on it."

"What?" says Loki, throwing his napkin on to his empty plate.

"Steve says—"

"I heard you!" A burst of orange light makes Amy look up. The napkin on Loki's plate is on fire.

One of his fingers is tapping agitatedly on the tablecloth. "I can't tell if you're lying because you don't know if you're lying."

"Ummmm ... " says Amy looking at the fire.

Smacking his hand down and extinguishing the flames, Loki says, "What we need is a teleconference."

Amy looks up and taps her chin with the pencil. "Well, I guess if we—"

And suddenly the light shifts and she's staring up at a ceiling much closer than the one in the restaurant. Her hands grip the table—she feels it under her fingers but when she looks down she sees empty air ... and tiny little black and white tiles. She looks directly in front of her. Steve is standing there, back to her, wearing only a towel. She blinks. Loki is sitting on a toilet across from her and next to Steve. He raises his eyebrows and smiles.

Amy looks down. She appears to be seated on the edge

of a bathtub.

"Are we in Steve's bathroom?" she says.

"No," says Loki, tilting his head.

Steve spins around, razor in one hand, his other hand going to hold the towel. Half his face is covered in shaving cream. He's actually … really well put together. Amy's eyes go wide, and she looks down at the floor.

"What are you doing here!" Steve says, his voice icy.

"Oh, don't worry," says Loki. "We're not really here. This is just illusions I've created for everyone's convenience."

"Convenience?" says Steve.

"Shhhhh … " says Loki. "Your little girl is in the other room. We wouldn't want to upset her."

Amy's eyes go to the door. That's right. Steve's divorced and has a kid.

Steve's staring at Loki. It's hard and frightening. "My daughter … " He points the razor at Loki. "If you … "

Loki's face goes livid; his upper lip starts to tremble. For a moment Amy swears she feels the air around her get hot.

And then Steve puts down the razor. His eyes narrow and he smiles, though it looks forced. "I forgot … you don't hurt women or children, right?" He turns back to the mirror and starts to shave.

The air seems to cool. Loki's lips purse. "Oh, I'd hurt a woman." He turns to Amy and says brightly, "I am a feminist."

"Errr … " says Amy.

But Loki's already turning away. "Now, Steven, I told you to arrange for surveillance around the gates to Vanaheim—"

Continuing to shave, Steve says, "And I'm trying to. You're suggesting covert operations in foreign countries. That requires coordinated efforts across multiple agencies—which is hard enough. Throw other countries into it—" He shakes his head.

Loki's nostrils flare. "And?"

Grabbing the edges of the sink, Steve bows his head. "And some people aren't convinced of the threat."

"Convince them," says Loki.

Steve turns and gives Loki a look that is completely withering.

Loki glares right back.

"Um … guys," says Amy. "We're all on the same team here, right?"

Both of them turn their glares on her.

"Or not … " Amy says.

A knock sounds at the bathroom door, and the muffled voice of a girl. "Daddy? Daddy? Is everything alright?"

Loki grinds his teeth, and the scene fades away. As it does Amy hears Steve saying jovially, "Everything's fine! I'll be out in a minute—"

And then Amy is sitting at the table in the Indian restaurant. She turns her head cautiously to the side. The manager, a waiter and a busboy are all staring at them with mouths agape.

Loki peers over. "Oh, yes, they've just been watching us have a three way conversation with empty air for the past few minutes."

Amy holds up a hand. "Check!"

A few minutes later they're out on the street, fine mist settling on their shoulders. Amy's staring down at her now damp notes. "I have a few more questions for you," she says.

"Proceed," says Loki.

They're standing in the middle of the sidewalk blocking

traffic, so Amy starts walking toward her intended second destination. "Steve's been doing some research on trickster gods—"

"That's not a question." Loki says.

Ignoring that, Amy says, "—Iktomi, Aunt Nancy, Prometheus ... Any of them ring any bells?"

Loki looks into the distance. "Prometheus."

"You know him?" says Amy.

"No, I just had a fondness for Greek literature." His voice gets quiet. "I named my daughter after Helen of Troy ... "

It's the first time he's mentioned Helen, or any of his family since before Beatrice's accident. They're all gone. "I'm sorry," Amy stammers.

Loki looks sideways at her, and then his eyes drift to the horizon. "You were saying?"

She swallows. "I ... so Prometheus is just a myth?"

He stops walking. "I don't know ... "

"Before your time, maybe?" Amy says. And then she notices his irises are doing that funny thing where they start to turn black.

Loki starts to tremble. "I don't know." The skin around his eyes and at the edge of his fingers is starting to turn blue again. Remembering how he fell last time, she slips her arm into his. He looks down at it and his lips quirk. Her stomach does an inappropriate little flip flop.

"Loki," she whispers, leaning closer. "You're starting to turn blue."

He shakes as though she's hit him. The blue recedes. The quirk of his lips vanishes. People are starting to stare, so Amy steers him down the street once more.

His face becomes pinched. "Amy, after discovering the elf queen's name was in one of your movies, I would hesitate to call anything just a myth."

Amy straightens. "I thought you said you didn't know her name?" But, actually, now that she thinks about it, he might have called her by name as they left the kingdom. Her brow furrows—yes, maybe, but she thought he was joking.

He shrugs, not releasing her arm. "It came up in conversation."

Her eyes widen. "When you left the banquet and came back without your shirt or your armor ... " She feels like two neurons in her brain have suddenly fired exceptionally brightly. "Did you and the elf queen ... "

He smirks.

Her mouth falls and her childhood smashes into a million pieces. "No ... with the queen of the elves?"

His eyebrows dance. The smirk widens to a leer.

Going hot, her eyes narrow. "Is that why she chased us out of her kingdom?"

Loki snorts. "No! Believe me, she was completely satisfied. In fact, I reminded her of a former lover. A *female* lover." He sighs happily. "My technique is very good."

Amy scowls. "So good we wound up on the run from knights trying to smash us with their hadrosaurs!"

"She didn't want to incur the wrath of Odin!" Loki says, his voice turning angry. "She had to make our escape look difficult."

"By setting her own knights on fire?" Amy says.

Loki seems not to have heard her. He is looking down the street at a group of people who have a thing for leather lingerie as outerwear despite the cold weather. "What have we here?" he says.

"Oh, they're probably going to the Alley," says Amy. "It's

a store for—"

Loki is already yanking her down the street.

"Hey! Stop! I wanted to go to the comic book store!" But he yanks her right by Chicago Comics and before she knows it she is standing among the black and metal studded clothing of the Alley, shopping center for all things punk and goth. Plastic skeletons and plaster gargoyles are grinning down at them. People with multiple piercings and tattoos look at them curiously. Modelling a black leather brassiere—thankfully *over* his clothes, Loki juts out a hip. "What do you think? A gift for Thor, maybe?"

Amy remembers her run in with Thor in Alfheim, how he suggested Loki keep her as a plaything, and how he waggled his finger at her as though she were a bird in a cage. "I'd rather not think of that ass at all."

Loki raises an eyebrow. "Oh, he isn't all that bad."

"He is an insensitive idiot and a clod!" says Amy, crossing her arms.

Loki puts the brassiere back on the rack. "No, not really." And then he looks away.

Loki is in Asgard. It is night and the streets are lit with jeweled lanterns of many colors. The streets are packed with Asgardians, Vanir, dwarves, elves, giants and even the occasional fire and ice ettin. It is the festival of the Changing of the Streets. Asgard is about to transform itself from an above-ground replica of dwarven jeweled cities to a city modelled after the Imperial City of Midgardian China.

Anganboða is at his side, her arm in his. Fenrir lopes beside them. Loki is holding Helen in his arms—an activity that surely labels him as argr and a fool among the Aesir; but he is called a argr and a fool for so many other reasons anyway, and he sees no reason to deny himself the pleasure of carrying his tiny daughter in his arms. Helen adores him. And she is so small and light, her bones as delicate as a bird, her limbs narrow and fragile. Eir, Frigga's lady-in-waiting and practitioner of healing, says Helen is as small as a child of one year, though she is nearly three.

In Loki's arms, Helen's misshapen limbs are easy to hide. The way her lips pull down slightly to one side, the blue color of half her face, the way her hair is half-honey colored, half-black, is another matter.

But tonight, everyone is too intent on the festival to pay Helen much more than a quick look of curiosity or disgust. Tonight Loki hears no whispers of how Aggie bewitched him into keeping a deformity, a monster. He catches no snippets of how Helen is a blight upon the court.

Not that these comments pain him much—though they pain Aggie. What is painful is when someone suggests he named Helen after Helen of Troy, the most beautiful woman on Earth, as a cruel jest.

Loki glances down at his little girl, the blue light of her magic nearly brighter than the lanterns above his head. Asgard is as blind to her beauty as they are to Baldur's ugliness.

Catching his eye, Helen gives him a lopsided grin, throws her good arm around his shoulder and buries her face near his neck. Loki can't help but smile.

"She has you wrapped around her little finger," says a familiar feminine voice from behind.

"Sigyn," declares Aggie happily.

Loki does not scowl as Sigyn comes over and embraces Aggie, or when she touches a finger to Helen's nose and Helen gurgles a laugh. No matter how much animosity he harbors toward Sigyn, she is one of Aggie's few friends, Helen likes her—even Fenrir likes her. And though her chiding would be an insult to another man's masculinity, he feels that it is completely good natured. So he bites his tongue.

As the women begin to chat about the elves' continued objections to Odin's order to remove the elven presence from Midgard, Loki's eyes go to the edges of the crowd. There are all sorts of gaming booths tucked in among the alleys. Loki loves gambling. He's married, he's faithful—despite the belief of everyone in Asgard, and despite being in Aggie's words 'an incorrigible flirt' ... he needs some games in his life. On Aggie's advice he stopped betting on sure things and started betting on surely not things; it allows him to put less money in for higher stakes. That increased his takings immensely. Odin says it's cheating. Loki says he's jealous.

But now that Helen's come along ... before her birth Loki could tell when fellow gamblers were lying or bluffing, but when Helen's with him he can feel what cards they hold in their hands, see the slightest unsteadiness in a horse's gait, and somehow knows what strategies are going through the mind of his opponents during chess. Now, in the alley closest to them, he sees a man sitting in front of a board. Smiling, Loki walks in his direction and whispers into Helen's ear, "Want to play a game of chess, Darling?"

"Nuh," comes the reply.

"But it will be fun. Daddy will win lots of money and buy you a sweet."

Thrashing in his arms, Helen twists her head. "Nuuhhhhhhhhhhhhhh!"

Loki scowls. But he turns back to Aggie and Sigyn. At that moment the ground at the foundations of the buildings begins to send off tiny sparks and the crowd goes wild. In Loki's arms, Helen squeals so shrilly he thinks he may go deaf.

The sparks begin to move up the side of the buildings, slowly at first, but then faster and faster. In their paths are ribbons of light of every color, roughly outlining the contours of the buildings beneath. There is a collective intake of breath, and then the threads of light slip down like a curtain. Instead of thick dwarven bejewelled brickwork and heavy green copper roofs, there are now white-walled pagodas accented with red and gold. Jewel lanterns are replaced by paper lanterns. The crowd roars. And then in the center of the street five plumes of smoke rise, about 40 paces apart from one another. Revelers run to get out of the way. Fire dances up to replace the smoke and smiling dragons slip out. They're not quite wyrms; they have sets of tiny legs with wicked claws every few lengths. The dragons begin to march along the street, the rhythm of their claws being matched by clapping hands. The crowd moves as one body to follow them. Somewhere drums begin to sound.

In his arms, Helen squeals in delight as they are carried along with the crowd. Loki shakes his head. Odin has outdone himself this time. It is then that he realizes he can't see Aggie. He projects himself upwards, sees her with Sigyn across the street from where he wades through the crowd with Helen. Fenrir is with them, so they're given a wide berth.

She's safe. Loki pulls back his apparition and concentrates on not letting Helen slip from his arms. Vendors are in the crowd hawking all sorts of mementos and alcohol. Loki sighs; with Helen bobbing in his arms, a bottle of mead is probably out of the question.

Loki follows the dragons and the crowds for what might be the better part of an hour. As he does he notices the crowd getting rowdier, even as Helen's body sags against his. After being knocked into for a third time, Loki scans for an exit. Seeing a break in the press of bodies ahead he slips forward ... and realizes why the gap exists.

Thor is walking amongst the commoners with his stepson Ullr, and Ullr's fiancee Skadi. The people are giving them space in deference to their station. Loki scowls and thinks about slipping back into the crowd. But by chance Thor happens to turn. He meets Loki's scowl with one of his own.

And then Ullr and Skadi turn also. Skadi's eyes narrow. Like Loki, she is a jotunn, and her skin is very fair. A consummate athlete she is tall and lean. Her father once repaired a large section of Asgard's walls. Since Asgard had no money at the time—due to fancy festivals like this—her father asked for Freyja's hand in marriage in exchange. Lopt told him he would have it, but only if the repairs were done in a ridiculously short amount of time. Skadi's father would never have succeeded if it weren't for his stallion Svadarvi. The creature could work both day and night and had the intelligence of a man. He led the other horses in delivering materials and made it possible for Skadi's father to concentrate on the actual masonry of the walls. But just before the task was completed, Svadarvi was distracted by a mare in season—human legend alleged the mare was Loki in disguise, but it was before his time. Mad with lust, the stallion ran off and the wall was unfinished. For daring to make a bargain of Freyja's hand in marriage, Skadi's father was slain, this despite the fact that Asgard had no death penalty. Svadarvi was never seen again, but 11 months later, Odin came into possession of the eight-legged realm-walking foal Sleipnir.

Skadi had come to the Aesir years afterwards to protest the treatment of her father. In compensation she was allowed to marry the man of her choice—but only allowed to choose based on view of their feet. She'd desired Baldur, but instead had mistakenly chosen Njörðr. She'd been furious and declared that unless the Aesir could deliver her happiness, she would relentlessly spread word of their unjust actions through the nine realms. It was Odin who declared if she was made to laugh, even briefly, her happiness had been achieved. One by one the Aesir had come forward with jests and tricks, but none even achieved a flicker of a smile. Loki, only a teen then, had held back. When two clowns were doing an imitation of a tug-of-war with an invisible rope he had slipped next to her and whispered, "Not as satisfying as seeing a tug-of-war with one end of the rope in the mouths of Thor's goats, and the other end tied to Odin's balls, is it?"

She'd laughed despite herself … and been angry at Loki ever since. Well, not so angry that they hadn't had sex after her divorce with Njörðr. The anger had been fun in bed; what hadn't been so fun were all her lectures afterwards on the importance of upright behavior, and how Loki disgraced his entire race with his cheap antics, and 'justified the Aesir's belief that jotunns are just slightly better than humans.'

Loki is snapped out of his reverie with the sound of Thor's hand smacking Ullr on the back. "If it isn't Scarlip," says Thor with a cruel smile.

Ullr snorts. He is the bastard son of Sif, and no one knows who his father is, but he looks remarkably like Thor. Had he not been born before Thor came to court, people might believe that he is the result of an enthusiastic coupling before Thor and Sif's marriage. But Thor had adopted the boy when he'd married Sif. Loki scowls. Thor still disputes Sif's reputation as a whore, even *with the evidence of her loose ways right before him.*

Skadi looks at Helen now asleep in Loki's arms. Her look is one of such unadulterated disapproval that the hairs on the back of Loki's neck stand on end. Loki should ignore it, but he's never been one for fine choices. "Something bothering you, Skadi?"

Skadi would never have let Helen live—she sees Helen's existence as a weakness, and just another blemish on the good name of all right-thinking jotunns in Asgard. "Yes, Trickster, the monster in your arms," she says. She's never been one to back down either.

Ullr's eyes go wide. Thor's face hardens. And for a horrible instant Loki's sharp tongue deserts him.

And then Thor says, "Ullr, look over there, a merchant is selling spun honey. Why don't you and Skadi go get some. I would speak to Loki alone."

The two depart through the crowd. Loki finds himself alone with Thor, revelers swinging around them drunk and oblivious.

"Out with it, Thor," hisses Loki. "Please, state your objections to my daughter's existence to my face rather than my back."

Thor steps closer, so close he is in the sphere cast by Helen's soft blue magic. "No, Fool, I will not, for I have none. It is good to see you so besotted." He snorts. "Perhaps now you will understand that no shame is too great to endure for a child's sake."

He blinks and straightens suddenly. He looks as though he is confused, like his own words are shocking.

Loki's eyes widen. He sees Thor's eyes go to Ullr. Sif and Thor have a daughter, but no sons. Loki remembers all the times Thor has declared Ullr his 'own son'. He remembers when Ullr was just Helen's age, how Thor had presented the toddler with a tiny wooden sword, and then let Ullr chase him around while feigning fear. And he remembers seeing the two in the training yards for endless hours, sitting next to each other at feasts, even sharing each other's cups of mead.

"You knew," says Loki, the realization so strong his mouth moves of its own accord.

Thor turns to him, his eyes tired. "Of course, I've known the boy's mother is a whore." He looks down. "But the boy doesn't, and that is what matters."

Loki suddenly feels very small. He looks on Thor—brash, quick to anger, sometimes thick-headed Thor, and sees nobility he will never possess, compassion, and strength of will enough to hold up all of the nine realms.

"Of course," says Loki. He can feel Helen's drool through his shirt, and she is just beginning to get heavy in his arms. But these things are immaterial. Her magic is so thick that the crowd moving beyond the little space allowed in deference to Thor son of Odin is almost obscured. Thor holds up a hand in the pale blue mist. "A lovely color magic for a girl to have," he says.

Loki has no words, and if he did his voice might crack.

"My head hurts," says Loki rubbing his temple. Amy takes a step closer; he does look pained.

And then he smiles, but it doesn't reach his eyes. "Melancholy serves no purpose," he declares. Suddenly, by the cash register a skeleton in Halloween finery starts to clatter.

Amy's eyes widen.

The skull begins to speak in a voice remarkably like Loki's:

To be, or not to be, that is the question:
Whether 'tis Nobler in the mind to suffer
The Slings and Arrows of outrageous Fortune,

Or to take Arms against a Sea of troubles,

And by opposing end them: to die, to sleep …

"What?" says the girl behind the counter, her eyes going wide.

"That's awesome!" says a kid buying a gargoyle.

"It's not supposed to do that," says the clerk.

"Loki," hisses Amy. But his eyes are focused on the skeleton.

The skeleton twists its head—or looks like it twists its head. Amy's sure it's an illusion.

"Am I dead or dreaming?" It raises a bony hand to its face. "Or both?"

"Auggghhhhh!" screams the girl at the cash register.

"Auggghhhhh!" screams the skull turning to her and the kid buying the gargoyle.

"Auggghhhhh!" screams the kid.

"Auuuuuuuuuuuuuuuuuuuuugggggggggggggggggggggggg ggghhhhhhhhhhhhhh!" Screams every gargoyle and skull in the store, whether on a t-shirt or made of plaster. The lights start to blink.

"Loki!" yells Amy as people start to run.

He turns to her and grins, lights blinking above his head. "Well, I feel better." He waggles his eyebrows. "My work here is done. Now if you will excuse me … "

And then he disappears.

The lights come back on. The skulls and assorted monsters go quiet.

A man with a shaved head and an intricate tattoo of a hammer on his bicep turns to her. "Did you just say Loki?"

"Ummm … " says Amy.

The man points his finger at her, his lip curling up in a

snarl. "He's evil! I'm a pagan; I know!"

From behind Amy comes a woman's voice. "I'm a pagan, too, asshole. Loki's not *evil*."

Amy turns to see a woman her age, with a 1940's retro hairstyle, wearing glasses with thick black rims. The woman is staring at the skin-head hammer-tattoo guy.

"Ummm … " says Amy.

The man snorts and rolls his eyes. "What is it with chicks and Loki?"

Grinning, the girl sashays her hips. "Maybe we just like his silver tongue." She winks at Amy and smiles. "Am I right?"

Amy blinks. "He's kind of funny, but I've never thought of him as particularly eloquent."

The woman's smile drops.

The guy is just staring at her.

"I mean, if he existed … " says Amy slowly. She's not supposed to talk about Loki.

They both scowl.

Amy's eyes widen. "Ummm … bye?" She practically runs out of the store.

It isn't until she's panting just inside the comic book store, in the mist that's become full-fledged rain, staring at a Captain America comic, that she realizes she hasn't asked all of Steve's questions … but she thinks she's learned something more important than all of his questions put together.

CHAPTER 6

It's 7:05 AM. In the elevator of the Presidential Towers apartment complex, Steve checks his email. There is one from Amy that he doesn't read past the first sentence—he's going to debrief her later in the day anyway, and several from Merryl, Brett, and Jameson. The one from Merryl about putting plastic explosives into goat carcasses before feeding the carcasses to trolls seems helpful.

The elevator dings, he puts his phone away, and he walks out of the building between another man and woman in business suits.

The streets are still wet from the rain Chicago had last night. The sky is clear and blue now, but unfortunately, not empty. Steve scowls. From over his head comes an all too familiar voice and the flap of wings. "Good morning, Steve, rawk, rawk."

"Did Claire get home safely, rawk, rawk?"

Steve narrows his eyes. The birds hadn't given him a rest over the weekend. They'd terrified Claire every time he'd taken her outside. Steve can feel the Glock he has at his hip. He swears it's calling to him. He clenches his jaw and keeps walking.

"Are those ravens tame?" says the business woman beside him.

"Nooooooo!" shriek the ravens.

"Just a couple of angry birds," says Steve.

"Steal their eggs?" says the man, laughing.

Steve's hands clench into fists. Fortunately the man and the woman both make a left as Steve and the ravens go right. He scowls at the birds as they hop along the pavement in between short bursts of flight.

"Shouldn't you be trailing Loki?" Steve asks as he walks down a stretch of street that is empty of passers-by.

Hopping around on the pavement about 10 feet away, one fluffs its wings. It is disturbing, but Steve's familiar enough with them now to recognize that as a raven equivalent of a shrug.

"Nope," says the bird.

"We've been assigned to watch you," says the other, flapping to the top of the mailbox—and leaving a crap.

Steve rolls his eyes. "And to what do I owe this honor?"

The raven on the ground flaps to the air. "We've wondered about that. Personally, I think, rawk rawk, Odin knows what Loki will do, but you are a mystery."

The hairs on the back of Steve's neck stand on end but he tries to keep his voice light. "What will Loki do?"

The raven lands on the ground and bobs its head. "What he always does, and then we'll catch him!"

At that point the other raven dives headlong onto the first and starts pecking at its head with a screech. "Huginn, you idiot!!!"

The two take off into the air, blathering in a Slavic sounding language the linguists at ADUO think may be related to Old Norse. Steve lets out a deep breath that isn't quite relief. He walks on for a few more minutes, falling into step with other people on their way to work. He lets his mind empty and just focuses on traffic lights and his fellow pedestrians.

He's only about a block away from ADUO when his cell rings. Pulling it out of his pocket he answers. "Rogers here."

"Sir," says Bryant. "I think we have a problem … "

"Wha—" says Steve, but then the ground beneath him trembles and from the sewer drain next to him comes a sound that makes his stomach drop. It sounds like a hiss, three octaves too low.

"We think something has infiltrated the tunnels," says Bryant.

"I'm on my way," Steve says, already breaking into a run.

Loki is sitting at his computer, a large coffee, assorted croissants, and little spheres of the Promethean netting no bigger than his palm on the desk next to him. Some of the spheres have the same sort of outgrowth that surrounds Cera, remnants of Loki's experiments with the stuff.

Picking up a croissant, he tosses its paper wrapper onto one of the mutated spheres. There is a soft pop and the wrapper sinks out of existence.

He tilts his head. They make attractive little trash disposals. And they aren't really dangerous at these small sizes. An infant could crush one and not be harmed. Too bad he can't market them at upscale interior design studios.

"When are you going to get me? I hate being locked up!" Cera whines.

Loki rolls his eyes. Cera is as impatient as a child ... or a human. "When I can get you out."

Unfortunately, the sphere containing Cera needs considerably more force than an infant to break it. He's looked at the feasibility of collapsing the Board of Trade on Cera's sphere, but Cera isn't quite at the epicenter of where impact would be—and the tunnel and building were reinforced post 9/11. If it did work—and Loki's not sure it would, he'd still wind up with an enormous pile of rubble to plow through to retrieve her.

His jaw tenses. He has to get to her before the Vanir. They are coming. They have to be coming ... and he can do nothing and go nowhere as long as the two gates to Vanaheim are unguarded.

He looks at his computer. It's nearly 7:30, almost market opening time and he's in the mood for some innocent distraction. The lack of progress with Cera is making him irritable. He starts opening his trading accounts when he feels the highrise apartment he is in start to sway.

He blinks.

"Something is down here," says Cera, sounding more annoyed than frightened.

Closing his eyes, Loki sends an apparition of himself into the tunnels. A serpent with a head so big it nearly fills the tunnel opens its mouth and tries to swallow him—and of course meets only empty air. Finding his projection in the belly of the beast, Loki withdraws back to his apartment.

Let ADUO deal with it. "Don't worry, Cera," he says. "It can't hurt you."

"It is pretty," says Cera.

"Hmmmmm," says Loki looking at one of the little algorithms he created to help predict the movement of the Brazilian Real. He smiles. A sure thing. Time to make a quick million or so. He purchases some futures of said currency and is about to divest himself of said contracts when the power goes out.

Steve is standing ankle deep in water in the tunnel system beneath Chicago's streets. The tunnels aren't supposed to be wet. There must be a leak somewhere. He's got one hand pressed to the headpiece in his ear, the other on his Glock. Several of the guys have their flashlights out, and there is also dim utility light behind him from one of the coal-loading platforms.

He and his team are beneath the intersection of LaSalle and Monroe, two blocks north of where the World Seed is, or as Loki calls it, Cera.

"Bryant," Steve says into the headset at his ear. "Any sign?"

Bryant's voice crackles back. "Negative." He's at the tunnel intersection of Clark and Adams, where an Internet substation and electrical power box went down minutes before. They've received reports of power going out all over Chicago's downtown.

"Gonna be hard to find whatever it is down here," says one of his agents spinning around, flashlight in one hand, M16 in the other.

Water ripples over Steve's feet. He looks down. The little waves are coming from the west. He looks up. His guys are all standing to the north of him. Blood running cold, he says quietly, "Incoming, 9 o'clock! Take cover."

Steve goes south and flattens himself against the wall; his boys go north, but one, Jones, the guy with the M16, turns and faces whatever is coming. Before he even has the gun raised a nightmarish shadow that looks like a giant gaping snake's maw streaks through the intersection.

Steve can't see his agents anymore; there is just a solid wall of dark gray something between him and them.

Over his headset he hears, "Jones is down!" And then Steve hears Brett say, "That wall has scales ... don't see any feet or nothing. I think it's a snake. Shouldn't be able to go backwards."

He thinks he might be sick.

A voice sounds by Steve's other ear. "It's a wyrm. And no, it can't go backwards; you're safe for now."

Steve jumps. There is Loki, in his armor, arms crossed over his chest, a flare of light dancing just behind him. Narrowing his eyes, Loki says, "Of course, since you're on a grid system all it has to do is make 3 right turns and then you're not safe anymore."

Steve's mouth drops. "It just ... "

"Ate someone, did it?" says Loki striding forward so he is just a foot next to the gently undulating scales. "They'll do that."

Turning back to Steve he scowls. "Never trust a broker

who doesn't have a fully functional mobile-trading platform, Steven. In the end low commissions ... Just. Are. Not. Worth. It."

Steve's brain draws a blank. And then his face goes hot. "Just tell me how to kill this thing!"

Loki runs his tongue over his teeth. "Try shooting it?"

Steve whips out his Glock and releases a whole clip. The scaly body twists and thrashes, the ground trembles, and something red trickles out. And then the scales resume their smooth slide. From the other side of the tunnel he hears the sound of more shots. The creature doesn't even writhe.

Loki shakes his head. "That's not going to work. I think you've just given it the equivalent of a bad paper cut."

"Well, what will work!" Steve shouts.

"I'm thinking!" says Loki, crossing his arms over his chest, the scales still slipping by in the tunnel before them.

Bryant's voice buzzes in Steve's ear. "Agent Rogers?"

"Loki's here," says Steve. "I'm fine."

"Normally," says Loki, "a blow to the heart is how to deal with these things. Their scales in their abdomens are more delicate."

"Did you hear that?" says Steve, pushing the headset against his ear.

"Yes," says Bryant.

Shaking his head, Loki says, "But the tunnel is too tight. You'll never be able get it to rear up high enough."

"What about a goat carcass with explosives!" Steve says.

Loki turns to him, eyes wide, and looking vaguely excited. "Oh, that might be fun." He squints one eye. "Of course, it would have to be a live goat ... .or goats ... And it might get out of the tunnels before you have an opportunity to procure said goats. Of course, then you could aim for the heart—"

There is a shriek from somewhere down the tunnel. Loki sighs.

"Who was that?" Steve screams into his ear piece. The scales are still sliding by. How long is this damn thing?

"Check in!" says Bryant. A few seconds later, Bryant says, "Not one of ours."

Steve closes his eyes. A civilian. Maybe a maintenance worker … His stomach falls.

"How do I kill it now?" says Steve, meeting Loki's eyes.

Loki's face is blank and unreadable for an instant. And then he gives Steve a tight smile. "Cera. We lead it to Cera and let her deal with it."

"It will eat the World Seed?" says Steve.

"No," says Loki. "But you and I will lure the snake to her. When it touches Cera, she'll … " he tilts his head toward the scales. "Do what she does to everything else."

Steve blinks. Cera is definitely the World Seed, just as Lewis suspected. His jaw tightens. Everything that touches Cera disappears. The hypothesis at ADUO is that anything that touches Cera's Promethian containment sphere gets sucked into a vacuum. Where that vacuum leads is a source of contentious debate.

"Cera's strong enough to handle this thing?" says Steve, backing away from the wall of shimmering scales.

Giving Steve a wicked, toothy smile, Loki says, "Oh, yes." Turning southwards, he shouts. "Come!"

Swallowing, Steve follows Loki and the ball of light just before him. They turn eastward on Adams and run two more blocks when Loki stops, turns northward and shouts, "Mr. Slithers! Come and get us!" He turns to Steve and starts to hop. "Start jumping up and down. It should be attracted to my light, but it will feel your vibrations, too."

Steve follows Loki's motions without thinking, although all he sees to the north is empty tunnel.

Only moments later, he's soaked through from water in the tunnel splashing beneath his feet.

He's telling Bryant where he is when he sees a glint at the end of the tunnel beyond Loki's light.

"Here comes, Baby," says Loki.

Steve freezes. A snake head taller and wider than him is moving down the tunnel. It's been a long time since Steve has been frozen in terror. This has to be just a nightmare ... if he just wills it to end ...

"Run!" says Loki, backing up. Steve blinks at the ginger-haired alien and remembers nightmares are real now.

Steve follows Loki as he tears down the Dearborn street tunnel, and then west down the Jackson tunnel toward Cera. Cera is sitting on a raised coal platform above the actual tunnel proper, lit from within with eerie blue light. The Promethean containment sphere around it is now just under 20 centimeters from touching the ceiling at the center of the platform. It's still growing, but only at a pace of a few millimeters a day now. The guys in tech say they've only got a few weeks before they have to worry about it touching the ceiling. And then what no one knows. It isn't sucking the ground beneath it away ...

In front of him, Loki, jumps the half meter wall up to the platform; Steve follows. Steve is closer to the tunnel, Loki is closer to the wall. Loki turns. Steve spins around next to him. The opening to the tunnel they just emerged from is about 20 meters away. He can't see the snake from where he stands, but he knows it's coming. He sees the gentle waves in the puddles at the bottom of the tunnel and the absolute pitch black of the tunnel where the reptile's body blocks all utility lights.

"When it strikes," says Loki, "dive." He nods with his head toward the edge of the platform and the wet tunnel shaft about a meter to Steve's left. "And then grab hold of the ladder on the far wall, lest you be pulled into the vacuum of the In-Between."

Steve looks over to Loki. "In-Between?"

Loki doesn't answer, just keeps his eyes focused on the tunnel opening.

Steve hears a hiss, and turns his head. It's too late at that moment to reflect on the wisdom of following the plan given to him by the so-called God of Mischief.

The head of the wyrm-snake-monster emerges from the tunnel. It has yellow eyes with round pupils set into the gray-green scales of its face. It slides its head up onto the platform, its long gray body still stretched out into the tunnel.

Steve takes a breath. Something long and pink flicks from the wyrm's mouth to just a meter before Steve's feet. He almost runs, but Loki says calmly, "Wait for it." And mutters. "Damnable thing cost me a lot of money, now it's going to die … "

Loki is here. If he can do this, Steve can do this—he has to do this … .

The snake's head draws back. There is a flash of white that later Steve will piece together is a bit of its underside.

"Now!" says Loki. Steve dives from the platform into the tunnel. There is a rush of air and his hands are hitting a puddle, fetid water is splashing into his mouth, and air whooshes over his head.

"Get to the ladder! Hold on!" screams Loki. Steve crawls toward the ladder on the wall, and air rushes past him, nearly knocking him over. He glances back for a moment and see the wyrm's mouth is stretched over the Promethean Sphere. For a moment Steve wishes the snake would devour it, and take the thing to the In-Between-vacuum-wherever. But then he feels air rushing faster and sees the snake's coils writhe as its head begins to vanish, the containment sphere and Cera remaining firmly in place. Cursing, Steve crawls forward, pulls himself upright, face to the wall, and wraps both arms around the ladder.

The snake is being sucked forward. It's ridiculous, but it reminds Steve of the automatic wind of a vacuum cleaner cord—a vacuum cleaner cord that is thrashing and is nearly 7 feet tall. As the wyrm disappears equipment from the platform and bits of trash from the tunnel get sucked forward into the ... whatever.

Loki is standing right in front of him. Steve feels increasing force pulling him toward the sphere. Loki can't possibly withstand it.

On instinct Steve reaches out. "Loki!" His voice is almost drowned out by the sound of air whooshing past him. His hand would have landed on Loki's shoulder but it passes through empty air. Loki looks down at its path and then up to Steve.

Steve's mouth drops. Of course. Loki was never here, never in danger. As that thought runs through him, he is ripped from the ladder. He lands in the puddle again, but this time he feels himself being lifted from the ground. Closing his eyes, he searches blindly in the water, trying to find anything beneath his fingers to grab hold of.

And suddenly something comes down on him, something solid and cold encasing his whole body. Is he gone—beyond … wherever? There is the sound of more air rushing past him and then there is a loud crack. The air stops moving. Suddenly, over the sound of his own labored breathing he hears Bryant shouting through his headset.

Steve shivers. He's so very cold. And there is pressure on his back and sides. He opens his eyes, tries to move, and then realizes the puddle he was lying in has frozen solid and he's frozen in it.

Loki is standing above him. "Thank you," he says.

Steve stares at him uncomprehending and then Loki says, "Sometimes it is the thought that counts, Steven."

As Bryant and the other agents race into the intersection he smiles tightly. "Now get surveillance on those locations I mentioned."

And then he disappears.

ADUO's offices are a little dark the next morning when Amy comes to work. It takes her a few minutes to realize they're running on emergency power. The rain must have damaged some power lines. She sits down at her computer and opens a browser. The T1 line is still up. She smiles. That's all that matters.

ADUO headquarters has changed a lot in the few weeks since Steve has been in charge. There are a lot of deliveries of new equipment, and a lot more employees. As Amy sits at her desk researching the hypothesis she formed the night before, a man who is the new department physicist goes by, then a woman who is an astronomer, and a doctor and two nurses who are setting up a trauma center on the floor above the main office. Apparently ADUO is worried about having to explain troll wounds to doctors at the local hospital.

She peers around her monitor. She can hear Laura Stogdill, the department's legal counsel, yelling over her phone through her office door. But where are the new agents she pegged as more muscle than brain? And where are Steve, Brett, Bryant and Hernandez? She checks her email. There is nothing about Steve being late.

Shrugging to herself, she goes back to her internet searches. It's nearly 10 a.m. when Agent Bryant comes over to her desk. He is wet, and dirty, and smells funny. He also looks a little pale. He's carrying what looks like Steve's gym bag. Leaning on the reception desk he says, "Meet Steve in the trauma center in 15 minutes for debriefing."

"Trauma center?" says Amy. "What happened?"

Walking away from the desk he says, "Ask your friend."

Amy's brow furrows. "Which friend?"

Bryant grunts and disappears down the hallway. 15 minutes later Amy is in the trauma center. She can't see Steve, but from behind a curtain divider at the end of the room she can hear him.

"With all due respect, Sir, I made an executive decision."

There is a pause, and then Steve's voice again. "There was no reason to believe Loki would want to destroy Cera—the World Seed."

There is another long pause and then, "One of our agents is dead, and we've got reports of a maintenance worker and several homeless people missing. Frankly, I am not particularly sorry that the football-field-long snake responsible isn't still around for scientific inquiry!"

Amy jumps and her eyes go wide.

There are a few noncommittal grunts. She thinks she hears a phone snapping shut. And then Steve's voice, "Where is Lewis?"

Stepping toward the curtains, Amy clears her throat.

The curtain divider is pulled away by Hernandez, and there is Steve sitting on a bed in a tight gray t-shirt that says Marines, loose pants, and gym shoes. His workout gear, Amy realizes. He looks a lot better than the guys standing around him in dirty wet suits.

Hernandez checks a magic detector and says, "Clear."

"Are you alright, Sir?" Amy says to Steve.

"I'm fine," he says in a bored voice. "Just got checked out for frostbite. Standard procedure."

"Frostbite?" says Amy.

All of the guys shift on their feet. Steve just raises an eyebrow. "Why don't you tell us about your run-in with Loki yesterday."

Amy nods. "I learned something really important, maybe the most important thing."

Steve sits up a little straighter and tilts his head.

Taking a step forward, Amy says, "The elf queen's name was the same as in our movies and books."

The room goes absolutely silent.

And then Bryant says slowly, "In the Lord of the—"

"In real life, too!" says Amy, turning to him with wide eyes.

"And this is important because … " says Steve.

"Because it means that there may be truth to all of our

myths, modern as well as ancient! That's ... " Amy lifts her hands, "huge!"

Everyone is quiet again.

Steve blinks, and then in a very slow voice he says, "Did you ask him the questions I gave you?"

"Sir," says Bryant turning quickly to him. "I think if what Amy says is true that it ... " He swallows.

"That it could be bad," says his brother Brett.

Steve and Amy both look at the two brothers.

Slipping his hands into his pockets, Bryant says, "We got a shiny glowy power thing underneath our feet, and Loki is trying to get it ... "

Steve and Amy both stare at him.

"Have you two seen the Thor movies?" says Brett.

Hernandez whistles low.

"It's been a while," says Amy.

"It's been never," says Steve.

Shaking his head, Hernandez says, "I'll paraphrase. An angry, entitled, arrogant, bat-shit crazy Loki steals a shiny glowy power thing and tries to take over the earth from the humans he declares ants on his boots."

Wringing her hands, Amy says softly. "Loki likes humans."

Bryant tilts his head. "In the movies, Loki is capable of astral projection ... and he turns blue because he is a Frost Giant ... like our Loki."

"He says Frost Giants aren't blue," says Amy weakly.

"Loki doesn't think we're ants," Steve says quietly, looking at something on his phone.

Everyone turns to him.

"He used you as wyrm bait and froze you in ice!" says Bryant.

Steve rolls his eyes. "We've been over this." There is silence in the room. Nodding his head in the direction of the door, Steve says. "Why don't you guys go find out how those home-less people managed to slip into the tunnels. I'll debrief Ms. Lewis."

No one moves for a minute, and then Steve fixes them all with what Amy thinks he should patent as a death glare. "Dismissed."

After the other agents file out, Steve pulls on a zip up sweatshirt.

"Did he really freeze you in ice and use you as wyrm bait?" Amy says in a small voice.

Steve raises an eyebrow. "He froze me in ice to save my life."

Amy lets out a breath of relief and smiles.

Not matching her smile, Steve tilts his head toward the door. "Let's walk, Miss Lewis, and you can tell me everything that happened."

They walk outside through a walkway that goes beneath the Board of Trade building and up Van Buren beneath the 'L' tracks that run through Chicago's downtown. They come to a stairway, and Steve leads her up to a wide open courtyard. There are pots of colorful cold-hardy plants, and a fountain of black stone, now drained for the season.

Steve sits down on a stone bench and looks up at the empty sky. He motions with his head for Amy to sit down next to him. She notices a few stares from businessmen walk-ing by. It strikes her they must make an odd couple, Steve in his forties, in his gym outfit, Amy in her business attire. She even catches a few glares, which is really surprising—is it because Steve's black? She gives him a sidelong glance, his eyes

flit to the glarers … but his face remains impassive. Amy's got
to hand it to him, the guy is a rock.

Looking upwards Steve says, "So you didn't get a chance
to ask him why he suspected visitors from Vanaheim when
we ran into that troll."

It isn't a question but Amy answers with one. "No?"

"Hmmm … " Steve raises an eyebrow at her, and then is
absolutely silent.

Amy swallows again. "Well, he did say that the sphere
thingy surrounding the World Seed Cera thingy is Vanaheim
technology?"

Steve's eyes narrow a little more.

Amy bites her lip. "And then there are the magic detector
doohickies; they are from Vanaheim, too," Amy says in a soft
voice.

Steve raises an eyebrow. The question is implicit. Amy says
weakly, "Loki told me?"

"But you didn't tell me," says Steve, his voice light, a faint
smile on his face. "Maybe because Loki told you not to tell
me?"

"No! It's not like that!" Amy says. "I was afraid of Bryant!"
Before she knows it, she's telling Steve all about her adventure
to the microbiology lab, about taking apart Bryant's precious
magic detector prototype, and even about Loki turning blue.

He doesn't say anything the whole time, but his eyes narrow considerably more and a frown settles onto his features.

By the time she's done, she's sweating despite the chill
weather, and she's wondering if he's going to fire her.

Looking off into the distance he says, "Ms. Lewis, next
time you do something like that, you tell me."

Amy starts to stammer, the sweat on her skin going cold.

"But … it is a $30,000 dollar piece of equipment and I took it apart with a nail file … and Bryant … and … "

Steve lifts an eyebrow at her. "You tell me, Ms. Lewis." He smiles. "I need to pass this on to higher ups, but don't worry. I can handle Bryant—and the rest of them." He winks. "They won't take away your nail file."

Amy's body sags with relief. At that moment her phone starts to buzz. Pulling it out of her pocket she sees a text from an unknown caller. Accepting it she reads: *Tell Steve I have disabled the gate Mr. Slithers used.*

She hands the phone to Steve. He blinks at it and then types back with surprising speed. It is her phone, so Amy doesn't feel too bad peeking over his shoulder.

Did u close troll's gate 2? Steve asks.

A text comes back. *No.*

Tilting his head Steve types. *Why not?*

Bye-bye, Steven. Loki responds.

Steve hands the phone to her. "Any idea why he would close one gate and not the other?"

Amy tilts her head. "Where is the wyrm gate?"

"I have no idea," says Steve, looking at the sky again.

"Do you have the troll gate under surveillance?" Amy asks.

"Of course," says Steve.

Amy looks at the phone. She remembers Loki staggering into her car after closing the gate to Alfheim … or redirecting it … or whatever. "Maybe he's afraid. I think it exhausts him. Maybe he thinks you'd try and catch him?"

Steve doesn't respond. Amy finds herself shivering.

He's quiet for a few long moments and then says, "So,

your theory about all stories being potentially true—"

"Partially true," says Amy. "Maybe."

"Is there anything in them about Loki that seems ... consistent?"

Amy looks down at her shoes. "Well ... he's a thief. And he brings about the end of the world." She bites her lip. Okay, that doesn't sound good. "But I've just really begun to research this ... so maybe ... I dunno."

Steve nods. "Why don't you continue to research it." He lifts an eyebrow at her. "Since you hardly answer phone calls and spend most of your time reading veterinary journals."

Amy reddens. He knew about that? "Okay," she says.

Looking away again he says, "Thank you for your insight, Miss Lewis. You're not our typical government agent, but I'm glad we have you."

A compliment? From Steve? The man of the patented death glare? She scratches the pavement in front of her with her shoe. She's actually flattered. But she doesn't quite feel like letting him know. Trying to sound plucky she says, "Just trying to earn enough money to get back into vet school ... you know, if I don't get my scholarship reinstated."

Steve laughs at that for some reason. For a few moments they sit in companionable silence and then two of the biggest ravens Amy has ever seen land in the empty fountain.

One starts to bob and squawk. "There you are, Steven! Rawk ... Rawk ... "

"Hey, Muginn," says the second one. "Is that Loki's girlfriend he's flirting with?"

Amy's eyes go wide and heat rushes to her face.

Bobbing, the first one says, "Remember what happened last time someone messed with Loki's girlfriend. Rawk, Rawk

… .Loki cut him to pieces and flushed him down the river!"

Scowling, Steve stands up. "Let's go."

But Amy's petrified … in absolute fury.

The second raven hops to the edge of the fountain oppo-site Amy and Steve. "What are you talking about, Muginn? That never happened … "

"You don't remember anything, Huginn!" squawks the bird that must be Muginn.

"Amy … ." says Steve.

But Amy is beyond hearing or caring. Picking up a rock from one of the planters, she hurls it at the closest bird—and hits her mark.

It gives an angry rawk and then both birds take to the sky in a flurry of feathers, one with noticeably more difficulty. "You whore! You hag!" they shriek.

Beside her Steve picks up another rock and throws it at them, just grazing one of their wings. With a shriek they both take off.

Amy turns to Steve. His face is a reflection of the fury she just felt. "Damn things have been following me everywhere," Steve says. "I still haven't figured out why me and not Loki."

Amy tilts her head. She knows who the ravens are. "Those are Odin's messengers … They're following you?"

Steve doesn't answer.

Amy takes a deep breath. "You're a scary guy, Steve."

CHAPTER 7

"Is that a poodle dyed pink, or a Midgardian animal I've never seen before?" says Loki, staring at the Star Trek Original Series episode on the television screen. He tilts his head. "Hoenir would approve of this evolution."

"Poodle dyed pink," says Amy, and he frowns. She and Loki are on her EZ Boy chairs, watching Star Trek and eating Chinese food. It's just a few days after Mr. Slithers graced Chicago with his presence. This isn't how she expected her evening to go, but it's great. Granted, seeing the line of caterers with pan loads of Chinese food outside when she got home from work was a little disconcerting—especially when they started demanding payment. But as soon as Loki stepped out of her apartment, it all made perfect sense.

"So you've never heard about the Three Billy Goats Gruff," says Amy. She has her list out. "I was sure there was a connection between that and the trolls finding goat meat irresistible."

Loki gives her a look that is almost sympathetic, or maybe it is just the headache he was complaining about earlier that is causing his brow to furrow. "It doesn't mean it didn't happen. It just means I've never heard of any goats speaking troll."

She looks down at her list. He can't animate statues, either—though he says Hoenir could do it. And he's never turned anyone into black-footed ferrets. Those were questions that Bryant and Brett said they'd snagged from the comics.

She looks at the last entry on her list. "Can you teleport?" It's something comic-book and movie-Loki can do, but myth-Loki can't.

Loki chokes on whatever he is eating. Thumping his chest, he sputters. "Teleport?"

"Yeah, you know … " She moves her hand in empty air.

He stares at her blankly.

"It's when—"

Pulling out his mobile phone he smiles triumphantly. "Tele as in telephone, and port, as in to carry or move! I only use temporary mobile services, but I always teleport. I thought you knew?"

Amy's brow furrows. "Actually, it means, um, like in Star Trek, when they dematerialize through the transporter … "

Loki gives her a look like she's kicked a puppy. "The only way my atoms will dematerialize would be with a rather large explosion … and there would be no putting them back together."

He looks down at the noodles he was just eating and puts them aside, looking a little disgusted.

"Right," says Amy. She'll put that down as a 'no.'

"Awww … the pink doggie died … " says Loki looking back at the pre-CGI pre-Muppet alien on the screen.

They watch several more episodes of Star Trek. It's kind of fun, like old times at Amy's grandmother's house. But with agents with guns parked outside, a portal to dwarf world's troll lands a few blocks off, and an apartment filled with surveillance devices. There's also lots of Chinese food—lots and lots of Chinese food. It was fun sampling all the dishes. Apparently if you can order in Mandarin, you really get the good stuff.

Abraham Lincoln is chatting with Captain Kirk, and Amy is about to fall asleep when she remembers one last thing. "Steve says to tell you those places in Europe and India are under surveillance."

Loki is silent. She turns to see him giving her a bright, mischievous smile, the tension in his brow completely gone. "Thank you, Amy."

Fenrir starts to whimper up at empty air and then runs over and jumps into her lap. Loki turns back to the screen but he's unusually quiet. Captain Kirk and Abraham Lincoln are saying their goodbyes when Amy suddenly gets suspicious. Picking up a chopstick, she throws it at his shoulder. It passes right through him and lands on the floor.

Astral projection Loki turns and sticks out his tongue and then vanishes. Amy looks to the door, wondering just how long he's been gone.

As soon as Amy tells Loki that the gates to Vanaheim in Europe and Asia are covered, Cera, who'd been whining all night, suddenly becomes irritatingly sycophantic. "You were right! They covered the gates to Vanaheim! Now Frey, puppet king and liege of Odin won't be able to get me! Oh, I am so relieved. You are so wise, Loki, so wise!"

Not that Loki trusts ADUO's word for it. He creates an astral image of himself in the chair, turns himself invisible and slips out the door. Cera follows close behind.

As soon as he's certain he hasn't been followed, he slips into a dark alley. Looking up at the sky, he creates an illusion of himself and lets it keep walking … just in case Heimdall is watching.

Cloaked in invisibility, he takes a breath, wills all the magic around him to himself, steps forward … and into the nothingness of absolute vacuum in the In-Between. It is beyond the reach of even starlight and there is only cold, darkness, and Loki's own magic. He panics momentarily. He needs a landmark at his destination to anchor to. Throwing out a hand, he imagines a stone in the ring wall of Visby, Sweden. Magic splits the nothing and pulls him forward and out.

He is suddenly falling forward and gasping for breath in a chilly Swedish autumn. His face hits the ancient stone wall that surrounds Visby's old city. Thankfully, it is very early in the morning. He's in a field next to the water, and there is no one about.

He staggers back and falls into the grass. His head is marvelously clear, and Cera's whining is gone. He lies back and closes his eyes. Tomorrow he'll check that surveillance of the gate inside the ringwall is adequately protected.

He throws an arm over his eyes, grateful he's in his armor and it has some temperature modulation. Only his chin and his exposed left arm are cold. His stomach grumbles despite the meal he's just consumed.

He's definitely sticking to air travel when he checks the gate in India ... Teleporting is just so exhausting.

Hopping off the 'L' at the Racine stop, Amy makes her way to Lexington Avenue just north of Arrigo Park and walks toward the statue of Columbus, two bags of groceries in her arms. The gate where the troll arrived is cordoned off with police tape.

Other than the police line there is no sign that anything unusual is afoot. It's a warmish fall day and there are people playing soccer on the open field. Kids and their parents are riding bicycles on the little trail that makes a large oval around the green.

It's been over a week since Amy has seen Loki. Her life is returning to its previous state of depressing normal. Her mother is still waiting to transfer Beatrice to another nursing home. Amy's waiting to hear back on her scholarship. She's still a receptionist for ADUO who moonlights as a vet tech.

She shakes her head. She's starting to worry about Loki. Or miss him. Or both. He showed up so soon in her apartment after Mr. Slither's visit ... she thought they were friends. Or something. But friends share phone numbers and email addresses, don't they?

She feels her face harden. He's the only thing in her life right now that makes her feel special and hopeful, and that can't be good. He is literally a mirage half the time ... but he's also the only person she can really talk to. She can't tell her friends outside of ADUO about anything that has happened in her life recently. Breathe a word about Loki, Odin, trolls, ravens, or wyrms and she could wind up in jail.

Leaving the sidewalk, she walks through a gate and steps onto the path that goes around the green of the park—and freezes. On a bench up ahead is someone she never thought she'd see again. He is alternately reading and watching the soccer match. He turns his head toward the cordoned off area where the troll arrived, and then back to his book.

Heart picking up speed, Amy turns off Lexington and almost jogs down the little trail.

"Liddel!" Amy calls when she is a few feet away.

The man looks up. Liddel was one of two elves Amy met in Alfheim who was not royalty. He and his wife Dolinar were planning to escape the land of the 'light' elves and journey to the dark lands to save their unborn child.

This man looks so much like him. He has blonde hair and brown eyes, and he is somewhat attractive ... and yet ... elven beauty is perfect. This man's nose is a little disproportionate and a bit crooked. One of his eyebrows seems a little higher than the other. His lips are a tad too thin, and he has a scar on one side of his mouth. His short haircut just barely covers the tips of his ears, but Amy doesn't need to see them to know that they're round.

He is just a vision of Liddel in a warped mirror.

His mouth drops for a moment, and then he says, "Pardon?"

Amy backs up a few steps. "I'm sorry ... I think I mistook you for someone else."

Closing his book, he stands up abruptly. "Well, no harm done. Have a good day."

He walks past her without giving her a backwards glance.

She's read that you've reached middle age when everyone starts looking like someone else you know. Is she middle aged at the advanced age of 25?

Adjusting her groceries, Amy starts walking home again.

A little more than a week after his hasty departure, Loki collapses gratefully into an EZ Boy chair in Amy's apartment. It's good to be back to his temporary home. Travelling by plane is exhausting, too.

Cera hums in frustration above him. "I don't see this visit is necessary. The gates to Vanaheim are under surveillance."

He sighs. Cera's Josef wasn't one for keeping oaths unless they involved killing or maiming someone and she just doesn't understand.

The little dog-rat beast jumps into his arms and growls at Cera's floating form. Smiling, Loki squeezes the shaggy creature to his chest and scratches between its ears. Fenrir yips and whines happily, giving an occasional angry bark in Cera's direction. Loki closes his eyes for just a moment. His mind feels fuzzy. A side effect of travel by plane—or just a headache from Cera's whining?

Cera hums angrily. "You don't even exchange genetic information with her like you did with the females in Visby and Chidambaram ... "

Loki tilts his head, remembering those encounters. They had helped him sleep, something that is more and more difficult to do. He dreams of Nari and Valli, Helen, Aggi, Sigyn, Hoenir and Mimir, but also of faces he doesn't recognize.

They leave him waking to the chill of his own sweat.

He feels as though there is something he is forgetting. Something just at the edge of his consciousness.

Loki looks at where the mist is thickest. "I still need to keep tabs on ADUO, and she's the easiest way to do that." And he likes not eating alone. He likes to be distracted from whatever it is hovering just at the back of his mind.

Cera withdraws with a misty equivalent of a huff until she is just a faint pink halo at the edge of his vision. Fenrir tucks her nose under his unarmored arm, and Loki rests his eyes, just for a moment.

He awakens to the sound of a key in the lock.

Loki puts his hand to his mouth to stifle a yawn and blinks. His hand is blue—just like when he woke up in Visby with that woman. Throwing Fenrir to the floor, he jumps from the chair, vaults over the half bookshelf and checks his appearance in the mirror by Amy's bed. He looks like one of the blue idols worshipped by the Indians in Chidambaram— blue skin, black hair, but eyes as empty as the void. Running his hands through his hair, he turns it back to ginger and pauses. Those idols ... if Amy's hypothesis is true ... could they have been suffering from the same affliction plaguing Loki? He's never met a Shiva, Brahma, or Krista ... or whatever. They're long gone if they existed at all. Could this affliction be the cause? Is he dying? He clenches his jaw and looks down at his blue hands. He will not die until he has his vengeance. Odin will kneel and all of Asgard will burn.

The blue in his body slips away like water leaching into sand. At just that moment, the door opens. Loki spins around and pulls a book from the shelf at random.

"Hey!" says Amy, her head between two bags of groceries

as Fenrir hops beside her. "Um ... nice to see you, long time no see ... .What are you doing?"

Smiling, Loki looks down at the book. "Oh, just reading ... How to Teach Physics to Your Dog." Holding it aloft he chuckles. "Is Fenrir benefiting from this?"

Looking far too smug she walks by toward the kitchen. "It's super simplified quantum physics for humans." She begins to unpack the brown paper sacks. "Since you told me magic is just basically quantum mechanics, I thought I'd read up a bit. I don't think Fenrir gets it, but I bet she'd have fun putting a cat in a box."

Loki actually laughs at the reference to Schrödinger's cat. Amy smiles and bites her lip. He wonders how long she's been waiting to tell that little joke.

Pulling something from her bag, she says, "Hey, I have portobello mushrooms—want a portobello mushroom burger?"

Loki purses his lips. "Let's skip the fungus on toast. Get changed. We have reservations at one of the premier molecular gastronomy restaurants in the entire world!"

"Molecular what?" says Amy.

His eyes widen. "How can you be oblivious to one of the greatest revolutions in your species' history? Especially when one of the best establishments for said revolution is in your hometown?"

Amy's lips quirk. "Do I need to bring a gun to this revolution—or explosive-laden goat meat?"

"Ha," Loki says dryly, fighting his lips as they turn up at the corners. "No. Just a nice dress." He rolls his head and bounces on his feet. "Come on. I'm hungry." The last comes out a whine.

Walking toward her closet Amy says, "Okay, Comrade."

And then suddenly Cera is filling the room and Fenrir is growling at the air.

"She is not a Comrade! She is a petty bourgeois!" Cera screams—in English. Of course being human, Amy can't hear her magical wail.

"Shut-up," says Loki, being careful to use Russian. And then he blinks. "When did you learn English?"

Cera retreats immediately and Loki scowls.

"Loki?" says Amy.

Turning to Amy he says brightly, "Nothing." He looks at the dress she's pulled out and the shoes. He purses his lips. "Heels, please."

"I fall down in the heels," says Amy scowling at him.

Loki smirks. "So earn your danger pay honestly for once." He looks down at the book in his hands as she glares at him and goes into the bathroom.

"Turn right!" says Loki. The cab driver turns sharply onto Ashland Avenue and Amy slams into the door so quickly that her high-heeled shoes fall off.

How did she let Loki convince her to wear heels again? She shakes her head, remembering overhearing Bryant in the hallway in the office. "Amy isn't a reliable go-between. She's got a crush on the guy, and he's dangerous."

Amy looks at Loki. He is looking out the back window, lips quirked in amusement, completely oblivious. "Brett must have significantly adjusted the sensitivity of the magic detectors," he says.

Amy sees the cab driver, an older guy with a little round cap and a long beard, maybe Indian, maybe Pakistani, raise an eyebrow in the rearview mirror. She shrugs at him.

Beside her, Loki's face pinches. "But I'm too hungry for games."

He turns his head northward. All of the street lights as far as the eye can see suddenly go green. "Drive faster," he says.

"Okay, Boss," says the cabbie in a thick accent. The cab jumps forward, and Amy falls back into the seat. She turns her head. As soon as they pass through a light it goes red and cars stop.

Loki leans back next to her and sighs happily. "Now where were we ... Molecular gastronomy ... where food preparation meets modern science ... "

The restaurant he's so excited about is *Alinea*. Amy's heard about it, but she's never been. It serves what Beatrice would call derisively, 'overpriced hoity toity food,' and once Amy might have agreed. But Beatrice would have turned up her nose at all the Chinese food she's been sampling with Loki at her apartment and the sushi, too. *Alinea* is located in an uber-rehabbed slate gray row house on Chicago's north side. Inside it's narrow. The decor is very modern, but with lots of rich browns and deep chocolate wood, it feels warm.

They're seated at a small table in a room with two small tables and one table set up for a large group; Loki takes the far seat facing the entrance. The large table is empty, the other small table, behind Amy, is already occupied by two men in suits.

The wait staff isn't hoity toity, they are all really friendly. Everyone smiles at them. Their waiter has dreadlocks and is very passionate about the menu, but Amy's too busy digging out her list to really pay attention.

"We'll take the 21 course option, and wine pairing," she hears Loki say. Hand still fishing in her purse, Amy grins and her feet do a little staccato dance step under the table. Loki raises an eyebrow at her as the waiter walks away. He looks businesslike this evening. He's wearing a dark gray suit over a green shirt—or well, that's what it looks like he's wearing anyway. He's probably in his armor. His hair is neat and brushed back, or looks like it is.

Leaning across the table she whispers. "I never have to feel guilty about ordering too much food with you … " She just takes a nibble of everything and then hands the rest off to him. It's so much fun sampling all the flavors and textures.

Staring at her chest he licks his lips. "Hmmmmm?"

Amy looks down, realizing that she's giving him a rather dramatic view of her cleavage. Face going hot with embarrassment and annoyance, she sits up. And Bryant is worried she's got a crush on him.

He shrugs and smiles without a trace of embarrassment as she glares at him and returns to fishing out her list.

An 'amuse bouche' of what looks like a foamy pink marshmallow on a graham cracker crumb with a single green chive atop arrives along with the first wine course. At just that moment she finds her list and pulls it out with a triumphant smile.

Loki snorts and picks up his wine.

"Hey, I want to get it over with." She puts her notes down on the table next to the pink marshmallow thingy. "Okay, the guys wanna know how creatures like trolls, which aren't the sharpest tacks in the box, can world walk when it takes extra effort on your part, and the Vanir, elves, etc."

Loki shrugs. "Birds don't understand aeronautics, but they fly." He takes a sip of his wine.

Amy makes a note and looks up to see him staring with wide eyes at the glass. And then he downs the whole thing in a single swallow and groans in a way that is slightly obscene.

Amy looks around. No one seems to have noticed. Looking down at her notes she continues. "So the whole invisibility thing—I'm guessing that is utilizing the theory of quantum entanglement ... you know two photons being in two places at once."

"Is that what you're teaching Fenrir?" says Loki with a grin and a wink. He picks up his little pink marshmallow chive thingy and pops it in his mouth.

He didn't say no. Excited, Amy sits up in her chair. "Am I right?"

But Loki's eyes are focused somewhere beyond her shoulder. They're very wide and he's chewing very slowly. Swallowing audibly, he pushes away the plate in front of him and then bangs his head on the table. Nose smashed against the tablecloth he sighs. "I think I just orgasmed in my mouth."

"But am I right about quantum entanglement?" says Amy.

Loki lifts his head just enough that he can glare at her. "By the Norns, woman! There is magic right in front of you. Eat! Or I'll eat it for you."

Amy narrows her eyes at him.

He narrows his eyes right back.

"Okay." She puts aside her list and takes a bite. Whatever it is melts on her tongue like cotton candy but it is savory and salmony and not sweet, except for the tiny bit of crispiness at the bottom. Her eyes go wide.

Loki sighs across from her. "Marshmallow of smoked salmon and cream cheese on carmelized rye crisp. Take a sip of your wine now."

Amy does. It's a dry white with a little kick that balances the salmon thingy perfectly.

She sets down her glass. "Wow. Well. I don't know that much about mouth orgasms but—" She stops. Loki is sitting up in his chair, eyes wide, obviously biting back a smile.

Why is he … ?

Oh.

She flushes from head to toe.

"Of course you don't," he says. Grabbing her wine he tilts his chair back and cackles maniacally.

Amy glares at him and hopes he tilts back too far. "You're perverted," she mumbles.

Giving her a leering grin, he drains her wine and leans forward. "No, that is not perverted. Sex with three dwarves at one time so that you can have a pretty bauble—that is perverted."

Amy recognizes the reference and knows which goddess' antics he's referring to. But opening her eyes as wide and as innocently as she can, she says, "You did that?"

Nostrils flaring, he sits up straight. "No! Freyja, the so called Goddess of Love and Beauty, did that—"

Amy bites her lip to keep from laughing, and his lips purse.

Looking to the side, he says. "Well played." When he

meets her eyes again it looks like he's fighting a smile. She can't help it; she sticks out her tongue.

He smiles and rolls his eyes. "And no matter what anyone says, I did not use my silver tongue to convince her to—"

His voice drifts off and his gaze drifts just over her shoulder. There is the sound of a large party coming in.

Amy turns around and sees a girl in a wheelchair. It's not the standard variety operate-it-with- your-arms-go-ahead-you-can-wheel-marathons wheelchair. It's a heavy-duty, electric machine. It has headrests at the top to hold the girl upright, and it's deeply padded. The girl's sitting oddly, slumping to the side. Her arms are curled upwards. Behind her is a man who looks like he's probably her father, and two sets of what looks like grandparents. Everyone is smiling.

The waiters smile, too. "Happy Sweet 16, Abby!" they say, and Amy feels her heart fall a little. The little girl Abby is so small she looks like she can't be more than 12.

Abby smiles back. Despite the gauntness of her face, it's a lovely smile. And then she laughs a little bit. Some spittle flies from her mouth, and she mouths a garbled, "Shanx you."

Behind her, Amy hears a disapproving sound from one of the businessmen.

She looks back at Loki. He's looking at the businessmen at the table behind her. His face is so emotionless it's frightening.

She's read myths about Loki's daughter Helen. The myths called her Hel. She was half alive and half dead in the stories, and banished to Nilfheim to rule over the dead. Loki told her Helen died, and her mother Anganboða …

She hears the businessman behind her summon the waiter and ask to be moved. Loki's eyes narrow as the man and his partner are ushered to another room.

Swallowing, Amy says softly, "Well. Now they won't ruin Abby's sweet sixteen."

Blinking as though he just realized Amy is there, he says, "Of course." His voice is inflectionless and impersonal.

Amy takes a breath. "I'd … I'd … like to smack that guy upside the head … but … don't … " She can't finish. The lack of emotion on Loki's face … the hardness in his eyes at the moment is terrifying.

"Don't worry. I won't ruin Abby's day either," he says as the first course arrives. Loki listens to the waiter, eats his and the remainder of Amy's in silence.

Amy tries to pick up the conversation. She's discovered some great stories, modern and ancient where Loki is the good guy. There is a short story called "Thor Meets Captain America" by David Brin where Loki saves the world from the Nazis. And another tale where Loki saved a little boy from a giant. But all Loki does is offer non-committal grunts. She realizes he is engrossed in the conversation going on at Abby's table. Amy hears snippets of, "And your second year of high school," and "we're so proud of you" and exclamations to the waiters of, "she's wanted to eat here for the longest time!"

It's difficult to understand Abby. Her words are drawn out and strange. Sometimes she grunts. But her father and mother seem to understand her. They translate for the rest of the table. Amy glances behind her and notice they help her eat, too.

Loki's eyes flick to everyone around them. He looks suspiciously at the waitstaff and incoming patrons, like he's expecting something from them and is prepared to lash out at any moment. And then abruptly at course 9 or 10 he says, "Amy, I'm full. I'm going to ask for the check."

She knows he's lying but doesn't disagree.

As soon as he's paid, Loki practically leaps from his chair. Face hard, he walks ahead of Amy toward the stairs. Which is odd. Normally he plays the gentleman—aside from the leering at her boobs.

And then it happens. Abby is laughing and a small bit of spittle flies from her mouth to Loki's perfect suit. He stops. Her table goes completely quiet. The smiles drop from her family's faces.

Amy can imagine what they're seeing. The cold business-man in the perfectly tailored suit looking down where the spittle landed - after someone else asked to be excused from the room. Amy sees Abby's grandmother swallow.

Loki suddenly flashes an absolutely disarming, dazzling smile. Holding up one hand he says to the room at large. "Look, nothing here!" Turning his hand around and holding up the other he says, "And nothing here!"

He puts both of his hands together, rubs, and then opens them as though he's about to catch a ball. Out fly dozens and dozens of butterflies. They're obviously illusions - they glow, and pass through objects, but they're beautiful, casting flick-ering lights through the room.

Abby and her family start to laugh. There's cries of "That's amazing." Waiters stop and stare and then begin to clap. Hearing murmurs of appreciation, Amy turns and sees other patrons crowding in the doorway of the room. People cheer and try to get the dancing mirages to land on their fingers.

Crouching down so he's at the level of Abby's face, Loki smiles brightly. "Happy Sweet Sixteen, Abby."

Abby smiles and grunts, and Loki just smiles wider and pulls a giant pink butterfly out of her hair.

There's a joint murmur of "Awwwww … " from everyone.

"I must go," he whispers to Abby. And then standing, he leaves the room a little too quickly. Amy just barely catches a look of strain upon his face.

She stands motionless, transfixed, in the swarm of swirling, glowing butterflies as people continue to murmur in wonder.

Forget worrying about developing a crush on Loki. She thinks she might have just fallen in love.

It is early afternoon on Wōdnesdæg, Odin's Day, the first day of the week. Loki is walking down the long path in the royal gardens that lead home, passing a few lovers, friends in conversation, and children at play as he does. They don't acknowledge him; he doesn't particularly care.

It is customary for Odin's Day to be a day of rest for Asgardians. But Odin and the Diar, the twelve judges assigned the task of helping Odin rule Asgard, were working on the final wording of a new treaty with the dwarves. They've been working on it nearly nonstop for the past month. Loki had been forced to be present the whole time, as he is, even in the words of his enemies, exceptional at finding loopholes.

He really should have told them the wording of the treaty was fine. Then he could have had the day off. But Loki has difficulty not pointing out the shoddiness of other people's thinking.

Now the sun is beginning its downward decline as he passes through the last copse of trees, turns a bend, and Anganboða Hall comes into view. Originally designed as a hideaway for Odin's mortal lovers, it isn't particularly large. When Loki won it in a wager with Odin, it had only a rather ostentatious boudoir, enormous bathing area, small kitchen and a few small servants' quarters. It had been in horrible disrepair—Frigga had been cracking down on Odin's trysts on Asgardian soil at the time.

Anganboða had occupied most of the early part of their marriage in restoring the place, procuring and placing magic rocks for the hot water heater, knocking down walls between the tiny, narrow, prison-like spaces that were supposed to be sleeping cells for servants they didn't have, managing the dwarven contractors fixing the plumbing, and painting the interior with her own hands.

On the outside it wears the same architectural style that is the fashion right now. It looks like an Alfheim country cottage, with walls of white gray stucco between beams of rough hewn logs beneath a curvy roof. Loki's not a fan of the current look. He thinks it resembles a small cluster of mushrooms. But it's theirs. Or Aggie's, ever since that unfortunate gambling incident.

As he approaches the home, Fenrir comes loping round the corner. Loki gives the wolf a scratch behind the ears and then walks up the steps illusioned to look like they are made out of living rock covered with green moss. He lets himself in the heavy, round wooden door, an illusion of a tree's cross section.

His wife isn't at the door to meet him. Nor does she call his name. She has been tired of late. Before this business of the treaty with the dwarves Loki had gone to Jotunheim with Thor to reclaim Thor's hammer. He was away several weeks. He thinks it's reasonable after such a long absence that Aggie might be tired … .and yet … he's been home over a month. She shouldn't be sick; she does have rights to one of Idunn's apples every year.

Tilting his head, he shuts the door and says softly. "Anganboða?"

Helen will be napping at this time, and he doesn't want to wake her.

Aggie doesn't answer. Loki wonders if she's asleep. He walks down the hallway and enters their room. Aggie sits up quickly on their bed. Her cheeks are streaked with tears, her eyes are red.

"Oh," she says. "You're home." Smoothing her dress, she drops her gaze to the floor. "Would you like some tea—or some mead?"

Loki tilts his head. "Has something happened, Aggie?" His voice comes out sharper than he means it to.

She drops her eyes to her hands. "Not really. Nothing unusual."

"Aggie … " He swallows. He hates … these things, but he has to fix this. "You're alone out here too often. Odin has kept me so busy."

Her friend Sigyn comes as frequently as she can, but she is a lady in waiting to Frigga and is often busy. Odin has also allowed her cousin Gullveig to visit a few times But Gullveig is a powerful sorceress, a chieftess in Jotunheim's Ironwood, and apparently threatening to the All Father. Odin finds reasons to deny Gullveig admittance to Asgard … and Loki finds it uncomfortable to have her under his roof. Gullveig looks so much like Aggie they could be sisters, but she radiates power. Loki finds the yoke of fidelity even more difficult when she's about.

Loki lets out a tense breath. "You know, we have money now … " He's been too busy to gamble, so instead of feast or famine Aggie's been able to keep the household purse at a little more than full enough. "Why don't you hire a servant?"

Aggie bites her lip and begins to laugh, or sob, Loki's not sure which. "Oh, haven't you heard, Husband? I'm a witch and a troll woman, mother of monsters … " She turns her eyes to him. "No one will work for me."

"No one?" says Loki dumbly.

"I have tried," says Aggie, looking away again, her face empty.

And suddenly he can imagine it. He's heard Baldur say she is obviously 'touched'—why else would she wed Loki—and see how he's cursed her with his cursed spawn? He's heard the ladies whisper how 'unfortunate' her situation is; but didn't she deserve it, not letting the little one go? He's heard the men about the court say Loki himself is bewitched by Anganboða; why else would he keep a woman who has borne him nothing but trouble? No matter how bad it is for Loki, it's worse for Anganboða, because it is the woman's soft heart that is 'always' responsible for babies like Helen not being 'taken care of'.

Loki goes and sits on the bed next to her. He pulls an illusion of a flower out of her nose. She stares at it but doesn't even smile. "Aggie," he whispers, kissing her forehead. "We'll take care of this."

He puts his hand on her back, strokes the line of her spine through her dress. He feels like she is slipping away from him, but to where he can't imagine. It makes him want her more. Leaning in, he kisses the shell of her ear. And then Helen begins to cry.

He pulls away. He and Aggie both let out a breath. It's been too long.

Aggie closes her eyes. "Loki, I can't take her out today ... " She swallows.

At three Helen can't walk or even crawl. She can only drag herself along on the floor. Aggie says she speaks and understands many words, but what comes out of her mouth is mostly garbled to Loki's ears. Besides finger food, she is incapable of feeding herself.

Nonetheless, Loki insists that he or Aggie take her out at least once a day. He will not be ashamed of his daughter, and he won't let anyone dare think he is. It is, of course, argr for a father to be out for a stroll with a child so young alone, especially a little girl. But when has he ever been one to let being argr bother him?

"Of course," he says. He wants to kiss her forehead, but Helen's cry becomes a wail. Standing up, he whispers, "I will think of something, Aggie ... "

Helen's wail rises and Fenrir whines. Loki hurries down the hall.

Whatever Helen's physical limitations, her mind is sharp. It is a blessing and a curse. She is easily bored, and just because her body is weak doesn't mean she will lie passively in a chair or bed all day—if neglected too long she will rage. Taking her outside every morning and afternoon feeds her mind and relaxes her.

Helen has a wheeled-chair built by Uncle Hoenir that Aggie uses to push her about. But Loki carries her. He likes the weight of his one beautiful creation in his arms. It reassures him that she is real. As they walk through the forest, Helen clings to his cloak with her good arm, and with her spindly blue arm she points to birds, animals and insects that even Loki doesn't notice.

The gardens are filled with plants and animals from all the realms, and quite a few from Hoenir's imagination. There was even a unicorn for a while, that Helen and the other children adored. But after it gored a member of Odin's elite Einherjar guard, Hoenir had coaxed it to leave. Still, there is plenty left to keep Helen entertained.

Something nags at Loki, and at one point he tries to go back. Helen bounces in his grip, presses her face to his shoulder, whines her displeasure, pointing down the trail where she wants to go. Loki might have ignored her, but at that moment, some young warriors walking through the gardens look askance at Helen and that eggs him forward.

They are quite a ways from home when Sigyn emerges on the

path, a blanket and a basket on her arm.

"Loki?" she says. "Where is Aggie?"

"Resting," says Loki tersely. Sigyn may be Aggie's friend, but Loki doesn't feel comfortable confiding in her.

Sigyn's brow furrows, but she says, "I brought a blanket. We can put it in the grass. Helen will like it. There are tiny violets just blooming; if you get down on the ground you can see them."

At her words Helen starts rocking in Loki's arm, and that settles it. They spread out on the blanket, Helen in the middle. Loki makes the violets appear to sing and dance, much to Helen's amusement. Some ladies pass, whispering, and Loki's eyes meet Sigyn's. It suddenly occurs to Loki that he's just given one more thing for the gossips to wag their tongues about. The court will have declared Sigyn Loki's mistress by the end of the day.

Sigyn turns to his daughter. "Come on, Helen, I want to see your mother. Let's go home."

Helen whines, but Loki picks her up anyway, suddenly anxious to be home.

"You don't mind if I come, too?" Sigyn asks. "I am worried about Anganboða lately."

"No, no, not at all," says Loki, but he doesn't slow his movements and Sigyn is forced to run to catch up to him.

Helen is not pleased to be leaving the gardens, and Loki finds himself making trees sway and rocks sing along the way. He also makes the keyhole belch, and the door open with a sound like a fart. Helen finds both delightful, Sigyn somewhat less so.

As soon as they enter, Sigyn says, "I'll go find Anganboða."

Loki nods, relieved that Sigyn is there. She'll know better what to say than Loki ever would. He sets about to entertaining Helen. He is just about to stand on his head when Sigyn screams.

Scooping up Helen, Loki half walks, half runs down the hall.

Sigyn comes out of his and Aggie's bedroom, shaking her head, hand on her mouth.

"Don't take her in there," Sigyn says.

Only half listening, Loki tries to run around her, Helen whining fearfully. Sigyn stops them with her body. "Give Helen to me, Loki. Don't take her in there."

The command in her tone makes Loki pause. He meets her eyes and sees the beginnings of tears. Wordlessly he puts Helen in Sigyn's arms and goes into his and Aggie's bedchamber.

Aggie is lying on the bed, facing away, just the barest hint of her profile visible. She looks almost peaceful. But the bedcovers are stained crimson and there is a long red gash running up her arm that crisscrosses first at her wrist. He screams for Sigyn to get Eir, the most gifted at healing of all Frigga's women, but when he sits on the bed and pulls Aggie to him, her body is already cold.

The cremation a few days later is a lonely affair. Aggie is laid out on a simple boat on the river Iving. Odin cannot make it. He is negotiating with the dwarves in their own land. Sigyn is there with Helen. Hoenir is in attendance, with Mimir mounted on his staff. Thor is there as well. And more surprisingly, Baldur with his most frequent companion, Tyre.

Loki is too empty to protest the attendance of the crown prince. Lighting the logs that lie beneath Aggie's body, he pushes the boat with Thor's help out onto the river. Helen is mercifully sleeping in Sigyn's arms.

He watches the flames leap into the air as the boat gets caught into the current. It is only when he can't see it anymore that he turns from the water, Thor and Sigyn beside him.

Coming forward, Baldur moves to block Loki's path. "This is all your fault, Trickster. You destroy everything that is beautiful, everything that is good. It is folly on my father's part to let you *remain here!*"

Loki is too shocked to be angry. Baldur is so ... sincere ... he can feel it as surely as he smells the smoke hanging in the air, or see the blue mist of Helen's magic.

The crown prince's face twists and he spits in Helen's direction. "If you hadn't given her that brat and made her keep it ... "

And then Loki is angry. His fists clench and the air shimmers, but before he can do anything, Thor steps between Loki and Baldur.

"That is quite enough, Brother!" Thor rumbles. "This jealousy does not become you."

Thor is defending him? Against Baldur? No one speaks ill of the crown prince.

Baldur's mouth drops and for a moment everyone is silent, perhaps even the birds in the trees. And then Baldur takes a step toward Thor. "You dare talk to me thus? You ... you ... bastard. It is only by my good grace that the court accepts you. My word could have you cast out!"

Thor's lips curl in a cruel snarl and he lifts Mjolnir between him and his half brother. "You could try. But I think you'll find my hammer is more valuable than your pretty face!"

Baldur backs up, eyes wide.

Thor tilts his head. When he speaks he sounds almost uncertain. "You look pale and unwell, Brother. Perhaps you should leave."

"That might be wise, Your Highness," says Mimir softly.

Baldur's eyes flick between the members of the party, and fall last on Helen. Without another word he departs.

Loki stumbles out of the restaurant. It's dark and chilly and the street is busy but not crowded. He catches a few curious glances in his direction just before he closes his eyes and massages his temples.

It's been so long since he last saw his daughter, he thought Helen's and Aggie's faces had gone blurry and indistinct with the years, but Abby looked so much like his own little girl ...

Or maybe she doesn't. Maybe she just made him feel the same way. He clenches his jaw. The whole scene played out like something from his own life, and yet ...

He hears familiar footsteps behind him.

"Hey," says Amy softly.

His hands ball into fists, and he scowls out of habit.

"You did great back there," says Amy. "Everyone thought so."

... and that is where the similarities to this scene and so many more end. Because on Asgard what he just did would have been an example of deviancy. And here ...

Amy slips an arm into his and squeezes. He stares down.

... and here his deviancy earns him the affections of the fair maiden. He almost smiles at the irony of it. Raising an eyebrow, he meets her eyes.

She swallows nervously, and her lower lip actually trembles. Her feelings are so amusingly transparent.

She bites her lip. "So ... " she says a little breathlessly. "You think you could make all the credit cards in the pockets of those jerk business guys look blank?"

It's a lovely idea, and Loki actually laughs. He pulls her close—because he can, and she is soft, and willing and here. Closing his eyes he concentrates, feels magic taking hold, feels it wanting to maintain its grip on the illusion he's cast.

"Done," he says and opens his eyes.

Amy's staring up at him and he feels his smile fade, his jaw harden and his skin heat. She is delicious and clever, and it would be so nice to have someone. Pushing a tendril of hair off Amy's face, he leans closer. The uproar it would cause at ADUO would be hysterical ... but he'd have to finagle another way to repay her. He drags his thumb across her lower lip and smiles at the short shallow intake of breath it elicits. And oh, how bringing her home would distract him from Cera; he can hear her whining now.

Loki drops his hand and stands up straighter. Actually ... why can't he hear her whining? She's been silent and invisible for hours—and left him blissfully headache free.

"Loki?" says Amy.

"Shhhh ... " he says. He creates projections of his consciousness across the city. Cera's physical presence is beneath the Board of Trade, but her mental presence is gone. He narrows his eyes; he thinks he knows why.

Pulling away from Amy, Loki hails a cab. One screeches to a halt and he opens the door for Amy to get in. Eyes on the sky he says, "Tell your handlers very bad things are on the way."

CHAPTER 8

Steve and Amy are sitting in front of the fountains on Van Buren again after Amy's post *Alinea* debriefing. Steve invited her out for coffee afterwards. Now they're both holding their hot drinks in chilly hands. Huginn and Mungin, who Amy has dubbed, "The Angry Birds," are sitting on the fountain a few yards down. Steve's told her to ignore them. It's hard. They're eyeing the blueberry muffin sitting between Amy and her boss with greedy eyes.

"Anything else you want to tell me?" says Steve.

Amy thinks about how she was sure Loki almost kissed her, how his pupils had darkened like they do when he's blue, how her heart had sped up, how her skin had felt electrically charged … .and decides she'll just keep that to herself. "No," she says.

"So no idea where he went." Steve sighs and takes a sip of his coffee.

Huginn and Mungin begin chattering between themselves. Amy narrows her eyes and lifts her cup to take a sip. A black shadow comes hurtling toward her muffin, but she snatches it away just in time.

Whichever raven it was gives an aggravated squawk and soars into the air.

Amy looks at the raven still on the ground and suddenly has an idea. "Hey, birdie … do you want a muffin?"

Steve meets her eyes. He smiles. "Mmmmmm … .I know I'd want some muffin. Still warm and everything, I bet."

"Yep, it sure is," says Amy. "Real blueberries, too."

The raven in the sky loops downward and lands beside its partner. They both hop forward.

"You know," says Amy eyeing the ravens, "I'd be willing to share some of this muffin if you told me where Loki is."

"Ha! You think you can trick us!" says one of the ravens.

"It's not a trick," says Steve. "It's a *bargain.* Your master gives you some discretion in accepting those, doesn't he? Or is he not as smart as I thought?"

Both ravens ruffle their feathers.

"Forget it, Steve," says Amy. "They probably don't know."

One of the ravens gives a ferocious rawk. "We do know, we do know!"

"Tell us then," says Steve.

"Give us the muffin first," says the raven.

"Half now, half after you tell us where he went," says Amy. The ravens dip their heads.

Splitting the muffin in half, she takes a deep breath. "Whoa, Steve, doesn't that make your mouth water?"

Steve leans in and inhales deeply. "My, my, it sure does."

The birds start yammering between themselves. Amy lifts

one half to her mouth when one raven squawks. "We'll talk! We'll talk!"

Amy pauses.

"Throw us the muffin!" says the other. Amy tosses it their direction, and one leaps and catches it with its talons. It brings it down to its partner and they make short work of it, yammering all the way.

Steve clears his throat.

One of the ravens lifts its head. Making the same throat clearing noise that Steve made, it lifts its wings to half mast and starts bouncing and singing. *"Loki's leaving on a jet plane ... don't know when he'll be back again."*

The other raven straightens and then briefly tucks its beak into its wing. Amy blinks. She has the distinct impression it's embarrassed.

"That's your answer?" Steve says. "That's not where he is, that's where he went! And you're off key!"

"I am not off key!" squawks the singer. "And that's all I know. We're not here to follow Loki. Give us the other half of the muffin!"

But Angry Bird 2 starts pecking at Angry Bird 1. They whisper a few seconds together and then Bird 2 turns to them and says, "We know something you don't know!"

Bobbing, the other one squawks, "And Loki's not here to see it!" With that they both let out some raucous rawk, rawks, and take to the sky.

"Uh ... " says Amy.

"I got a bad feeling about this," says Steve, echoing her thought precisely.

Where could Loki be?

"Stop," Loki says to the jeep driver in Tajik, his heart beating fast. Finally. It has taken him six days to find this place, retracing the path of Cera from Chicago, to the United States west coast, then to Karachi and now Herat, Afganistan. He feels something off here ... a gathering in magic that is too strong to be human.

They are on Herat's Millionaires' Row. The new houses are an eclectic blend of Iranian and Afghanistani architecture. They've stopped outside a home with a massive fence the same yellow brown as the dust on the road. It has a very ornate but very solid wrought iron gate. Just visible through the gate is an enormous, box-shaped house painted deep cobalt blue. The house has ornate gold and white trim around the front door and balconies where men pace, guns in hand, faces grim.

He sends an invisible astral projection of himself to sweep through the building. On the inside, it is a sparsely furnished and perfectly functional fortress. He sees rooms filled with weapons and ammunitions, and other rooms filled with packets of white powder. As he slips deeper into the compound he hears shouting in a language that makes the hairs on the back of his neck stand on end.

"We can feel you!"

"We know you're there!"

"She wants us, us, us!"

"We will succeed where you failed!"

They are speaking Jotnar.

His projection slips to where the voices are coming from and he finds himself in a barren prison cell at the center of the compound.

Eight jotunn—seven men, and one woman—are locked to the walls at the wrists and ankles.

Loki almost laughs. His kinsmen hold humans in even less esteem than the Aesir. What a blow to be captured by such lowly creatures.

The male Jotnar beat against their chains as they stare past his invisible projection. But the woman, wearing silver armor, her hair a gleaming white gold, looks directly at his astral form.

It's Gerðr. For centuries she was wife of Freyr, chieftain of the Vanir—Loki may have slightly exaggerated Freyr's position to incite Cera. Freyr and Gerðr have been divorced for centuries now. With the divorce, Gerðr sacrificed her right to Idunn's apples of immortality, though she looks not to have aged much. Loki's eyes narrow. He'd known she'd become strong in magic; he hadn't realized how strong.

"Who are you?" she whispers. "Show yourself."

Loki lets himself fade into view and gives a shallow bow. Her eyes widen. "Loki, help us," she whispers. "We'll rise up, take the power, unite Jotunheim … unite the worlds, make all equal."

Loki tilts his head. She wants Cera, obviously. He looks at her and her party, caught in human chains. This is what Cera has abandoned him for? He'll kill them all and show Cera how foolish she is.

"Save the exploited! Save the exploited!" chant the other jotunn.

Snarling, Gerðr thrashes her head. "No! Not all are equal … get out of my head! Get out of my head! Loki, help!"

He frowns. "Save you? And share Cera with you? So you can waste her on your frozen world?"

"Please … ." she screams. "We'll kill Odin for you."

He sneers. "I'll kill Odin."

Outside on the street, two guards standing at the gate come toward the car. They both carry beaten-looking M-16s. "What are you doing here? Move along!" one shouts. The other just raises his gun.

Letting his apparition in the prison fade, Loki hops out of the jeep and onto the dusty street.

Turning back to the man at the wheel, he says, "Drive if you want to."

As he expects, the driver takes off without a second's hesitation. Loki smiles grimly. The jeep will draw the guards' fire. Loki slips into invisibility and runs toward the gate.

One of the guards screams, "Another djinn!"

Loki's ears are suddenly flooded by the sound of gunfire, and he is knocked off his feet as his armor absorbs the impact of incoming bullets. Dust rises around him as he hits the dirty pavement.

Recovering from his shock he concentrates. He tries to form a weak magic shell around the arm without armor, and simultaneously pulls that arm toward his stomach to protect it, but he's too late. He feels a flash of pain, and then his arm *is* pain.

Pulling himself up and forward, he steps into the In-Between and exits to his apartment in Chicago. Gasping for breath, he falls onto his bed. Closing his eyes, he stops the flow of blood in his arm before he passes out.

When he opens his eyes, the shadows have gotten longer. His arm is screaming for attention.

Cursing, he pulls out his phone and texts Steve the location of the captured jotunn expedition force in Herat. Brain foggy, he falls into unconsciousness again.

The Aesir man standing before the World Gate to Vanaheim is beautiful, his head high, his hands bound with a golden rope. The man looks familiar ... but so young. Beside him is a jotunn Loki recognizes instantly. It is Mimir, but he is whole and walking upright.

Loki tries to dart forward, but a hand grasps his shoulder. The man with bound hands turns his eyes to Loki and nods.

"Hoenir!" Loki screams. But it is not his voice; it is the voice of a woman.

He turns to the man holding him back and meets the single eye of Odin. "It is necessary for peace."

The World Gate pulses with light and Hoenir and Mimir vanish. In their place stand Freyr, chief of the Vanir, and his sister, Freya.

The air ripples, and then the world bursts into flames.

Loki wakes up, face pressed against the duvet on his bed. He looks down. The fabric is dyed red-brown where his blood spilled before he closed his wounds.

His arm is in agony. Closing his eyes, he concentrates. There is a bullet lodged between the bone of his upper arm and an artery. He grits his teeth and presses his head against the soft bedding. If he hadn't tried to protect his arm with the magic shell, it might have passed right through. Now it's going to have to come out the way it went in—through the back of his arm. He can extract projectiles from his body by convulsing his muscles, but that method is crude, and the bullet is in a perilous position. If he accidentally ruptures the artery he may not be able to close it before he loses the limb ... or his life.

CHAPTER 9

"Amy, it's dead in here. I'm going next door to get some lunch," says Dr. Terry.

Pulling a mop from the vet clinic closet, Amy lifts her head. It's the late night shift, and 'lunch' for Dr. Terry means a soup and muffin at Dunkin Donuts at 4 A.M.

"Sure," Amy replies. "I'll call you if anyone comes in."

Throwing a jacket over her lab coat, Dr. Terry gives her a smile. "Thanks."

"No problem," says Amy as the doctor steps out the front door. She sighs. It's been a quiet evening. Amy should be glad for all the little critters in Chicago—and she is! But no emergencies means no exciting surgeries, stitches, or casts, refreshing her skills, or learning anything new.

She walks by Fred's perch. He's been here since Fenrir decided to knock down the cage and have Fred for lunch.

Thankfully, Fenrir doesn't have opposable thumbs and couldn't open the cage. But it terrified Fred … and got pigeon poop all over Amy's floor. Right now the cage is covered with a cloth so Fred can sleep, but she finds herself talking to him anyway. "Another exciting day at the office!" Fred does not respond as she passes by and heads into the first examination room.

Mopping up the clinic isn't so bad most nights, but tonight she'd rather not have time to think. It's been 7 days since she last saw Loki. 7 boring days for her—but exciting for everyone else at ADUO. No one will tell her what's going on; but the office was a whirlwind today. She hears whispers of 'Guantanamo' and 'Afghanistan' and wonders when they started worrying about normal security issues—especially when two new trolls have popped up on the south side in the past three days, and someone on the news was swearing they saw a griffin over Lake Michigan.

She's just wringing out the mop and is about to take her first swipe at the floor, when she hears the backdoor of the clinic slam. That door is an emergency exit only. Chill going up her spine, she straightens. "Dr. Terry?"

There is no answer. Amy's grip on the mop tightens. She peeks out the door at the back of the examination room. It leads to the pharmacy, lab, operating room and boarding area in the back. She swallows. The back door of the building is in the boarding room. She hears the animals in their kennels start to whine and mew.

Amy's eyes go to the pharmacy. Maybe someone is here for the drugs? She pulls out her phone—and for a moment is paralyzed. Should she call the police or ADUO? The ADUO agents are across the street. All she has to do is …

Through the boarding room door a shadow stumbles forward. Amy almost hits speed dial, but then the shadow's eyes meet hers. It's Loki, his hair and eyes are black again, and he's completely blue.

He grins. "Hi."

Amy puts her phone away. He's wearing a t-shirt and jeans, a black leather coat thrown over one shoulder. What catches her eye is his left arm; it's hanging at his side, and he's holding his elbow with his right hand—as though to keep it from bending.

Questions about where he's been drop away. Going forward quickly, Amy looks at his arm ... it looks unmarred from the front but Loki looks pointedly backwards and Amy walks around him. Just below the edge of his t-shirt his skin isn't fair or cerulean, it's an ugly shade of dark purple.

"What is this?" Amy says, not touching it.

Loki straightens. "Miss Lewis, have you ever extracted a bullet?"

"Several. From a cow, a horse, and a pitbull." She wants to know who shot him, but it's secondary. "I don't see any point of entry, just the bruising." Which looks three shades of evil.

"I healed it," he hisses.

Amy walks around to his front. "It has to come out."

He meets her gaze. "Obviously."

She tilts her head. "ADUO has a trauma center—"

Scowling he says, "No ADUO, no hospitals."

For a moment she stares into the black of his blown out pupils. Comprehending what he's saying she shakes her head. "No, Loki, no."

"I have confidence in your abilities," he says through gritted teeth.

She narrows her eyes. "It's not my abilities I'm worried about." It comes out harsher than she intends and she swallows. "I don't know how anesthesia will react to Frost Giant physiology ... "

He smiles. "I've lived through much worse."

Amy stares at him. Of course he has—but she doesn't want to hurt him.

His smile softens. "Do you think, Amy, that if I walked into ADUO that they would let me go? And if I walked into a hospital, and ADUO found out ... " his voice drifts off.

Amy opens her mouth. She wants to say Steve needs Loki and is willing to work with him. But she's heard things whispered in the halls of ADUO: how furious Director Jameson is about their cooperation with Loki, whispers of how if it weren't impossible to arrest Loki there would be a warrant.

Her jaw hardens. They're idiots and wrong. "Okay." She takes a breath and nods her head. "This way. I think you'll fit on the surgery table. I'll get the supplies."

Rolling his eyes, he follows her lead. "All you'll need is a sharp knife. I'll be able to patch myself up just fine when you're done."

Her stomach falls at his words. She's really going to do this, without anesthesia. She looks over at him. His blue face is blank.

Loki jokes about pain.

She suddenly knows what to say. "That's a shame."

He raises an eyebrow at her.

She forces herself to smile. "I do the *best* stitches."

He actually looks a little relieved when he smirks at her.

In the end, all she needs is a sharp scalpel and forceps. Loki shows her exactly where to cut, and he somehow temporarily stops the blood flow and helps her hold the tissue back; she doesn't even need clamps.

His stillness as he lies on the the cold operating table is more eerie than his blue skin, and Amy can hear her heart beating in her ears. Oddly, she's more worried about Dr. Terry coming in than about the surgery. The vets often let her practice on rescue animals that are brought in, she's done things like this more times than she can count, and Loki isn't trying to bite or kick her.

Loki has his head turned the opposite direction. "It's right—"

"Between the brachial artery and the humerus. I see it." She narrows her eyes at the slightly reflective surface of the bullet. The brachial artery crosses down the front of the arm. The bullet came in at an angle from behind and is lodged right where the artery passes next to the humerus. He's lucky it didn't hit the bone or the artery.

Reaching in with the forceps she says, "You're going to feel pressure." When she operates she sometimes feels like her hands aren't really her own; the unsteadiness she feels in her life in every other way disappears. Now as she grasps the base of the bullet with the forceps, her grip is sure and firm. Pulling it out in one smooth motion, she holds it up in the light. "It's out."

Loki gasps and presses his head against the table. Before Amy's eyes, his tissues begin to mesh themselves together.

She looks at the bullet smeared with blood. It is long and wicked looking. "Did the very bad things do this to you?" she whispers.

"No, they don't have guns. That was just an unfortunate misunderstanding. Some Mujahideen drug runners I think."

Amy looks at him with alarm. Afghanistan. Guantanamo.

He rolls over on his side and leans on his arm. And now that the imminent danger is gone, it's as though he is suddenly there, all sky blue, 6 feet and 5 inches stretched out on the operating table, feet sticking off the end, his hair now dark and dishevelled, his eyes black. It strikes her that the last few times she's seen him in his more human guise he's had a furrow between his brows and has looked tired, but now his face is completely smooth.

He looks good. She's suddenly aware of all 5 feet 5 inches of awkwardness that is her. Swallowing, Amy looks down at the bullet in her hands, grabs a piece of gauze, and begins wiping away the blood.

"You did that remarkably well," he says, sitting up on the table and slipping to the floor.

She raises an eyebrow in annoyance. "Of course I did." Did he think she'd be unnerved by a little blood and raw muscle?

He takes a step closer. "It's kind of sexy when you're so … " Smiling, he tilts his head and drawls. " … .competent."

Amy promptly drops the bullet. She fumbles but it's Loki who kneels and catches it before it hits the ground.

Standing, he narrows his eyes and presses it into her hand … and then doesn't let go.

She's dressed in scrubs, she is not at all sexy, and he's being mean. "Don't want to keep it as a souvenir?" she says, trying to ignore how quickly her heart is beating.

Leaning down, he whispers near her ear. "Thank you, I think I would."

He squeezes her hand, releases a bit, and then lets his fingers pulse feather light on hers. Her body goes hot, her mouth drops and her limbs feel like they've turned to wet noodles. And suddenly some thoughts in Amy's brain crash together at once. He kissed her palm when he was blue in the micro lab, and after *Alinea* when she swore he was going to kiss her, his eyes had blown out to completely black like they are right now. "You're flirty when you're blue!" The words just pop out of her mouth—embarrassingly breathily.

Pulling back, he stares at her a moment and then drops her hand and gazes down at his own. Looking somewhat disgusted, he says, "That might explain why the taxi driver was so frightened … "

She silently curses herself; why did she open her mouth?

He lifts his eyes. "But it doesn't frighten you. In fact … " He tilts his head, and his black hair falls to the side. She wants to touch it, but of course stands stock still.

"Kinky Amy," he says shaking his head. He sounds vaguely disappointed … or disgusted. Which makes her scowl. She wants to protest, wants to tell him no, he looks better when he's blue. Healthier. More alive. But from the front of the clinic comes Dr. Terry's voice. "Amy, I'm back!"

The blue in Loki's skin melts away, the furrow returns to his brow, and there are dark bags under his eyes, too. He puts his hand to her temple. "I have some memories to give you," he says.

"What?" Amy's eyes widen, and she pulls back away from his hand. "Didn't you tell me that you're not very good with memory manipulation?" It was before she really knew who he was, back before they'd even gone to Alfheim.

"Amy?" says Dr. Terry, this time from the examination

room.

Lowering his voice he says, "That's memory *erasure*—I tend to take the whole she-bang." He smiles grimly. "This is memory addition. I need someone at ADUO to talk to the very bad things and find out where the gate is."

"I don't think that I—"

She hears the door to the examination room opening to the back, and Dr. Terry's footsteps. There is suddenly nothingness in front of her, but she's pulled forward by one arm, a gentle pressure lands on her opposite temple. Something warm and soft falls on her brow. "You'll be fine," she hears as the warmth on her brow fades.

"Amy?" says Dr. Terry.

The warmth on her temple and the weight on her arm disappear. Amy takes a stumbling step forward, her vision blurs for a moment, and she puts her hand to her head.

"Are you all right?" says Dr. Terry.

Amy turns around and blinks at her. "I think I just had the world's biggest headrush," she says.

"Do you need to sit down?" Dr. Terry asks.

"No, I think I'll just finish up my mopping." Turning, she practically runs into the exam room. What was that?

CHAPTER 10

Amy comes to the office a bit bleary eyed the next morning. No one pays her the least bit of attention. The tension in the air is almost palpable.

Sitting at her desk, she watches Laura walk quickly and purposely from Steve's office to her own. Brett, Bryant and Hernandez are in the conference room …

Everyone is so busy, she's not sure she should bother anyone. But Loki tweaked her memory … and okay, she doesn't know how, she doesn't seem to have forgotten anything—but if she had, would she remember?

She bites her lip. Approaching Steve's office she notices that his door is slightly ajar. A woman's voice, slightly hissy, like it's a bad recording echoes into the hallway.

"You filthy fuckers of polar bear dung, let me go! You blight on the tundra of Midgard! You slow-eyed pieces of snow weevil snot! Arrrrggggghhhhhh!!!! You again!"

Amy blinks and knocks.

The recording clicks to a stop. "Come in," says Steve.

Amy pushes the door open. "Whoa," she says. "Someone's mad."

Steve stares at her a moment as though she might be from Mars. "Pardon?"

Amy looks to the side, "Ummm ... the recording. I don't even know what a snow weevil is. Is it a tundra thing?"

Steve puts his elbows on his desk and leans forward. "Amy, we've had every linguist in the FBI and a handful who aren't listen to that recording and none of them understood it. Are you telling me you can?"

Amy pushes a stray piece of hair behind her ear. "Errr ... but it's in English?"

Steve stares at her for a moment. And then pushing a key on his computer he says, "Listen again."

And then instead of just *understanding*, she *hears* it: harsh guttural consonants that remind her of German.

Steve tilts his head.

Amy swallows. "So Loki came to see me last night."

Raising an eyebrow, Steve motions toward his chair with a nod. "Have a seat."

As Amy sits down, Steve clicks a button, and the recording starts to play once more.

"Get out of my head, Cera! Fuck you and your Josef!"

Amy shivers and feels her heart beat quicken. The strange voice is verifying something ADUO has been trying to find out from Loki: Cera is conscious ... And apparently, she gets "into the heads" of magical creatures.

"There she is," says Steve. Amy peeks in the window of Steve's office. It's four days since the giants were taken into U.S. custody. Three days since all but one of them managed to get themselves killed, either in escape attempts or by banging their heads against their cell walls. And it's the first day the one remaining survivor has been in Chicago's ADUO office. Steve's office is now a makeshift hospital room. The sleeping giantess is in a straight jacket and bound to a medical gurney at the chest, waist and thighs. Her definitely not-blue face is beautiful, heart breakingly symmetrical, framed by pale gold hair. Amy shivers. It's like some twisted version of Sleeping Beauty.

She swallows. Amy suggested to Steve that Cera was wreaking havoc on the magical matter in the giantess' brain, and that maybe in a place with Promethean shielding she'd be able to be coherent and less dangerous to herself.

Steve actually thought it was worth a shot. Amy takes a deep breath. Loki, on the other hand, thinks that Amy is bonkers—he has insisted that the giants most likely scrambled their brains in a 'wonky world walk' because they're 'obviously amateurs.'

She tilts her head. Since his visit to the clinic, he's been coming to her house every night. She knows it's because he wants to find out if they figured out where the gate to Jotunheim is; but that can't be his only reason for showing up. He stays for hours—or they go out for hours. She's never eaten so well in all her life, and they have such great conversations. Last night they were discussing epigenetics. Amy's sure there is no way that Frost Giants, Aesir, elves and humans are simply a product of convergent evolution—according to Loki they can interbreed. Why do all the other races have more magic matter in their nervous systems than humans? Amy wonders if it may be environmental, a switch they can turn on. Loki isn't positive, but says it's a possibility because the Einherjar, Odin's elite guard, are allowed Idunn's apples and afterwards—

"Amy?"

Amy blinks at Steve's voice and meets his eyes.

"She's waking," Steve says, inclining his head to the giantess. "You're on."

Amy takes a breath and a guy with a big gun opens the door. She walks in, two guards behind her, two in front, and two doctors.

The giantess stirs on the table. Her pale blue eyes blink open and widen. She strains at her bonds and then shrieks a string of harsh guttural syllables. "What are you doing to me?"

Without thinking Amy responds in the same guttural language as she unfolds the questions she's supposed to ask. "Um, hi. We're really sorry about keeping you, um, tied up. But we don't want you to hurt yourself. We thought that you might be safe from Cera in here, but we weren't sure so … "

The giantess stares at her a moment. Her eyes narrow. "How do you speak my tongue, human scum?"

Amy takes a deep breath. She will not be like pretend jailers in those psy experiments in the 1970s who became all crazy and sadistic. This woman just went through something horrible, and Amy will be nice and honest. Damn it. "Loki fiddled with my memory," says Amy.

The woman on the table glares at her, and then she laughs. "Odin's lackey? And what are you? His slave? His whore?"

Amy's nose wrinkles. "That's not nice, and no."

The woman blinks at her, and then spitting in Amy's face she shrieks. "I will not fall victim to your wicked mind games, you retarded spawn of a yeti!"

The rest of the 'interview' goes about the same.

It's Friday morning. Amy is at ADUO headquarters. She's had 5 days of unproductive interviews with the giantess. Now she's sitting in on a surprise teleconference with Steve, Laura Stodgill, and two of ADUO's new linguists. Director Jameson's face is hovering on a large monitor in front of them. Everyone but Amy is wearing a dark suit. She's wearing a great big warm comfortable green sweater over a pair of yoga pants and slippers. Jameson is listening to their progress, or lack thereof.

Fenrir is sitting on her lap, out of view of the cameras. Obviously having Fenrir here is strictly against protocol, as are the clothes she's wearing, but Amy's upstairs neighbor Jan is away on vacation, and she is not dumping Fenrir in a kennel.

Also, having Fenrir here makes things more bearable. Whenever Amy's not been with Evil Not-So-Sleepy Beauty, she's been in intensive sessions with the linguists trying to teach them Jotunn. In between, she's slept on a couch, loyal little Fenrir at her feet.

It would probably be a good idea to leave Fenrir outside of the conference room right now—but the call was a surprise. Also, away from Amy, Fenrir barks. A lot. So now Amy is running her hands through Fenrir's fur as she faces Jameson.

Her phone vibrates and she sees a text from Loki. It's been

days since she's seen him, and she misses him.

All the text says is, *Find out Sleeping Beauty's name yet?*

Amy scowls. He knows the answer to that. Still she types back. *No.*

And then tilting her head she asks. *Do u know it?*

His answer is immediate. *You keep asking me that. ;-)*

Amy's eyes narrow. That isn't a straight answer, but why would he hide it?

Before she can reply, Jameson says, "Well, Ms. Lewis, you won't have to worry much longer about interrogating our guest anymore. It sounds like our linguists will be ready to take over soon and the subject will be in far more capable hands."

It's a lot less insulting than being told to have sex with snow monkeys by the giantess. Nonetheless, Amy's hand tightens on Fenrir's back. And then Fenrir growls.

All of the ADUO agents in the room ignore the sound and stare pointedly at the camera.

"What was that?" says the Director.

Amy tries to hold onto Fenrir, she really does, but the angle is awkward and her little beast slithers up from Amy's lap and onto the table.

Bristling what little hair she has, Fenrir bares her teeth. "Rrrrrrrrrrr … ."

"Is that a rat?" says Jameson.

"Uh … " says Steve.

"Rrrrrrrrrrr … ." growls Fenrir. "Rrrrrrrrrrr … ."

Straightening, Jameson says, "Well, I can certainly see why you haven't made any progress, Agent Rogers."

Steve responds in a bored voice. "As I discussed with you, we have a number of unique assets in this situation, flexibility is necessary—"

And suddenly Amy's had enough. Standing up, she puts her hands on her hips. "No progress? You just said yourself the linguists would be able take over soon. And Steve's been fighting trolls and wyrms, and almost dying, and throwing off the media! What have you been doing? What progress have you made?"

Out of the corner of her eye, she sees Steve nod at Stodgill.

In front of her, Fenrir barks and wags her body, nails clicking on the conference table.

Jameson stares at Amy as though she's sprouted an extra head.

A hand comes down on Amy's shoulder. "This way, Ms. Lewis," says Stodgill pulling her from the table.

Fenrir follows them both with a yip.

As the conference room door closes, Amy hears muffled shouts as Jameson yells at Steve.

Laura doesn't say anything, just guides her to her desk. Amy sits down on her chair, gathers Fenrir in her arms, and starts to spin. She's chilled with the flush of sweat she had during her outburst. And she's humiliated. They've been trying so hard to win Sleeping Beauty over with niceness ... they've released her from her straight jacket, given the giantess clothes to wear, and decent food, and no one's ever raised their voice even and—

Amy straightens in her chair. Why have they been so nice to Not-So Sleeping Beauty? ADUO must want something more than simple answers delivered under torture. It's as though they need her *trust*. And of course the giantess can't trust them because they've got her locked up—for her own protection—but she doesn't *know* that. Not-So Sleeping

Beauty can't believe humans have mastered magic enough for them to protect her from it. Amy has no idea how Sleeping Beauty rationalizes the fact that she hasn't attempted an act of self harm since she's been in Steve's office. All the giantess does when Amy talks to her is toss insults.

Head bowed, Amy spins in her chair.

She's still spinning in her chair when she hears Steve's footsteps. Before he can admonish her for her outburst, Amy says, "Let Not-So Sleeping Beauty out of the Promethean magic shield thing—put the place on lockdown so she can't get to Cera … but let her see what happens. She'll trust us then. It's probably the nicest thing to do in the long run." Because they'll torture the giantess if she doesn't cooperate, won't they?

She hears his fingers tap on the desk. "If we put the place on lockdown, I suppose it can't do any harm."

Amy pats Fenrir nervously. It won't harm any of the *humans* . .

Steve pats the Glock under his suit and looks through the window of his office. The Giantess is standing, poised as a statue and just as cold, between two male guards, two female guards and a linguist.

Steve's not sure about this, but Lewis was right about the Promethean containment field protecting the giantess from Cera—or if Loki is to be believed, from magical scarring incurred during her world walk.

One of the guards nods at him, and Steve opens the door.

Walking between her captors, the giantess steps out into the hallway. Wearing a simple a-line cotton dress, wrists handcuffed, she stops before him. She's just a few inches shorter than he is. The dress' short sleeves reveal arms that are strong and muscular—but not too muscular. Her pale legs are the same way.

Steve fights the urge to stare. Loki may wax a little off-color about his admiration for Miss Lewis' breasts, and Steve will admit, Amy has nice ones—he's her boss, not blind. But Steve has always been more of a leg man. He doesn't like skinny legs. He likes them long and strong and the giantess' legs are perfect.

He jerks his head up. She is staring at him, those gray-blue eyes unreadable beneath her white gold locks. Her skin is so pale it's nearly translucent. Normally that isn't a look that does much for Steve. He'll admit he does have a preference for women of his own race. But on her, it looks good—otherworldly. A pre-Raphaelite painting come to life.

He blinks. It's been decades since he's thought of anything from that Art History course he took to meet a credit requirement.

She looks to the ceiling and smiles. "Da," she says. "Da."

She brings her smile back to him. "Would ... take off?" she says holding up her handcuffed wrists.

Steve looks at the handcuffs. She is unarmed. What was the point of them again?

"How come she's speaking English now?" says one of the female guards.

The giantess winks. "Magic." She lifts her wrists again. "Take off?"

Steve smiles. "Oh, yes, sure."

"Sir," says one the female guards. "Is that really a good idea?"

Ignoring that question, he reaches for the keys and remembers belatedly one of the guards has them. He scowls and is about to order the guard to take off her cuffs, but the man is already there, unlocking them. Steve's scowl intensifies as he watches the other man's hands brush the giantess' skin. He shakes his head.

"Look around?" says the giantess, rubbing her free wrists.

"Of course," says Steve. The office is empty of personnel—just in case she becomes violent like the other giants did. But she is so calm, that seems like a needless precaution.

She walks toward Amy's empty desk. And then turning, she walks toward the back, the guards staying in step, Steve just behind them.

The giantess peeks into cubicles and stares up at the fluorescent lights in the ceiling, saying nothing. But every now and then she turns and smiles at Steve or one of the guards.

This is going really well.

As they get closer to the back of the office and the door that leads to the tunnels, she turns to one of the guards. "May I have your sword?"

The guard stops short.

The giantess smiles. "Sorry … mean may I have your weapon?"

Well, that sounds reasonable.

Steve reaches into his holster, about to give her his own, but the guard beside her is ahead of him—he has his gun in outstretched arms and is just about to drop it into her hands, when one of the female guards races forward. "What are you doing?" she screams. What is her name again? Jones? Steve tilts his head as she lunges at the man and is distantly aware of her shouting to the other woman, "Stop them!"

The giantess turns to Steve and shouts, "Kill the women!"

He wants to. He really does. Steve's fingers tremble on his Glock, but another instinct is stronger. "That seems excessive. Regulations specifically state—"

The giantess screams. Turning to the door, she starts yanking at the handle, shouting in a language Steve can't understand. Steve stands still as a statue and the guards wrestle. Failing to unlock the door, she beats her fist against it. Steve just stares like he's watching a movie.

And then she starts pounding her head against the door. He hears a crack. Somehow he knows it's her skull. And then it's like a light has gone on in his brain. Running forward he wraps his arms around her torso and rips her away, his vision filled by the blur of her face and hair rapidly turning scarlet.

Amy walks into Steve's office, holding Fenrir. The giantess is strapped down on the bed again. Her head is wrapped in bandages. There are bruises all over her face. Her nose is taped, her lips bloody.

Amy's seen the security footage. She seemed to have possessed enough control to use magic to speak English ... and there was that weird spell she'd seemed to cast on the men in the group. And then she'd gone crazy.

Amy takes a deep breath. Those injuries, they're her fault, but it is better than the alternative ... isn't it?

Staring at the ceiling, the giantess says, "I will talk with you now—"

Amy bites her lip. Well, that's promising.

"—human scum. But I will not play your games!"

Amy blinks and sets Fenrir down. Did she hope to be friends? "Sure. Want to start with your name?"

Turning her head, the giantess screams. "Impudent mortal filth! You know my name from Loki!" Thrashing at her bonds, she hisses. "No. More. Games."

Stunned, Amy takes a step back. In her arms Fenrir growls. Amy's breath hitches and she squeaks. "He actually never told us." Sagging into her chair, Amy wipes her eyes. No wonder the giantess didn't trust her. "He's not ... not very reliable."

The giantess begins to laugh. It's not a pretty sound. "Oh, you can always rely on Loki." The woman's lip is turned up in a snarl. "You can always rely on Loki to deceive and destroy!"

Amy draws back in her chair, and Fenrir sits upright, a growl erupting in her throat.

Staring at the ceiling the giantess' eyes go wild. "For the sake of Jotunheim and Jotunheim alone I will talk to you!"

"Ummm ... okay," says Amy. "What should we call you?"

Straining against her bonds, the giantess raises her head as high as she can. "You may call me Gerðr."

Later that day Amy meets with the Steve in the conference room. Brett and Bryant and some of the new linguist guys are there, too.

She feels wiped. It worked. Her super duper plan to let

Gerðr out proved to the giantess they were protecting her—
even if they were only idiot magicless humans. Amy's telling
herself the fact that Gerðr tried to beat her brains in to get
through the back door to Cera isn't really her fault. Even if
she knew, or at least suspected it would happen.

...and it's better than sending her to Gitmo, or Egypt, or
Iraq to be "interviewed."

She bites her lip and looks around. Everyone else looks
happy and elated. Steve's even smiling a bit and *humming*.

Fenrir hops up onto her lap and Amy runs her fingers
through her fur. Steve hits a button on his computer and
Gerðr's voice fills the room.

Several sets of eyes look to her. Amy blinks. "That's where
she is explaining that a magical creature can use objects of
power as sort of ... well, a battery. It takes energy to collect
magic to direct, but with something like Cera, all the magic is
collected and ready to be directed." She scowls. "Or as Gerðr
said, 'all the magic is ready to be directed, you deficient mortal fool.'"

"Nice, nice," says Steve, looking at the transcript.

Amy raises an eyebrow but says nothing. Fenrir presses her
nose against her palm and Amy closes her eyes. They learned
a lot from Gerðr today. About magic, Asgard and the other
realms, and about Loki.

Amy scowls. According to Gerðr, Loki is only tolerated
by Thor, Odin, 'the mute gardener' Hoenir, his wives and his
children—one of them a child that was a 'disgraceful disfig-
ured blemish on the jotunn race.'

Gerðr also says that Loki is a womanizer, murderer, gam-
bler and a drunkard. Amy can't quite reconcile that image
with the man who conjured butterflies for Abby, the little girl

in the restaurant.

... But hadn't Loki told her during their trip to Alfheim that he'd seduced Sif, Thor's wife? And by Gerðr's accounts Thor was the closest thing besides Hoenir and Odin that Loki had to a friend.

"Amy?" says Steve.

Blinking, she looks up and meets Steve's eyes.

"Thought we lost you there for a moment," he says.

She smiles tightly. "I'm just tired."

At exactly that moment the phone in the conference room buzzes. "It's Jameson," Steve mutters, hitting the accept button.

Jameson's voice fills the room. "Agent Rogers, is your team there?"

"On speaker," says Steve.

"We've had another breakthrough." Jameson says. "One of our agents in Visby just happened to overhear a woman in a bar say a recent one-night stand turned blue after their encounter. The agents interviewed her. He fits Loki's description perfectly. I can pipe the video in to you."

Amy suddenly feels all eyes in the room on her, and it's like they have physical weight. Swallowing, she tightens her grip on Fenrir. "It's not like he is my boyfriend or anything." It comes out much softer than she intended. But she's never thought that. Not really. And this shouldn't make her feel weird ... or disappointed.

Jameson's voice cracks over the speaker. "Well?"

Steve's voice sounds tight when he says, "Maybe we can get to it some other time."

Amy feels a flush of relief and gratitude as she looks up

to her boss.

But then Jameson's voice crackles through the air again. "This is important. As I'm sure you'll recognize when you see the footage."

Amy goes cold. Standing, she says, "I think I'll just take a break."

Turning, she leaves the room without bothering to shut the door, Fenrir at her heels. She's not quite to her desk when she hears Steve say, "We still need her to interface with Loki."

She almost laughs to herself—and there she thought for a moment Steve cared about her feelings.

Bryant runs back into the conference room. "Lewis just left the office, Sir." Steve scowls.

Making a noncommittal noise, Jameson says, "Get your vid screen up, gentlemen."

Bryant hastens to comply. The video screen flickers to life. A woman in her late twenties or early thirties sits on a chair. The first thing Steve notices is that she is "well endowed." She is sitting, wearing a short blue dress and heels, legs primly crossed. Her hair is blonde and brushed over her shoulder. In one hand she is waving a cigarette.

A man off screen asks her a question in Swedish and she says, "I speak English."

She proceeds to tell them how she met Loki at a bar, thought he was cute and funny and took him home. She doesn't go into details about what happened between the sheets, just says, "and afterwards, you know he fell asleep a little bit and I looked over and his hair is black and his skin is all blue. I screamed and he woke up. You're blue, I told him, and he changed back. He put on his clothes and left."

"Was there anything else unusual about the encounter?" an ADUO agent says offscreen.

The woman smiles. "Jah."

"Would you elaborate?"

She laughs so hard she doubles over. Lifting her head she licks her lips and grins. "It was amazing."

Someone in the conference room coughs.

Taking a drag on her cigarette, she blows smoke at the camera. Her top leg starts to swing, and she runs her free hand down her thigh. "I don't suppose you have his number?"

The video ends.

Jameson's voice cracks on the conference phone. "And now gentlemen we can discuss our plans to bring Loki into custody."

"What?" Steve says. "Is that really a good idea? Gerðr may be informative but she's useless in the field—"

"We'll only bring him in for questioning," says Jameson. "Show him who's boss."

Steve can hear the smile in his voice; it makes the hair on the back of his neck stand on end. Cera's growing. They're 11 days away from having to evacuate the Chicago Board of Trade Building—and a very awkward explanation to the public about why such drastic measures are necessary. Meanwhile, Steve's boss wants to get in a pissing match with the one being who might be able to help them.

CHAPTER 11

When Amy gets home Loki is there, of course. His back is to her; his head is in her refrigerator. Fenrir immediately gives a happy yip and runs in his direction. For a moment Amy just stares. Some women he uses for sex. He uses her for food, and maybe company. And some women he just uses. "You could have at least told me Gerðr's name!"

Not turning around, he snorts. "Where would have been the game in that?"

She waves her arms. "She got hurt, *badly, horribly,* because *I* suggested she leave Steve's office!"

"Couldn't have happened to a nicer giantess. I still don't understand why the locking mechanism on that door frustrated her so much." He turns around with a pint of milk in his hand.

Amy throws up her hands. She shouldn't care at this point, but she does. "Frustrated? Frustrated? She bashed her own head in!"

Ignoring her, he takes a swig of her milk right from the carton. He immediately makes a face and spits it out in the sink. Grimacing, he turns to her. "When was the last time you went grocery shopping?"

"Loki—Cera will kill you … it wants destruction, it wants death … " Gerðr told her as much.

Closing one eye, he peers into the carton. "She hasn't killed me yet, though with her whining … " He makes a tsk, tsk, noise.

Amy's shoulders fall. "Maybe you're just stronger than the other giants."

"Did Gerðr suggest that?" Loki says taking a whiff of the milk and grimacing.

Amy crosses her hands over her chest. "No." Gerðr said just the opposite.

He smirks at her.

"But Gerðr did say you are supposed to bring about the end of the world in Frost Giant prophecies … just like in our myths, which doesn't jive with the being unpowerful thing."

He looks heavenward, and says bitterly. "Oh, Amy, flattery will get you nowhere."

Swallowing, she brings up something more positive. "And in our myths you're sometimes described as part of a trinity with Odin and Hoenir, which would make you very powerful, too."

Loki freezes. For a moment she thinks she sees a tinge of blue in Loki's skin. Then he shakes himself. "Cera doesn't want destruction, she wants revolution."

"Close enough," mutters Amy.

He raises the milk carton at her and tilts his head. "Exactly.

When I figure out how to get her out of your *custody*, she and I will get along just fine."

Amy shakes her head. "Cera will destroy you." Fenrir starts to whimper at her feet.

Loki just snorts.

She clenches her fists in frustration. "Why do you have to make things hard? Is destroying Odin reason enough to destroy yourself?"

For a heartbeat Loki just stares at her. And then the carton of milk goes hurtling past her and crashes against the apartment door with a splash. Amy's eyes follow it and she gasps.

"Yes!" Loki screams. Amy turns back to him; he is full-on blue.

"This is your urgent matter?" Putting the goblet down, Loki rolls his eyes. "I can't go troll hunting with you, Thor."

Smiling, Thor leans across the worn wooden table in the public house. "It will only be for a few nights."

Loki looks around. The other patrons are eyeing them curiously. They are common people and not so accustomed to see Thor, son of Odin, in their midst.

Thor, in his cunning, probably brought Loki here because the big oaf knows Loki is disenchanted with the court. This is the sort of honest place filled with honest criminals they'll find themselves in if they go troll hunting.

Loki looks down at some rude runes carved into the table. If rumors rippled like breezes before Aggie's death, now they are a full blown whirlwind. Baldur declared Loki's wife should have been named Angrboða, bringer of sorrows, instead of Anganboða, bringer of joy—and of course it stuck. Thor says it's because Baldur was drunk at the time and it was grief talking.

Loki's jaw clenches and the dead candle at their table suddenly leaps into flame.

Thor lifts his eyebrow at the candle and turns back to Loki, his smile replaced by a look of concern. "It would be good for you to leave for a while."

Taking out a knife, Loki begins to scratch at the table. "It's out of the question. Right now Odin has me trying to arrange a contract with the dwarves to get the south wall repaired—and he's not authorized me to pay them a reasonable amount . . ." He brings his knife down with a thwack.

Thor grins. "So did you know there is a story among the humans on Earth about how you managed to get the wall built in the first place?"

Loki stabs the table again and begins to absently carve a rune. "Yes, Thor, I am aware of the story of me turning myself into a mare and getting raped by a giant's horse—"

"And giving birth to Sleipner!" says Thor, gleefully bringing up Odin's eight-legged, world-walking steed.

Loki narrows his eyes and makes a silent oath: humans will tell the tale of Thor dressing himself up as a woman to get Mjolnir back. Turning his attention to the tip of his knife he says, "And even if there wasn't the matter of the wall, I cannot leave Helen."

Thor shrugs. "But surely Sigyn wouldn't mind watching her . . ."

Loki blinks to where he has carved, 'Baldur will die'. Frowning, he scrapes it away quickly. That is the sort of sentiment that will get him killed. He looks to the window where the sun is just setting. "Speaking of Sigyn, I have taken advantage of her kindness long enough," he says rising from the table.

Standing beside him, Thor sighs. "Can't you go? These things are always so much more fun when you're along … "

Ignoring him, Loki strides out of the public house, leaving Thor to pay. Thor catches up to him, and together they enter the royal grounds and head toward Frigga's palace, passing Tyr and his wife, Vord, several months along in a pregnancy, on the way. Tyr doesn't acknowledge Loki—and Loki snorts. The man also barely nods at Thor. Keeping company with Loki isn't winning Thor any friends in the court, especially after Thor's outburst at Anganboða's funeral. But there is little outward hostility toward the hammer wielder. Thor was right, his hammer is more important than Baldur's beauty.

As Vord and Tyr pass, Thor says in a perplexed voice, "Vord was eyeing you funny, Loki."

Some months after Aggie's death he had a brief tryst with Vord. It was stupid. He wants to hurt Baldur but can't. Hurting Tyr, by sleeping with his wife when he was off hunting wyrms, felt like the next best thing at the time. It was petty and unproductive—the baby in her belly isn't even Loki's and she'd hopped right back into her husband's arms on his return. Loki shrugs noncommittally at Thor's comment and keeps walking.

They meet Sigyn in Frigga's hall. Helen is asleep on her lap, and Sigyn is singing to her softly, face aglow with Helen's blue magic. Fenrir is lying at their feet.

It makes Loki's chest tighten. Just because he is a father does not mean he has escaped his duties as Odin's retainer. Finding someone to care for Helen has been difficult. One nurse left her to scream in her bed all day. When Sigyn heard, she offered to help with Helen's care—and she does it well. Today Sigyn has tied Helen's hair up into elegant braids. Helen's face is clean; there is *a ghost of a smile on her features.*

"Lady Sigyn!" Thor says—it's a whisper, but nonetheless the sounds seems to reverberate through the room.

Sigyn looks up and smiles at Loki. The whole court thinks they are lovers. They could be, and he even wants her, but does nothing. He doesn't know precisely why.

"It was my fault that Loki was detained," says Thor, dropping a fist on Loki's shoulder and nearly knocking him over. "An urgent matter of troll hunting."

"Thank you for watching her today," Loki says, trying to end the topic of trolls. He goes to take Helen from Sigyn's lap.

Standing, Helen in her arms, Sigyn says, "Don't. You'll wake her. I can carry her; she weighs nothing." She kisses Helen's head and it hits Loki like a physical blow.

Loki nods, and they walk toward the exit of Frigga's great hall together. Fenrir lopes at their side and Thor falls into step with them, too, going on about trolls again, though Loki and Sigyn both roll their eyes.

They are nearly at the foyer when Fenrir begins to growl. A servant opens the front door and Baldur comes in, Tyr beside him.

Smiling at Thor, Baldur says, "Brother!" Thor nods back. Thor doesn't smile back, and that is odd. Not that Baldur has given Thor any reason to trust his smiles again, but everyone but Loki forgets Baldur's cruelties when Baldur turns on the charm.

Baldur's eyes slide toward Sigyn. His smile widens. "And Lady Sigyn - it has been a while."

"Yes," says Sigyn. She is unsmiling, too. Loki tilts his head.

Stirring in Sigyn's arms, Helen's eyelids flutter.

For a moment Baldur's smile slips, but then he smiles again and bows. "But trust me, Lady, I have not forgotten you, all your beauty, *or any of your charms."*

*Baldur's none-too-subtle allusion to his conquest of Sigyn makes
Loki bristle—and Baldur sees it. He smiles at Loki. It is not a nice
smile.*

"Baldur, Brother," says Thor suddenly. "You look ill."

Sigyn tilts her head. "Your complexion is off…"

*Baldur's smile drops completely. Loki should restrain his smirk, but
can't quite manage it. The crown prince excuses himself and goes to find
his mother. Thor thankfully leaves not long after that.*

*Sigyn is still carrying Helen when they reach Loki's home. They put
Loki's child to bed and Loki offers her a drink, just to be hospitable.
He is pouring blue elvin wine into a glass when Sigyn says, "You know
I was showing her runes today—I do believe she understands them."*

Loki says nothing, only turns away to pour wine into his own glass.

*"I believe when the time comes, we should consider getting her a
tutor," Sigyn says.*

Smiling a little mirthlessly to himself, he says, "We?"

*Sigyn comes up very close behind him. "You know it can be we if
you want it to be."*

*Glass in hand, Loki turns back to her. Sigyn is more traditionally
Asgardian than Aggie. Her hair and skin are golden, her eyes are wide
and clear blue, her cheeks pink. She's soft, curved like a fine instrument,
and her body has beckoned his for a long time.*

*But his tongue seems to form words of its own accord. "You're cast
off by Baldur and now you're interested in me again."*

*Sigyn's face goes hard. "That was a long time ago, and as I recall
very soon after you were cutting off Sif's hair."*

*Instead of acknowledging her statement, he continues. "And you'll
take me despite my crippled daughter."*

*Sigyn's hand connects so hard to Loki's cheek that the glass he's
holding falls to the floor. Shaking, she says, "Why must you always*

make things hard! I love you because of Helen! You condescending,
cruel, selfless, twisted, brave—"

Grabbing her shoulders, he pulls their bodies together and silences
her with a brutal kiss. "I know," he whispers, as he pulls back for air.
"I know." Closing his eyes and pressing his forehead to hers, he lets his
hands drift to her elbows. Her mouth comes to his again. This time they
kiss gently, almost tentatively, as their hands dance over the fastenings
of each other's clothes.

The milk container crashes against the far wall. He will
not be lectured to by a human … even if he's heard her words
before.

Cera is screaming. "The Frost Giants are not dead! They
are gone. She is speaking falsehoods!" He can feel Cera isn't
lying. Nor is the girl. Both believe their words.

Cera came back to him the day ADUO 'broke' Gerðr. Her
return is both pleasing and annoying.

"Let us leave here," says Cera, yet at the moment she
sounds so far away …

Miss Lewis, on the other hand, seems so close. She is
breathing heavily, as though she is frightened or angry. "What
do you want?" she says. "To know the location of the gate the
giants walked through, right? Right?"

Loki smiles at her indulgently. He wants quite a few things
really. He remembers the smell of her hair, and the softness of
her skin as he'd pressed a kiss to her forehead a few days ago.
He shakes his head.

Taking a step forward, Amy says, "Well, we got it. Steve's

working on a joint project with the Afghanis to bury it under a ton of bricks." Her hands go to her hips, and Loki licks his lips. She's quite fetching when she's mad.

Oblivious, she goes on. "Do you know *why* Gerðr told us where the gate is? Do you know *why* she is helping us block her only way home? So that other giants don't destroy themselves like her companions did! Like she tried to do! So that if you get Cera you won't take that gate to Jotunheim and slaughter your own people!"

Any more potential competitors for Cera who might have come through the Afghanistan-Jotunheim gate will be blocked. Loki blinks. His cooperation with the humans is progressing excellently. "Well done," he says.

Straightening, Amy says, "Now. Get out."

His jaw twitches. He is hungry and tired of eating alone. He smiles. "Why don't we *both* get out? Get some food?" He shrugs and flashes his most disarming grin.

"No," says Amy. "Leave."

He tilts his head. "We'll order in then—"

"No!"

He blinks. "What is wrong with you?"

When she speaks her voice is a whisper. "I gave you the information you wanted ... I've *interfaced* with ADUO for you. I'm done. Get out!"

He sighs happily. Her displeasure is just a little game—even if she doesn't know it. "But if I leave how will I repay my debt to you?"

Amy blinks. "Repay your debt?"

Proud of his cleverness, he shrugs and gives her a triumphant, toothy grin. "Why, of course! Why do you think I am so often in your company? I arranged with Steve for you to get danger pay whenever I am in your presence. It was the only way I could repay you without them confiscating the payment … or tracing it."

Her anger washes away and she stares at him for just a moment. And then she swallows. "That's why you spend so much time with me?"

He's almost won this game. "Why, Amy … Why did you think I was here?" He leans in close. "Did you think I was, as you Midgardians put it, 'your boyfriend'?"

He expects a playful slap on the cheek—or even one that isn't so playful. But backing away she says, "No, actually, I guess I really didn't think *that*." His brow furrows at the not-quite lie.

Her face falls, and for the first time he notices her eyes are starting to well up with tears. Pathetic. Pathetic that she is starting to cry and pathetic that his stomach is starting to fall.

A tear slips from her eye. "I knew you were using me … but I thought at some level we were friends … "

Suddenly he knows what he could say to make this all better. But that would be too much like losing. Loki scowls at the tear. Waving a hand at her cheek he says, "Don't do that."

Her lips turn up in a snarl, even as more tears fall from her eyes. "Get out of my house!"

He doesn't move. "I don't renege on my oaths."

Picking up a random book and hurling it at him, she says, "Fuck your oath, I absolve you! Get out of my house!"

He lets it hit him, and she throws another, and another. He's actually a little bemused; he didn't think she had this much passion in her.

Picking up her phone she says, "If you don't get out, I'm calling ADUO."

For the first time it occurs to Loki that she isn't really playing. He rolls his eyes and makes himself invisible.

"I know you're still here!" Amy shouts. She throws a book at his invisible form and hits him in the stomach.

It falls to the ground with a soft thud and he stands immobilized with fury—fury at her and himself. He knew he was pushing her limits, and he did it anyway. His fingers clench and there is a clicking noise.

Amy's head turns and she screams. Loki follows her gaze. Every eye on her stove is alight. As she races over to put the flames out, he backs toward the door and then with an angry snarl—at her or himself—takes off into the night.

CHAPTER 12

It's late afternoon on Monday, nearly a week after Gerðr started talking to Amy. Amy is on the 'L' train heading north. She told Steve that she wasn't coming in today. There are plenty of linguists to talk to Gerðr now, and Amy needs a break.

She looks down at the book in her hand. It is *Young Stalin* by Montefiore. She exhales sharply. She should have picked up something a little lighter.

In the course of her discussions with Gerðr the giantess commented that Cera had 'imprinted on a human named Josef.' Also in Gerðr's words, 'Josef seems to have been an exceptional creature for a human.' The fact that Cera's first language was Russian … well, with Cera's *charming* personality, Amy immediately thought of Josef Stalin. She feels her skin crawl. Stalin was the man who drove Beatrice and her family from the Ukraine and who had made Hitler look like a rank amateur at mass slaughter.

Most of the office thinks Amy's paranoid. They point out that Cera is a new thing and Stalin died decades ago. Steve points out he was also Georgian ... But Amy's pretty sure by the time Stalin was the Big Bad the language he used most often was Russian. Beatrice understood Russian, and she'd overheard Loki talking to Cera. He'd mentioned Tunguska— a place in Siberia where a meteorite hit in 1908. Amy has wondered if that might be where Cera came from. She and Steve worked out a hypothetical scenario where the meteorite was picked up by the Tsar's regime and locked up until after the revolution. After Stalin came into power, he had somehow come into contact with it—her.

Amy swallows. She doesn't know how much Steve believes in the scenario, but he doesn't discount it. He says in cases like this it's best to consider all the possibilities. But there is a possibility he won't entertain—that Cera is evil. Steve doesn't believe in evil.

Amy thinks when it comes to Stalin, saying he wasn't evil is kind of splitting hairs. Steve suggested she read *Young Stalin*. And okay, she kind of gets where he was coming from. Stalin was a bright young boy, born into poverty under one of the most repressive and simultaneously ineffectual regimes on the planet. He was scarred physically by illness and emotionally by an absentee father and a mother who was probably a whore. He was sent to the most fundamental of seminaries to become a priest—a seminary where boys were spied on, beaten and raped. Most of his peers left the seminary atheists and joined him in the revolution. She sees where he was the product of the perfect storm of genetics and a personal and political environmental whirlwind.

She still thinks saying he wasn't evil is splitting hairs.

Amy's phone beeps. Pulling it out she scowls. It's an email from Loki. He has been sending her little things about odd appearances and occurrences all week. She really wants to ask questions—but she just forwards the emails onto Steve.

She stares at this email's subject line: Spider Mouse! She opens it up. She should just forward it …

She reads Loki's message anyway.

Amy, I thought these were just one-offs created by Hoenir. But apparently there is an infestation in DC. So far people are attributing them to genetic experiments. Cute, no? Or do you not like spiders?

There's a link to an article and a jpg attachment. Amy stares at the attachment; against her better judgement she clicks on it.

… And finds herself staring at the most adorable little gray mouse with eight velvety black legs. He is upside down, and hanging by what at first she thinks is a tail, but then realizes is spider silk.

She types: *I want one!* And then squeezes her eyes shut. Resisting the urge to send it to Loki she forwards it to Steve.

Her boss responds almost instantly.

Interesting. Wouldn't have thought Cera's route to Chicago would have taken her through DC. Hope that your visit with your grandmother goes well.

So nice, thoughtful and polite. Because Steve still thinks he needs her. She slips her phone back into her pocket, looks at the book in her hands but can't bring herself to read it. Leaning her head against the cold glass of the window she watches Chicago's dreary landscape blur by.

Not quite an hour later she walks into Beatrice's nursing home facility. Joy of joys, Amy's mother is at the front desk.

"I'll be back to pick her up tomorrow!" her mother says, too bright and too cheerful.

"Yes, we'll make sure she's ready," says the nurse.

Amy's mother Anna turns around. Beatrice had Anna late in life. Anna had Amy very young. Her mother is only in her mid forties. Everyone tells Amy they look alike, but Anna's hair is bleached blonde in the front and she wears a lot more makeup. They stare at each other a moment.

"You're welcome to come with Doug and me when we take Beatrice to the new facility, Amy," her mother says.

Amy's lips turn down in disgust. Doug is Anna's boyfriend—again. They'd been together before in Oklahoma and are back together.

"Yeah, no, I would rather not be stuck in a car for 3 hours with Doug," says Amy.

Her mother rolls her eyes. "That was just a misunderstanding."

Amy feels her face heat. After all these years her mother still doesn't believe that the reason Amy ran away in high school was because Doug tried to sneak into her room one night. "Fenrir misunderstood, too," says Amy coldly. If it weren't for Fenrir …

"Fenrir hates all men," says her mother dismissively.

And you just hate the idea that a man would be more interested in me than you. The words are on the tip of Amy's tongue but she doesn't say them. She just walks past her mother down the hall toward the elevator banks.

She's out of the line of sight of the lobby when she hears Loki's voice. "Amy, I caught up to you."

Amy turns around and sees her mother smiling up at a surprised looking Loki. He looks human, like his ginger haired self. He's wearing nice looking trousers and a navy blue peacoat over a pink and navy blue striped sweater.

"May I help you?" says Anna, smiling and gently putting a hand on Loki's arm. With a sharp exhale of breath, Amy turns and dashes into a waiting elevator.

The door closes and she sags against a wall with relief. She's escaped them both.

The elevator dings at the top floor and she walks to the desk. As she signs in she thinks she hears a scream from the lobby that sounds strangely familiar. She blinks, then shakes her head. Turning, she walks down the long beige hallway to Beatrice's room, resolutely ignoring the smells of urine and disinfectant, the empty eyes of the patients, and the feeling of despair.

When Amy arrives, Beatrice is sitting on a chair by the window. She doesn't look up when Amy walks in. Her hair hangs long and unbrushed.

"Hi, Grandma," says Amy. Beatrice doesn't respond; Amy didn't expect her to. Putting down her coat and bag, she goes over and whispers in Beatrice's ear, "Grandma, I'm going to do your hair up now, okay?"

Beatrice's eyes flick to her, but then she looks to the window again. Is she dreaming of the trip they took to Alfheim with Loki? The elves had loved Beatrice, dressed her up in a beautiful gown, and done her hair up with pins that glittered like stars. And Beatrice had loved the elves—she'd told them the story of her life, things even Amy hadn't heard of, about of growing up in the Ukraine and escaping to the States. The elves had hung on every word. And okay, maybe they loved Beatrice because the tragedy of her life was caused by a 'land without kings and queens' and validated their worldview. Still they made Beatrice feel like a queen and let Amy touch a hadrosaur.

The trip was dangerous but magical and wonderful. Running a comb through Beatrice's hair, Amy swallows. And it was all Loki's doing.

Her eyes flit to the door of the room. He's gone by now, it hardly matters ... and she should be grateful. She pulls back Beatrice's hair, fastens it with a clip, and steps back. Her grandmother looks a little more present now—but she isn't.

There is a knock at the door. Expecting a nurse Amy says, "Come in."

"Beatrice!" says a sunny voice.

Amy jumps. It's Loki, and he's flashing his most rakish grin in Beatrice's direction, though there is the familiar tightness in his brow, and something about the tug of his lips that feels forced. For a moment, Amy's heart lifts. Loki is magical, maybe—

Heart beating fast, she turns her head. But Beatrice is still staring out the window.

"Beatrice?" says Loki.

Amy turns to him. He stands in the doorway, head tilted. Somewhere down the hall a patient starts screaming. Loki doesn't move.

"If you're coming in, shut the door," says Amy.

Gently shutting the door, he comes further into the room. There are dark circles under his eyes, and if it is possible, he looks paler than usual.

Amy sighs. "Don't feel bad, she doesn't respond to anyone." Beatrice drools a little and Amy wipes it away and then sinks into a chair.

Loki sits down on the bed. He swallows. "I had no idea ...

we don't … magical creatures don't suffer from neural damage … magic matter has memory and heals injured neural tissue."

"Must be nice," says Amy, her voice thin and bitter. And then she remembers why he is here. "If you're wondering why Jameson has moved into the Chicago office, and what all the extra agents are for, I have no idea."

"Oh," says Loki. But he doesn't move or speak.

Neither of them says anything for several minutes. And then through the door Amy hears more screaming down the hall. Just to not think about the noise, Amy says, "So you met my mother."

She hears, rather than sees, Loki turn toward her. "Yes."

"She flirted with you," says Amy.

"She was … .friendly," says Loki.

Amy snorts and looks at him. "She was being more than friendly, trust me—and don't let me stand in your way."

Loki draws back a little. "Believe me, I wouldn't."

"Yeah, guess not." She swings her feet. "The whole office knows about the thing in Visby."

One corner of his mouth turns up completely without humor. "And that is your business because—?"

Chastened, Amy sinks into her chair. "It's not."

"Hmmm … " says Loki.

Amy drags her foot across the floor.

"Your mother wasn't so friendly when I showed her the gift I have for you."

Amy blinks and looks at him. He reaches into the pocket of the peacoat and pulls out something small, gray and wiggling, and walks toward Amy.

Loki opens his hand and she gasps. On his palm is a little gray mouse with eight black spider legs. Standing on the four back ones, he wiggles his whiskers at Amy.

"He likes you," says Loki.

Stifling the 'you should never give animals as gifts' that has been drilled into her for years, Amy exhales in wonder and holds out her hand. The little mouse spider hops over and rears all the way up on two legs. He has little paws at the end of his spider limbs. Amy gently reaches toward him with a finger. Clasping her finger in his two most forward paws, he shakes it and Amy laughs in delight. "Oh, Mr. Squeakers! So nice to meet you."

"Your mother didn't appreciate him as much," says Loki.

Amy tilts her head. So that was the scream she heard when she was signing in. "She doesn't like mice or spiders."

Mr. Squeakers rubs his head against Amy's fingers. He's warm and soft. Smiling, she scratches behind his ears. And then she remembers why Loki is here again. "I really don't know anything about why Jameson is at our office. You don't have to stay."

Loki sinks onto the bed and tilts his head at her. He sighs and scowls. "You know just because I have ulterior motives when I come to visit you, it doesn't mean that I don't enjoy your company."

Amy bites her lip and Mr. Squeakers nuzzles against her finger. Oh. Not knowing what to say, she turns to look at Beatrice.

"Is Beatrice your mother's mother?" says Loki.

"Yes," says Amy. Feeling defensive, she says quickly, "Sometimes good people have bad kids."

Slipping his hands into his coat pockets, Loki stares at Beatrice. "And the opposite is true as well."

Loki is wiggling on the floor of the nearly empty throne room, one of the few places in Asgard where all the splendor is real, not illusion. Golden buttresses hold up a ceiling so high from below it seems to be made of clouds, the floors are decorated with mosaics, and the walls are dwarven crystal that make the great hall nearly as bright as day.

Lying next to Loki is Helen. Helen is nearly 36 years old. She is so small that she barely looks older than 12. And although she is intellectually as accomplished as an adult, magically, and emotionally, she is still 12.

All of the children of the Asgard are stunted this way. There is a lot of debate about the cause. Some say it is a curse. The more educated say Idunn's apples have changed the magical code within the Aesir bodies that transmits traits. Aggie's sorceress cousin Gullveig says that it is the effect of Odin's magic, growing unchecked. For Helen this extended childhood is probably for the best. Sigyn says that she will want someday to have independence and "adult" relationships—but neither Loki nor Sigyn expect any Asgardian man to have her. And even independence is a bit of a dream. Helen still can't walk and barely crawls. What she will do if something happens to Sigyn and Loki … Loki banishes the thought from his head … .

Loki is lying beside Helen because Helen wanted to get close to the mosaics on the floor.

"Wha' is dis?" says Helen, running her fingers over a picture of a blazing man, his skin so black it is almost blue, flames leaping

from his skin and hair. Next to the man is a voluptuous woman whose skin and hair are glowing pale gold. Circling around them are two beautiful young girls. The picture is stylized, the girls' arms are entwined, and they appear larger than their parents. "The woman is Glut, or glow," *says Loki.* "The man is Laugatjanaz, the Blazing One. The two girls spinning away from them are their daughters, Einmyria, or ashes, and Eisa, embers."

Loki traces the girls. Einmyria's skin is as pale as his own, and she has black hair. Eisa is dark brown gold, her hair black braids with glowing yellow and orange flames. "The girls spun away from their parents. Einmyria became the planets and Eisa became the stars of the World Tree."

"Prettie sistas," *says Helen softly.*

"A pretty metaphor," *says Loki.* "Hoenir told me once that Glut was the soul of the universe, trapped and condensed as matter. Laugatjanaz was the the spark that set her—and the universe—free." *He smiles softly.* "Hoenir told me they had a son, too. He was more powerful than either of his parents. He became the magic that holds the World Tree together." *Loki tilts his head. He couldn't find that story documented anywhere—and as a child, when he was interested in such myths, he looked obsessively.*

Helen traces Eisa's cheek with a blue finger. Loki thinks for a moment he hears laughter and the crackle of flames. He pulls back and takes a breath. And then he hears footsteps fast and light coming from behind them. Loki puts an arm protectively over Helen's head.

"Arrrrggggghhhhh! Die!" *screams a child's voice.*

"Never!" *screams another child.*

Loki scowls. His sons are at it again.

"Nari, Valli, watch where you are going!" *Loki shouts. He and Helen both duck as shadows vault over their heads.*

The two boys slide to a halt. "We were watching!" shouts Nari.

"We jumped over you!" shouts Valli.

Heart beating fast, Loki narrows his eyes at them. They are fraternal twins. Their conception was only a few decades less difficult than Helen's. Sigyn had even consulted Frigga's healing lady Eir for help and fertility herbs. And then one night after they'd given up, Loki had come home briefly from a campaign for just one night. It wasn't Sigyn's time, and they'd both been extremely drunk, but despite the odds, Sigyn had conceived.

The twins are nearly 15 now, but they are only the size of 5 year olds. Their skin isn't quite as tan as Sigyn's Aesir gold , but it's darker than Loki's pallor. They are both blonde, their eyes are the same gray as Loki's, and they are healthy and hale. Nari tends toward the thin side, and Valli's physique is more traditionally Aesir. They are, according to all who look upon them, beautiful.

They are also monsters. Nari is a bit of a coward, but he is so clever, he hides his cowardice with words. With words he can soothe every insult, and talk himself—and more often his brother—out of any scrape they get into. Valli is not a coward. He is brave to a fault, protective, loyal—and vicious and violent.

"And now I will destroy you!" Valli shouts again, raising a sword toward Nari.

Laughing, Nari takes off through the hall, Valli whooping on his tail.

"Now where were we?" says Loki, looking down at his hands. They're blue in the glow of Helen's magic. Helen is tired … it is strange, but that is when her magic seems strongest. It's as though she holds back during her more wakeful moments. He is about to rebuke her, to tell her to just let go, when a voice booms from behind. "What are you doing on the floor, Fool!"

Loki rolls his eyes at Heimdall's familiar disappointed tone.

Snickering at Loki's eyeroll, Helen says, "Showin' me pictas."

"It is disrespectful," says Heimdall, his heavy footsteps coming closer.

Loki rolls to his back, puts his hand behind his head, and scowls up at Heimdall. "How precisely is being prone on the throne room floor disrespectful? It's not as though we're bouncing in the Big Chair." Scratching his chin, Loki says, "Although, perhaps it's next—I'll let the All Father know it was your idea."

Heimdal stops, just a pace away. Standing as rigidly as ever, he stares down at them, hand on the pommel of his sword, his hunting horn hanging at his side. Loki is expecting some sort of argument, but instead Heimdall's mouth drops. When he speaks, it is a stammer. "It just isn't done."

Loki sighs in vexation. Of course, lying on the throne room floor with one's child isn't done. Fathers spending time with their daughters is hardly done, but there are extenuating circumstances. Helen's wheeled chair is a few paces away. It is hard for her to control her head movements while sitting up, and she gets a much better view lying down. Heimdall has watched her long enough; surely he must know this? But then again, this is the Aesir whose meddling created the social classes among mortals—he can't stand a universe without order. However ...

"Does it really matter?" Loki snaps.

Heimdall swallows. "No, in this case, I suppose it does not."

They stare at each other. Heimdall upright and rigid as ever, Loki sprawled out on the floor. It strikes Loki at that moment that the person most trapped by Heimdall's inflexible nature is Heimdall himself. Loki is suddenly, oddly, overcome by sympathy for the man who vexes him almost as much as the crown prince.

Heimdall clears his throat. "Prince Baldur noticed the illusion of

Alfheim turrets failing at the south gate earlier."

Loki tilts his head. "We rested there earlier and I noticed it flickering. I could not discern the nature of the problem though."

Beside him Helen makes a small sound.

"Will you look at it again, Loki? As I passed it, it seemed fine, but the Prince was insistent." Heimdall shakes his head. "It is beyond my skill."

Loki blinks. An admission of weakness … and a compliment? Normally in Heimdall's presence Loki casts true and untrue verbal barbs, but he finds himself speechless.

Rolling back over, he clambers to his knees and picks up Helen—waiting for the reprimands that Heimdall throws at him for 'coddling his warped daughter.' But none come. Loki puts Helen in her wheeled chair and they set out to the gate in a silence more uncomfortable than Heimdal's insults.

The sun is just past its zenith, and it is hot. From a distance, the gate looks fine—white stones, with climbing flowers, and green turrets atop. But as they get closer it begins to flicker, gray blocks of poured cement showing through the facade.

"Schtop me here," Helen says as they approach.

Loki tilts his head. He sees sweat upon her brow. "I can stop you by the gate, in the shade."

"No, schtop me here," says Helen. She's wobbling in her chair and Loki's skin is bright blue. They've been out since early morning and she's very tired.

Not stopping, Loki starts to argue. "But—"

And then the illusion drops completely at the space of wall just before them and everywhere in the reach of the blue glow of Helen's magic.

Helen gasps. "Letchs go home." Her fingers tremble on the chair's armrests.

Baldur's voice rings out from behind. "Heimdall, what is Loki doing here?"

Heimdall and Loki both turn and bow—though Heimdall's bow is deeper and longer. "My Prince, I just brought Loki here to help."

"He's probably the cause of this malfunction," Baldur snaps, wrinkling his nose as he steps into the glow of Helen's magic.

Smirking, Loki winks at Baldur and waggles his eyebrows. Loki sometimes flirts with him just to get his goat.

Baldur narrows his eyes. He's never made an attempt to bed Loki. Which is a pity. Loki would be well within his rights to defend his honor to the death for the insult, crown prince or no. Loki's very sure he knows who would win. Just for fun he lets a jet of flame rise from his hand.

Oddly, Heimdall ignores Loki's theatrics. Instead, raising his head he says earnestly, "My Prince, are you well? You look pale."

"I am fine, Gatekeeper," Baldur snaps again.

"You do not sound yourself, either," Heimdall says. Bowing again, Heimdall says, "My liege, far be it from me to offer advice, but please, I beseech thee, go to the healers. Your color and countenance seem off. I fear enchantment."

Baldur backs up a few paces. His eyes fall to Helen. How long has it been since he has been in the presence of Loki's daughter? Loki blinks, not since that time in the great hall with Sigyn and Thor—when they both had remained uncharmed by the prince.

Loki sneers. Baldur meets his eyes and then turns and strides away. Loki's eyes slide to Helen and he begins to laugh. "It's Helen. Helen is bringing down the illusion!"

"Father ... " says Helen.

"Is this true, Helen?" Heimdall says. "Can you see through all illusions?"

Helen looks at Loki, and he smiles encouragingly.

She nods, and looks down. "And liez. Is getting stronger." She meets

Loki's eyes.

Loki stares at her in wonder. He can sense lies, but his daughter exposes them to all. He laughs again. "The humans will call you the Goddess of Truth, and the Judger of Souls!" Breathlessly, Loki shakes his head. The Goddess of Truth—his daughter! It makes no sense, but there it is.

Kneeling before her he smiles, new possibilities spinning out before him. "The All Father will make you an ambassador, he will put you before the dignitaries of the realms to judge their fealty!" She may never find love, but she will be valuable, she will have purpose, respect, and power—independence even, if she wants it.

Overwhelmed, and relieved, Loki pulls his Helen into his arms. The Goddess of Truth ... how could such a beautiful creature even be his?

"A dangerous gift," Heimdall says. But he sounds a million realms away.

Chapter 13

Mr. Squeakers climbs up Amy's shoulder and settles by her ear. Amy looks back at her grandmother; Beatrice is crying. Amy sits up straighter. Does she understand them? She takes a sharp breath, and then Beatrice stands up and starts yelling in Ukrainian.

"She's saying 'Don't take him, don't take him'? But I sense no magic ... What is she talking about?" Loki says, wide eyes meeting Amy's.

Mr. Squeakers gives an alarmed squeak and Amy shakes her head. "I don't know. Something from her childhood maybe?"

Beatrice screams and backs toward the window. The look of fear in her eyes is heartbreaking.

"Grandma," Amy says. "It's me. Grandma!"

But it's as though Amy isn't there.

Loki speaks a few words softly in Ukrainian. Beatrice

lunges at him. He catches her easily and spins her around, pinning her arms against her chest. She shakes, and thrashes, screaming in Ukrainian, her eyes filled with anger and horror.

Loki looks at Amy with wide eyes. "What do I do?"

Amy runs to the door to call a nurse; they are already running down the hallway. The first nurse in the door has a needle in her hand. "Hold her!" she says to Loki. She has the sedative in Beatrice's arm just a few moments later.

The other nurse, a middle-aged man who talks with an African accent says, "She has been doing this these past few days. None of us speak Russian or Polish, though, and we don't know what she is talking about."

As Beatrice calms down, the nurses take Beatrice from Loki's arms and put her into bed. And then they leave.

Loki stares down at Beatrice. "All I said was that she was safe and that we wouldn't hurt her. But then she called me a liar and accused me of killing her baby brother." He looks at Amy.

She closes her eyes and rubs her temples. Beatrice never told her or the elves about having a little brother. But then she was from a breed of people who wouldn't talk about such things.

The nurses didn't close the door and from the hallway comes the sound of someone crying.

"Is this better than death?" Loki asks.

"I don't know," says Amy.

"I'm very good at killing things, Amy. And people."

She turns her head to him sharply. Gerðr's voice rings in her head, 'Everyone knows Loki killed Asgard's golden son.'

Loki's just staring down at Beatrice, a hopeless expression on his face. "But when it counts, when it is a kindness ... "

He shakes his head. "I can't."

He says it as though it is such a weakness. She wants to reach out and put her hand on his arm, but doesn't.

They stand in silence for a moment, but then Amy notices the sky outside is starting to darken. Biting her lip she says, "I have to go now."

Walking over to Beatrice, Amy whispers, "Goodbye, Grandma," and wipes away a few tears. She has no idea when it will be before she sees Beatrice again, now that her mother is moving her out of the city. Taking a deep breath, she looks over to Loki.

Walking over to Beatrice, he picks up her grandmother's hand and kisses it but says nothing.

"Well," says Amy.

Loki shakes himself and blinks at her. "Is it bad form to ask you if you'd like to get something to eat?"

"No, not really," says Amy.

He perks up ever so slightly, and Amy feels sad for what she is about to say. "But I can't, I have plans this evening." Amy was very careful to make sure she had something to look forward to after this visit—now she sort of wishes she hadn't. She is very glad he is here … and doesn't want him to leave her. But he is unreliable, and she has to nurture relationships she can depend on.

Loki scowls.

"I'm going to a lecture on REM sleep in rhinoceroses at the University of Chicago. James's wife is hosting it."

Loki stares at her as though she's just started speaking another language.

"Do you want to come?" Amy says, feeling slightly uncomfortable.

"Will there be food?" Loki asks.

Amy shrugs. "Yeah."

"We'll take my car!" says Loki, heading toward the door. "It will be much faster."

A car would be much faster, the University of Chicago is on the far south side of town. Before she goes there she has to stop at home to let out Fenrir—and to find a proper nesting spot for Mr. Squeakers—she'll have to switch trains at least two times. As they step out into the hallway, Amy's heart leaps a little, and then she stops herself.

"You have a car? And you can drive it?" Loki made Beatrice's Subaru a permanent load-bearing part of Beatrice's garage wall.

Smiling, he says. "I drove it here. Though technically it isn't mine."

Amy stops short. "I'm not going anywhere in a stolen car!"

Waggling his eyebrows at her, Loki smiles and says, "Relax, it's a rental."

A few minutes later Amy is staring down at a sleek ice blue sports car parallel parked on a nearby side street. "What sort of rental car is this?" she says.

"A Maserati Gran Turismo—from the Second City's First Exotic Car Rental." He holds up a key, and the car beeps, which is kind of reassuring. He has the keys! It isn't stolen. She scowls. Maybe.

As he opens the door, Amy looks at the parking job. There isn't much more than a foot between the front and back bumpers of the surrounding cars. "Ummm ... you don't have much room to get out."

Loki shrugs, and slips into his side of the car. Blinking, Amy gets into her own seat. Noticing a "Second City's First

Exotic Car Rental" brochure in the door pocket she relaxes a little—at least when he crashes before they even get on the road it isn't a *stolen* car.

To her surprise Loki pulls out of the impossible space without a hitch. She's still craning her head back, not completely believing he's done it, when he says, "So what is REM sleep?"

"Beak and feet like a duck, body like a beaver, and it lays eggs? It's a magical creature." Inside the car, Loki turns his head to her and gives her a triumphant grin, but his forehead is still tight and pinched. Outside the cars on interstate 90/94 are whizzing by in a blur.

Heart in her throat, Amy cries, "Look at the road!"

Shrugging, he faces forward very slowly, as though deliberately trying to tick her off. Which he probably is.

"I don't think the duckbilled platypus is magical," Amy says.

"I think it is," says Loki.

"You didn't even know what one was until I explained it to you!" says Amy.

"I still think it is magical."

"Maybe in the sense that all creatures are magical," says Amy, trying to get to her point.

Loki snorts.

She scowls. "*The point is* ... unlike marsupials and placental mammals, it doesn't have true REM sleep. Therefore we know that REM sleep is a more recent adaptation."

"Maybe it doesn't need REM sleep because it is magical. Maybe that is its magical power!" says Loki.

Amy stares at him and then rolls her eyes. "Fine. Maybe it is a magical creature."

"Ah - ha!" says Loki.

Rolling her eyes again, she looks out the side window.

But thinking of magical creatures has set her mind off in worrisome directions. "Do you think Mr. Squeakers will be okay?" When they'd stopped at her house to let Fenrir out, the spider mouse had jumped from her shoulder and dashed under one of her cabinets.

She turns her head back to Loki … and screams. The car right in front of them has just slammed on its brakes. She braces her hands on the dash for the impact … but it never comes. There is a skid of tires and a crash as the car right behind them barrels into the car that was right in front of them, but Loki has already swerved into the outer lane between two SUVs, with barely more room than he'd had when he parallel parked.

Hearing another crash, Amy looks back and sees a three-car pile up where they just were. She looks in front of them … traffic is slowing down everywhere.

Loki eases onto the brakes and then turns to her as though nothing has happened—and as though he isn't driving a car and supposed to be watching where he is going. "I'm sure Mr. Squeakers is fine. He probably just spied a cockroach—they're his favorite food. Hoenir can't kill so he created the spider mice to deal with his cockroach problems."

His face is so wide open and earnest. And then his brow tightens again and he looks back to the road. "*Couldn't* kill. *Had* exotic animals."

The air pressure in the car seems to drop. Outside traffic slows to almost a standstill. Neither of them says anything for a moment. Amy thinks of Beatrice and Hoenir ... sighing, she turns on the radio and starts flipping stations.

"None of your modern music," says Loki. "It's too vulgar."

Amy pauses. "Vulgar? You, Mr. I Like Big Boobs, is calling our music vulgar?"

Huffing, he says, "I have never called your divine bosoms anything so *vulgar* as boobs."

Amy snorts and hits "Scan". Over the radio speakers the Kings of Leon's, "Sex on Fire," suddenly blasts.

Loki snickers.

And okay. It is sort of funny. And it is good to see Loki happy again. Still, her face reddens as the singer belts out about his lover's "sex" being on fire.

Loki snickers again.

"Maybe he has a rash?" Amy says.

Loki stares at her, face completely expressionless. And then he bursts out into cackles, his forehead colliding against the steering wheel. Thankfully they're only going about three miles per hour and the next car is a good distance in front, so if Amy grabs the wheel ...

Before she's grabbed it, Loki must hit the gas because they suddenly plow into the car in front of them ... thankfully not hard.

The car in front comes to a stop.

Loki is still laughing.

Amy swallows. "Um ... Loki ... "

And then her head jerks as the car behind them hits them, again, not terribly hard, but still ...

Loki wipes his eyes. "Hmmm ... ." he says.

Amy sighs. "I guess I'm not going to that talk."

The man from the car in front of them gets out and starts walking toward his back bumper, looking none-too-happy.

"Will the police be coming?" says Loki.

"Probably," says Amy.

Loki grabs her hand and looks into her eyes. "You will get to your lecture on REM sleep in rhinoceroses on time! I give you my oath."

Amy looks at the stalled traffic. "You know, even if we weren't in an accident, I don't know if—" She blinks ... Loki suddenly isn't there. She looks down at her hand—she isn't here either, she's invisible.

"No!" says the disembodied voice of Loki. "We shall! It shall be a grand quest! Get out of the car!"

"Um ... okay," says Amy, grabbing her mittens and opening the car door as the door on the opposite side opens.

She slips out into the parking lot their side of the freeway has become and is immediately assaulted by cold, the smell of gas and exhaust and the sound of car horns. An invisible hand lands on her arm.

Speaking in the direction she thinks he's in she says, "But what about the police?"

Dragging her toward the median, he says. "I'm sure they'll be able to handle it. Come on, hop over."

"Ummm ... " she says as she's forcefully pulled over the median.

"I gave you my oath!" says Loki, dragging her away from the scene. "You will get there on time!"

"Well ... " says Amy.

Pulling her firmly, invisible Loki says, "Also, the car is stolen, so it would be best if we were far away when the police arrive."

"You told me it was a rental!" says Amy, slapping the invisible hand.

The hand withdraws and Amy is looking at a woman perhaps in her twenties. She has brown hair and large, doe-like brown eyes in a gentle rounded face. "A stolen rental," says the girl in Loki's voice. Amy looks her ... Loki ... up and down. This new illusion isn't voluptuous, or scantily clothed. She's wearing a long white sweater wrapped at the waist, and an A-line baby blue skirt that hits just below the knee. On her feet she's wearing ballet slippers.

Amy's mouth drops. "You look so wholesome." Last time Loki adopted a girl disguise he'd been a scantily clothed Amazon.

The girl Loki smiles charmingly. Clearing her throat she speaks in a voice that is delicate and light. "I know." She holds up a hand as though to flag down a taxi. "Believe me, every man with an ounce of chivalry in his bones is going to want to rescue us."

Amy's eyes widen as several cars slow, nearly causing an accident. "Are you sure we're not just fishing for psychopaths?"

Girl Loki turns to her. "Oh, yes, they'll stop, too. But don't worry, I'll have no qualms about killing *them*."

Amy blinks at that, just as a taxi skids onto the median just in front of them. A young driver of indeterminable ethnicity jumps half-out and starts gesturing wildly for them to get in. "What are you doing! You'll be killed out here! Get in! Get in! You don't even have to pay!"

"Rats," says girl Loki, dragging Amy by the hand. "I don't think my killing skills will be needed."

"No," Amy is saying to the cabbie as Loki sags in his seat. "We—I—can pay, really."

Loki wishes she'd be quiet. The sound of Cera whining in his ear, and the cab driver's radio tuned to a weather report, is adding to the headache he's had all day.

"You could go to Vanaheim right now," Cera says, as though privy to his thoughts.

Loki inhales sharply. He'd made a goal for himself ... if he hadn't cracked the outer containment sphere by this day he'd travel back to Visby, slip through the World Gate, and risk being arrested by the Vanir mages at the Royal Library.

... of course he *could* have left sooner. But as much as Cera annoys him, the thought of leaving her unprotected makes him feel faint and slightly nauseous.

Also, he just hates giving in to her petulant demands. He made it a point to book his plane flight for *tomorrow*, and he came out today, to be distracted from his burdens, partly just to annoy his whiny child.

"You can't do it! You are a liar and a failure! Others are coming! They will help me." Cera screeches.

Loki puts a hand over his eyes. He's heard this before.

"No, really," Amy is saying, her voice far off and distant. "It's alright. I can expense it."

On the radio an announcer says, *"This just in, a storm is brewing in Iowa. It's taking meteorologists completely by surprise."*

Cera starts to hum. "Someone else has come. He's stronger than you! He'll help me lead the revolution. You'll see!" Her misty form fades to pink and then vanishes.

Loki sits up in his seat, eyes wild, his heart beating in his ears. Over the radio the first announcer says, *"None of our models forecast this weather pattern ... "*

"Loki, are you alright?" says Amy, her eyes wide.

Loki blinks. And then he smiles, his headache melting away. He has nothing to fear by who has come. Laughing, he snatches one of Amy's mittens and swats her with it. "The man doesn't want your money, Girl!"

Amy scowls and swats his cheek with the other mitten. "It's not my money, it's ADUO's!"

Swatting her right back, Loki says, "Are you challenging me to a duel?"

She scowls. "Give me back my mitten!"

"Here!" says Loki, swatting her against the shoulder and cackling.

Leaning in, she tries to snatch the mitten from his grasp. Snickering, Loki leans back and holds the mitten just out of reach. She falls against him, delicious and soft; she hardly weighs anything ... in fact, she's quite comfortable. Sighing happily, he switches the mitten to the opposite side.

"Gimmee!" says Amy.

"No," he says with a snicker. Glancing up into the reflection of the rear-view mirror, he notices the cab driver's eyes are wide ... and the man is licking his lips.

Loki's eyebrows go up ... of course, he looks like a demure young woman. What a delicious opportunity for mischief! In the most dulcet tones possible, he coos, "Oh, no, a button on my sweater has come undone ... now my bra is showing!"

"You faker! Give me my mitten!" Amy shouts, redoubling her attack.

"Oh, there goes another button!"

The cabbie swallows audibly, the car careens dangerously, and Amy's breasts press just below his chin.

Excellent.

"And that concludes the question and answer segment of our lecture. Thank you, Dr. Grossman," says Katherine.

Amy claps as the lights in the conference room come on. Sitting next to her, a dozen muffin wrappers and a cup of coffee in front of him, Loki is whispering. "You mean you can also measure brain activity, not just sleep cycles?"

"Yes," Amy whispers back. "Different equipment though."

"Do they have such equipment here?" He's back in male form and leaning very close to her ear. He seems ... happy, almost bubbly. He's seemed so since the Great Mitten War.

"I'm sure they do," Amy whispers.

He looks contemplative. "How big is it? How much does it weigh?"

Amy blinks. "Well, there are different machines used, too—" Her eyes widen. "You're not thinking of stealing it, are you?"

Waggling his eyebrows, he smiles mischievously and she tries to scowl. Before she can give him a lecture about property rights, Katherine materializes behind her. "Hey, Amy, I'm so glad you could come."

Amy turns and smiles. "Hi, I'm so glad we could make it—sorry we were late. This is Loki, Loki this is Katherine."

Amy tilts her head as Loki shakes Katherine's hand. Katherine is one of those people who can only be described as classically beautiful. She has wide brown eyes, a delicate nose, bow-shaped lips, and thick chestnut hair. She is usually the epitome of graciousness, too, but tonight Katherine's face looks pinched, and her movements are a little jerky.

"How are you doing?" Amy asks.

Katherine shakes her head. "I'm ... " She rolls her eyes. "I could really use a drink. Want to go to the pub?"

Before Amy can respond, Loki shouts an enthusiastic, "Yes!"

"My boss said he'd clean up. I'll get my coat," says Katherine, running to the door.

"Um ... Okay," says Amy. Loki is already hopping out of his chair and following Katherine.

A few minutes later they are stepping out into the chill night air. Loki is quizzing Katherine on the weight and size of various neuroimaging devices while Amy gives him dirty looks. Hearing rapid footsteps, Amy turns around to see James, Katherine's husband, running up to them.

Breath rising up in a cloud, he doesn't stop until he is right in front of them. "Katherine? Where are you going?"

"I'm going to drink with Amy and Loki," says Katherine. She says it like someone might say I am going to war.

Amy stops short. And so does Loki.

"Are you sure that's wise?" says James, as though Loki and Amy aren't even there. "I mean since we're trying—"

"I don't care if it's wise!" Katherine interrupts, her voice cracking. "I just found out today that my chances of getting pregnant without time-consuming, invasive procedures are less than 1%! I. Want. A. Drink."

James draws back. Amy's mouth drops. Katherine stops, and her shoulders droop, but she meets James' gaze head on.

Amy bites her lip, suddenly feeling like she's invaded their privacy. She's not sure of what to say, even if she agrees a little with James.

"Your wife deserves a drink," says Loki. Amy thinks that he might be the little devil that sits on cartoon characters' shoulders—though he doesn't look cartoonish in the least. He isn't wearing his trademark smirk, and the humorous edge to his voice is gone. Everyone looks at him. The corner of his mouth turns up, but it isn't precisely a smile. "Trust me, I've … had friends in your situation."

Amy tilts her head, suddenly hit with the realization he isn't talking about a friend. He may look like he's only a few years older than her, and sometimes his behavior might seem years less mature, but he's much older than any of them. He's lived *lives*.

Loki looks down, and then lifting his head again, he claps a hand on James' shoulder. "First round is on me."

As they head toward the pub, the wind picks up around them. Amy thinks it carries the scent of rain.

CHAPTER 14

Steve's door is open and the office is humming despite the late hour. He has a weather map open on his computer. The freak storm that arose in Iowa is moving toward Chicago. Steve is one of the few privy to the knowledge that there are fighter jets scrambling above and around the storm's epicenter as close as they dare.

"We traced the car," says Bryant, knocking on the door but not bothering to stop.

Steve meets his eyes.

Bryant shakes his head. "The Second City Exotic Car Rental is owned by a Frank Galuzzo."

Steve raises his eyebrows at the name.

Bryant nods smugly. "Yeah, of the Galuzzo family. He's got mafia connections ... but seems relatively clean himself. Frank borrowed the car from his business for the week; apparently he likes to do that. He's out of town, though—spending a few days in Paris with his girlfriend."

Steve snorts. "Must be nice."

Nodding, tiredly, Bryant says, "Yeah, near as we can tell, Loki must have stolen it from his garage. No alarms or anything went off, though … technically he could have borrowed it from Frank—we haven't been able to contact him yet. Anyway, it hasn't been reported stolen."

Rubbing his eyes, Steve sighs. "Frank's going to be real happy when he gets home."

"Yeah, Loki's probably endeared himself to some very unsavory characters," says Bryant.

"He's good at that," says Steve. Just at that moment, Steve's cell buzzes with Jameson's phone number.

Meeting Bryant's eyes, he says, "Rogers here."

"Got word he's out with Lewis again," Jameson says without preamble. "Where are they now? What are they doing?"

Amy dropped her phone on the way out of her apartment—or Loki dropped it for her. The tail Steve had on them lost them on the freeway after the accident.

Steve scowls. "I have no idea."

"It doesn't matter," says Jameson. "When he brings her home he'll head off to get a late night snack."

"If he follows his standard routine, yes, Sir," says Steve. He knows where this conversation is going. He doesn't agree with it, but his opinion has been discounted long ago.

"Are our operatives in place?" says Jameson.

"Yes, Sir," says Steve, looking at the computer monitor showing the storm's progress.

The smile is audible in Jameson's voice over the phone when he says, "Loki will be in our custody by the end of night, Agent Rogers."

Steve's hand tightens into a fist as the line goes dead.

Bryant is still in his office.

"What?" snaps Steve.

"I don't like that we don't know where Amy is," says Bryant.

Steve doesn't roll his eyes, but his nostrils flare. He has an idiot boss to contend with and Jiminy Cricket here trying to be his conscience. "I'm sure she's fine."

Bryant glares at him. Narrowing his eyes, Steve says, "Pranks aside, have we ever had reason to believe that Miss Lewis isn't safe in Loki's company?" And even if she wasn't completely safe, who else is going to talk to Loki?

"He's going to take advantage of her," says Bryant.

Steve sits back in his chair. "Your fears to the contrary aside, Miss Lewis has so far been very adept at keeping her head on her shoulders when it comes to Loki."

Bryant snorts. "Yeah, right."

Steve steeples his fingers. "I'm sure we have nothing to worry about."

Rolling his eyes, Bryant turns and leaves the office.

The pub is very loud. And very crowded. Amy leans on the large round table James, Katherine and a half dozen of their *very close* friends managed to commandeer. She stares into her empty glass. "How many of these have I drunk?"

The chair she's sitting on shifts beneath her—because it's not really a chair, it's Loki's knee. And that's okay. It's just friendly. And practical. The place is packed and there aren't enough chairs. Across the table April is sitting on Mark's lap, Samantha is sitting on Todd's, and Katherine is sitting on James's lap—okay, maybe the last isn't the best example.

A warm hand settles on Amy's hip, and Loki speaks into her ear. "Only your second, I think." She absolutely doesn't shiver at the warmth of the hand. She squints at her empty glass. Lust is just a biological joke played by evolution to get her to participate in an awkward disappointing activity that has the added disadvantage of the potential for unplanned pregnancy and disease.

Loki rubs his hand absentmindedly on her hip, and she closes her eyes. It feels nice. Very nice.

Just an evolutionary joke. Remember that Lewis.

"Can I trust you?" she asks, and she's not sure if she's talking about the number of drinks she's had.

"No," says Loki, and she can hear the grin in his voice.

Amy tilts her head and turns to him. His face is very close, but that's okay. She is absolutely not attracted to car thieves—although his explanation, that with ADUO chasing him he can't legally rent or buy a car without being traced, is compelling.

Scowling, lips quirked, she says, "But if you say I can't trust you, does that really mean I can trust you?"

"Don't overthink it," he says. Smiling, glowing almost, he tightens his hand on her hip and leans close to her ear. "I'm very nearly drunk." There's a few baskets with the remnants of chicken wings next to him, and a glass of Guinness is in front of him, brand new and foamy. He's idly tapping a spoon on the table with his free hand.

"You look soo 'appy," she says. She can't tell if she's slurred the words or if it's just too loud.

His grin widens, if that's possible. "I just got in an argument with a philosophy major and a physicist about the Quantum Zeno effect."

Amy blinks. Oh, yeah, April and Mark. Giggling, she summarizes the argument. "If a photon hits a tree in the forest and no one's around, does it make any sound?"

He drops the spoon and she can barely hear it hit the table over the din in the room. Before she knows what's happened, he's scooped up her hand and is kissing her knuckles.

Warmth shoots through her and Amy laughs. It's just a kiss. On her hand. She's too buzzed to bother to pull away. He drops the hand from his lips but doesn't release her fingers.

"So flirty and not even blue!" she says before she's really thought about it. For once he doesn't seem mad, but he lets go of her hand and picks up the spoon.

"It's been happening, but I keep watch on the back of the spoon," says Loki. Oddly, he's still smiling.

Amy pulls closer. "Do you know what's causing it?" Gerðr doesn't turn blue, it's definitely not a Frost Giant thing ... and since he's in a good mood about it ...

Leaning back on his chair, he shrugs and smiles. There's something genuine and open about it. "I think I'm dying," he says.

Her face drops and the air rushes out of her lungs.

Loki straightens so he's close to her again. "Don't worry, Darling. It feels good, better than good." As he says it, he runs his fingers down her spine, and heat and urgency shoots through her. She wants to grab him by the head and hold on to him, press her forehead to his, and not let go. She wants to protect him, from what she's not sure.

Amy meets his eyes. They're very close to her own. He has

the barest hint of a smile on his lips. It strikes her that failing to protect him from the vagaries of the universe, kissing him would be a really nice second. Jokes of evolution be damned.

Loki pushes his forehead against hers. Their noses are just centimeters apart. Around them the collective clamor of conversation, silverware and glassware clinking, and bodies and chairs moving rises around them like a wall.

She's going to kiss him. She's as sure of it as the taste of Guinness on her tongue, or the feeling of rain-heavy air in her lungs.

"Hey, Loki!" someone shouts. "How do you feel about *American Gods?*"

The wall falls. Amy and Loki both turn dazedly to Thomas, the classics major sitting to Amy's left.

"You have gods?" Loki asks loudly, taking a sip of his drink. Several people at the table laugh.

"No," says Thomas. "You know, the book, where you and the other gods are figments of our collective imaginations."

Loki snorts and chokes on his drink. Smiling, he thumps his chest and says, "You humans think highly of yourselves, don't you?"

Everyone in earshot laughs. Loki has been 'in character' all night, 'pretending' to be himself, and everyone thinks it's *hilarious.*

Holding up his drink Loki says, "You don't have *that* much power over us. Now figments of the universe's consciousness as it tries to understand itself … ." He tilts his head. "Yes, maybe. All of us, Frost Giants and humans alike!"

"Hear, hear!" someone shouts. Around the table everyone takes a drink—well, not Katherine and James, they're making out. Amy stares wistfully down at her empty glass. Loki pushes his own into her hand. Amy grins at him, takes a long sip. As she puts the glass down he wipes some foam off her upper lip away with his thumb.

She laughs. The world seems really bright and beautiful.

"So, Amy," someone says, "The Rhodes Scholar over there says you did better in comparative anatomy than he did and that you'd make a great researcher. What are you doing becoming a veterinarian?"

Turning to her questioner, Amy shouts back, "Someone has to do the real work."

Half the table groans, and the other half laughs. Loki's hand tightens around her and the world gets even brighter.

"You take the first cab," says Loki to James and Katherine.

Arm around his wife's waist, James looks up at the rain. "But you ordered them ... and are you sure? You two have further to go—"

Loki laughs and shakes his head. The way James and Katherine have been at each other for the past hour, he sees make-up-us-against-the-universe sex in their futures—far be it from him to stand in the way of that.

"Get in!" says Amy, swaying dangerously under Loki's arm. He grins down at her and then feels Katherine's lips on his cheek. "Thank you for the drinks," she says.

Loki nods and blinks as James shakes his hand. The two get in the cab, and the cab driver is just about to pull away when Loki knocks on the window.

Looking puzzled, and maybe a little annoyed, James rolls

it down. "What?"

"May your aim be true, James!" Loki says.

James blinks and then laughs aloud, and so does Katherine. They wave at Amy and Loki as their cab pulls from the curb. Loki stumbles back—or Amy pulls him back, he's not sure. The second cab Loki called screeches to a halt at the curb.

He doesn't get in so much as fall in after Amy. As he shuts the door he lifts his head and barks "Downtown!"

The cab veers onto the street so fast Amy topples over, her head falling in his lap. She laughs, and so does Loki. They're both drunk. And it feels wonderful.

"You had a great time!" she says.

Loki shrugs noncommittally, but he can't keep from grinning.

"Youknow," she slurs. "In some of the ancient myths you're the god of the hearth fire ... " She takes a deep dramatic breath. " ... and unrestrained intellect. Youfitrightin." She grins back at him.

He smiles too as the driver hits the gas. The lights of Chicago's downtown skyline glitter in the rain. In the daytime the city's rough edges show, the garbage and pollution. But by night, the human metropolis looks more like a city built by gods than any city in the nine realms.

He's had a grand night—he doesn't remember the last time he's felt so comfortable, since he's laughed so much, had such good conversations, or felt so much like he *belongs*. He feels ... .content. Cera hasn't made a peep in hours, and he's not even worried. Looking down at Amy, he knows that if he wishes, he won't have to sleep alone.

He wishes.

Amy's wearing her coat, and beneath it a heavy sweater. He imagines peeling both away and falling between crisp white sheets. ADUO will be furious—there will be repercussions. But when has that ever stopped him before?

Eyes half lidded, her mouth opens as though to make a silent oh. Finding one of her hands, he brings it to his lips. Smirking, he says, "What?"

She smiles. "You're blue again."

Loki looks up and catches the faint reflection of his blue face, black eyes and black hair in the bulletproof glass between the backseat and the driver.

Putting a hand to his cheek, Amy whispers, "If it feels good, don't change. Just tell him it's for Halloween."

Raising an eyebrow, he leans into her hand. "It does feel good." He doesn't want to bother with maintaining an illusion of looking normal ... because his ginger hair and pale skin, those are the lie now, aren't they?

He drops her hand; the girl smiles up at him.

"What address?" barks the cab driver.

Loki looks down at Amy, her head pillowed in his lap, and gives the address of a hotel.

"That's not my address," Amy slurs, her eyes going wide. "We can't go to your house—they'll find out where you live!"

She's trying to protect him. How touching. Running his free, very blue hand through her hair, Loki whispers, "It's not my home address."

"Mmmmmm ... ." Her eyes close. "Where is it then?"

"Someplace we can be alone and unwatched." An address that he won't mind being revealed to ADUO. "Would you like that?"

Eyes still closed, she smiles. Loki would kiss her, but

the angle makes it impossible. And her head on his lap isn't unpleasant in the least. He lifts her knuckles to his lips again instead. Smile still on her lips, her head lolls to the side.

Loki runs his hands through her hair. She makes no sound. He kisses her knuckles again, and there is no reaction. Loki tilts his head and stares at her a long moment. Gently he disengages his hand from hers. Taking her chin, he rolls her head back toward him.

Amy doesn't respond at all.

"Amy?" Loki whispers. "Amy?"

Her eyelids don't even flutter.

With a groan, Loki leans his head against the window.

"Are you okay, man?" says the cab driver.

"Yes," says Loki, head against the glass.

"Please don't throw up in my cab," says the driver in another language.

"I'll do my best," says Loki in whatever tongue it is. He's more frustrated at the moment than drunk. He considers pushing Amy off of him, the state of semi-arousal suddenly no longer enjoyable.

"You understand Polish?" says the driver.

Loki makes a non-committal, "Mrrrmmmmffff."

"Cool Halloween costume," says the man.

Ignoring him, Loki starts gently shaking the girl. She doesn't rouse.

By the time they get to the hotel's driveway, Amy still hasn't so much as snored. With a sigh, Loki gives the driver Amy's address.

As they pull past the not cleverly-concealed ADUO agents, Amy is still 'dead as a door moose.' Or something. Poking her, Loki says, "Up, Miss Lewis."

She doesn't respond to that. Or when he shakes her again.

In the front seat the driver coughs.

Loki stares down at the sleeping girl. There is a faint smile on her lips, as though she is in a happy dream. He, on the other hand, has sobered up enough to contemplate his marvelously bad luck.

"Do you need some help?" says the driver.

Grumbling, Loki throws some money into the front seat and opens the door. Putting his hands underneath Amy's shoulders and knees, he awkwardly maneuvers her out of the cab. "No!" he huffs belatedly. Kicking the door shut with his foot, he stumbles down the steps to her apartment—not because he's drunk, but because the leg she was sleeping on is numb.

Or maybe he is still a little drunk.

The cab screeches away and Loki opens Amy's door with a flamboyant puff of green magic. Fenrir starts yapping excitedly and runs happily between Loki's feet—nearly knocking Loki over, but he manages to drop Amy on her bed unharmed.

He scowls around the room and feels the presence of new surveillance devices. Closing his eyes he concentrates … from every corner come little pops and sparks as he blows their circuits. A few light bulbs also explode. He's almost sure they aren't bugged, but his aim is apparently a bit off. Fenrir gives a yip and runs around in a little circle. Bowing to the animal, Loki says, "Let me know if any of them start a real fire." And then with a happy sigh he flops down beside Amy and puts his blue hands over his eyes.

Beside the bed Fenrir starts to whine.

Amy suddenly sits bolt upright. "I have to let Fenrir out!"

Loki peeks between his fingers and watches in a sort of

horrified bemusement as she takes the animal to the door, seemingly oblivious to his presence. Without as much as a, "Hello, why are you in my bed?" Amy lets the dog back in, shuts the door, and falls down beside him, her eyes instantly shut.

Rolling onto his side beside Amy, Loki gives her a poke. "You know, I am very dangerous." There is no response.

He sighs. "You really know how to stoke a man's ego."

Amy does not even have the decency to snore, but across the room Fenrir cocks her head.

Loki rolls his eyes at the dog. "All right, it's true. We had a lovely evening." He looks down at Amy. She's curled in fetal position, her face away from him. She isn't as tall as a typical Asgardian woman. She looks very small and vulnerable in the dark.

If a photon hits a tree in a forest and no one's around, does it make any sound? He finds himself smiling. With a disgusted sigh he sits up, moves down the bed, and slips off her shoes. Fenrir sits up and makes a little noise that sounds almost like a growl.

"Relax," says Loki. "Only her shoes. I will not dishonor your mistress."

Fenrir lies back down.

"If I had any sense at all, Fenrir, I'd stay here with her." He takes the blanket that's at the bottom of the bed and pulls it up over Amy. "I would give up my hunt for Cera, I'd start over, make more babies." He runs his hand over the curve of Amy's hip, covered now by the blanket. His blue hand should be a shadow, but he thinks it's almost glowing. Dropping down onto the bed, he curls up behind Amy. She is soft, and warm—even through the blanket.

A good long fuck would have been very nice. But this isn't horrible.

Tracing a hand up her side he whispers, "I'd stay here on this beautiful world with your charming mistress ... convince some university to give me a degree, become a professor ..." His eyes widen. "Or maybe become a professional poker player!"

For a moment he can almost imagine it, and then he scowls, skin crawling at his own lie. There is no future for him here. Even without Idunn's apples, as a magical creature, Loki has at least a few hundred good years before him. But all the humans around him are going to wither and die—because Odin is selfish with his apples, and because Hoenir never gave them magic.

"Fenrir, don't listen to me, I'm drunk." Loki says bitterly.

Closing his eyes he inhales the scent of apple shampoo. Hoenir is dead, and Odin will pay. He pulls himself closer to the girl. He knows enough to claim what comfort he can while he can.

CHAPTER 15

The wind whistles through the cliffs above the world of Vana-heim's Great Road. On the cliff's edge, Loki holds the dwarf by the collar of his armor. "Who ordered this!"

The dwarf's eyes are wide. His lips tremble. "I don't know."

Behind Loki, Thor says, "Loki has ways of making you speak, don't you, Loki?"

Loki does have ways. But then, they all do: Thor, the Valkyries Freyja and Brynhildr, and the half dozen Einherjar that accompany them.

Loki is so angry he is shaking. He is not injured, but he is dirty and he stinks like blood, sweat and the excrement of his enemies. Pulling a knife out of his sleeve, he slits the dwarf's throat and drops the small man.

"What are you doing?" Brynhildr hisses.

Snarling, Loki wipes the knife on his tunic and slips it into his belt. And then with a grunt he kicks the dwarf's corpse in frustration. "He wasn't lying, he didn't know."

Freyja walks among the bodies of the five dozen dwarves, dark elves, jotunn and human warriors that litter the cliffs. This month she has dark green hair, olive green skin, and disturbing white eyes. The falcon cloak she wears has wings that are the same green as her hair. She shakes her head, "See how they had arranged their camp? They were expecting travellers from the East—we came from the West … "

Thor reaches down and lifts a bag from the ground. "They all are low on provisions, the camp has been here for many days … there have been many travellers coming from the East, they could have robbed from anyone."

"But they chose to wait for us," says Nahal, one of the Einherjar. He is nearly as tall as Thor; his skin is ebony. He is African, or was. Odin chooses the best human warriors from all Midgard to join the ranks of the Einherjar, his elite guard. Once chosen, the humans must leave their world and their tribes, but they are granted access to Idunn's apples of immortality.

Loki spits. That their party came from the West is, as most unplanned things are, indirectly Loki's fault. It started with a seedling Loki had brought back for Hoenir from a troll-hunting expedition on Midgard. Loki hadn't seen the plant before. The humans called it 'Mistletoe.' Knowing Hoenir would be interested, Loki took a small potted specimen back to Asgard with him.

Hoenir had been interested, but of course, Loki's potted specimen was dead by the time he got it to his friend. So he'd gone with Hoenir to Midgard to get another—right before a very important gathering of mages at Vanaheim's Hall of Records. The gathering happened only once every century, and Hoenir was planning on attending. Things on Midgard hadn't gone as planned—-the gate had shifted, the ground was frozen. They were delayed and managed to delay the departure of the healer Eir, the other Asgardian headed for the mages' gathering.

To make up for it, Hoenir did something that Mimir had only whispered about. He created and then opened a World Gate that went directly from the backdoor of his hut to a forest not a day's march west of Vanaheim's Hall of Records ... World Gates were strictly forbidden to alight anywhere closer to the Great Hall. Considering that Asgard's main gate opened 3 days to the east, it actually spared them time. And it was an amazing display of magic. Loki asked Hoenir if he'd ever be able to do such a feat. Mimir said Loki would probably never be able to create a branch, but that someday he might be able to traverse them—if he was willing to hole himself up in a cave and practice for a hundred years or so. Which was the same as saying 'no.'

However, Loki got to spend some of the time saved on the journey in the Hall himself and to learn some tricks for applying magic to weapons—tricks that didn't take hundreds of years to learn. He also got to look at some choice elven erotica before he, Thor, Freyja, Brynhildr and the Einherjar left Hoenir and Eir to enjoy a three-month long sojourn in the great Hall.

He stole a book of said erotica, too. He's carrying it beneath his armor. They are a half day away from the main World Gate—without Hoenir in their party they must use the normal routes. Loki was looking forward to sharing the book tonight with Sigyn.

Loki doesn't love Sigyn the way he loved Aggie. With Aggie Loki had been idealistic and blind. There is something hard edged about his marriage to Sigyn. Which doesn't mean he doesn't like Sigyn, but it's different. More practical. One of the things he does like about her is that she is curious enough to enjoy things like elven erotica. But the investigation of this attack is going to put those plans on hold. A ball of flame rises in one of his hands. Cursing, Loki waves it away.

From across the cliff comes the sound of pebbles falling. Loki looks up quickly. He sees no one but there is a boulder large enough to hide a hominid. He pulls out a knife he modified with some of the tricks he'd learned in the Hall of Records and aims it at the boulder.

Beside him Thor says, "What are you—"

The knife hits the rock and explodes, shattering the rock into pebbles and revealing a human man who had been hiding behind it. The man takes off along the narrow ledge. Loki pulls out another knife, but Thor grabs his hand. "Wait."

"We've got him!" Brynhildr and Freyja shout, launching themselves into the air and across the chasm. Wide eyed, the human turns, and seeing them, he throws himself from the ledge. Freyja and Brynhildr scream and dive.

Beside Loki one of the Einherjar, the one with dark brown skin and eyes that look almost Asian, says, "Even with their numbers they were not a match for us. Whoever sent them didn't mean for them to survive."

Thor grunts in assent as Brynhildr and Freyja rise from the canyon bottom, the broken body of the human in Brynhildr's arms.

Thor steps forward, Loki and the Einherjar close behind. With wild eyes the human laughs, blood trickling out of his mouth. "We were promised eternal life if we killed the man who carried a second head and the woman among the angels."

It takes a moment for Loki to comprehend the man he means is Hoenir, and the woman is Eir. Breathing heavily, Loki rushes forward, dry brush around them bursting into flames. Throwing her cool arms around him, Freyja whispers in Loki's ear. "Easy, Loki, easy!" It is only thanks to her compulsion over men that Loki doesn't set the human aflame.

"Who promised this?" shouts Thor, ripping the man from Brynhildr's arms and pressing Mjolnir to the man's side.

The man's body convulses and he screams as electricity courses through the hammer.

When Thor pulls Mjolnir away the man laughs. "The god of gods!" And then his eyes grow dim, and foam and blood leak from his mouth.

"Liar," says the first Einherjar. "Odin made us all swear to protect Hoenir and Eir with our lives."

"Who would do this?" Loki hisses.

Turning her head, Brynhildr says softly. "A rider approaches from the the direction of the World Gate." Unfurling her wings, she leaps into the air.

Thor's eyes meet his. "Why would anyone want to kill the two most powerful healers in Asgard?"

Loki's stomach sinks as Brynhildr alights beside him. "It is Sigyn. She rides Sleipnir and has your boys with her."

Loki feels himself go cold. He looks down the cliff walls and sees Sigyn approaching below. Running to a narrow path that leads to the road below he calls out, "Sigyn! Sigyn!" Behind him come Thor's heavy footfalls.

A few minutes later he is panting at the bottom of the cliff at Sleipnir's side, Sigyn and his boys still astride. Freyja and Brynhildr circle cautiously above them in the sky; and Thor is holding Sleipnir's bridle. His boys are staring wide eyed at his filthy armor. Sigyn's golden hair is wild and windswept; fresh tears are making trails through the grime on her cheeks. Pushing Valli into Loki's arms, Sigyn says, "There is plague in Asgard! Magical plague … They've taken her, Loki! They came to our house, Anganboða's own Hall, and took her!"

Loki's eyes widen. Magical plague. Such a thing hasn't occurred in centuries—and is never a natural occurrence. His mouth is dry. He holds Valli like a doll in his arms. "Taken who?" But he knows.

"Our little girl!" Sigyn says, the words spitting out of her mouth. "Take Nari!"

Loki takes his second son as Sigyn gets off the Sleipnir "They're banishing all the afflicted to Niflheim! Odin sent me here to tell you, and to bring Nari and Valli to safety … We must get Eir and Hoenir … "

Niflheim is cold and barren. Banishment there is the same as death.

"I will get Hoenir and protect your family, Loki," Thor says. "I swear on my life. Go! Before your daughter is banished!"

Loki is already swinging up onto Sleipnir. He turns the beast back to the east and the World Gate. Before he's dug in his heels into the horse's flanks, Sigyn grabs a stirrup. She looks over her shoulder at Thor, walking away with Loki's boys. And then she beckons for Loki to lean close. "I saw Baldur and Tyr near Helen just before her maids took her home … they all got sick. I was across the field with the boys … Baldur did this, Loki. I know it. Make him pay!"

Loki scowls up at the cliffs, the air shimmers around them, and Sleipnir whinnies. Loki nods tightly. Sometimes he loves Sigyn.

Loki wakens to the sound of Fenrir's growling, and for a moment thinks he is back on Asgard, approaching Odin's throne. But he snaps into the present quickly. On instinct born over centuries, he slips invisibly out of his sleeping form. Leaving an illusion of himself on the bed, he crouches behind the low bookshelf that sets the bedroom apart from the front of the apartment.

The doorknob turns and Fenrir takes off in an explosion of yapping. Without bothering to see who is there, Loki vaults over the bookshelf, knocking over some books. He bites back a curse as they fall to the floor with soft thuds. He is still slightly drunk, apparently.

A beam of light flashes through his invisible form, briefly blinding him before landing on the bed where his illusion and Amy sleep. Agent Bryant McDowell stands in the doorway. His hair is slick with rain, his coat is drenched; Fenrir is tearing at the cuffs of his pants. "Miss Lewis?" says the agent looking vaguely confused. "Is everything alright?"

He carries a heavy duty black electric torch in one hand, a Glock upraised in the other—both pointed at Loki's sleeping form on the bed ... the form that is immaterial, that will not shield Amy from the bullet when it comes. Baldur's words come to his mind, "You destroy everything beautiful, Loki ..."

Loki feels his skin heat. Not this time. His lips curl up in a snarl and he closes the distance between himself and the agent as silently as a snake. In one fluid movement he wraps an invisible hand around Bryant's wrist and aims it at the ceiling, popping the flat of his palm into the man's elbow at the same time. The bone breaks with a satisfying crack and Bryant screams. There is the sound of fast footfalls from outside, and the voice of his brother. Vision still dancing with the afterspots of the torchlight, Loki shakes his head and casts a hand toward the approaching figure, shrouding Brett's face in light to blind him.

"Bryant? Bryant? Are you there? I can't see you!" Brett

says, voice panicked. "Is the girl okay?"

Loki blinks at that. Something in this scenario is off …

"I'm here," Bryant says, cradling his arm. Spinning in Amy's doorway, he says in the direction opposite Loki. "Show yourself, you fucking coward!"

In the bed Amy stirs at last. She sits up in bed. "Bryant?"

"Is fine," says Loki from a point near Bryant's elbow.

"What the—" But Loki has already shoved him out the open door into the rain.

"Go back to sleep, Amy!" Loki says cheerily. She falls back into bed and he steps out into the cold night, casting the same light around Bryant's eyes that surrounds his brother.

"Ahhhh!" Bryant screams.

"Do yourself a favor, close your damnable eyes or you may find yourself blinded permanently!" Loki hisses.

Brett raises his gun in Loki's direction even though he's blind. Loki steps around, touches the Glock and it goes hot. Brett drops it with a curse.

Blind, and with a broken arm, Bryant rushes in the direction of the sound of the dropped gun, but Loki easily steps aside, holds out a foot and pushes Bryant to the ground.

Snapping the still-blind Brett roughly against the wall, Loki pins his arm against his back. "You came to arrest me— when the girl was unconscious and helpless and you wave a gun around without once announcing yourselves!" Trembling, he shoves Brett harder against the wall. "Why shouldn't I kill you?" If Brett and Bryant weren't soaked through, they would probably be in flames.

"We're not here to arrest you!" Bryant hisses from the ground. He is sitting, cradling his arm, but otherwise making no effort to move.

Face pressed against the wall, light dancing in front of his eyes, Brett says, "We were worried about the girl!"

The words crash into Loki like a bucket of cool water. They are telling the truth.

Loki's grip on Brett slackens, almost against his volition, his state of semi-inebriation affecting his control. "But why now? I've been calling on her for weeks … "

"She's never been passed out drunk before," Bryant says through gritted teeth.

"And Gerðr has told us about Asgardian morality," Brett snarls.

Oh. Loki rolls his eyes. "Yes, I suppose some men would find Amy being unconscious a convenient accident."

"Here we'd call it rape," Bryant hisses.

Loki goes hot with the mortal's insinuation. "I don't need to get a woman passed out drunk to spread her legs. I'm not *Odin*!"

Letting Brett go, he steps over Bryant's legs—and almost trips in the process. He snorts at his own clumsiness. "And besides, sex with an unconscious woman would be so … so … boring."

Suddenly in a forgiving mood, he drops the blinding lights hovering around their eyes.

Above them the lights of Amy's neighbors come on. A man, the fiance of Jan, Amy's sometime dog sitter, comes out, a broomstick in his hand like a baseball bat.

Loki makes himself visible—and gives himself and Brett and Bryant the guise of police officers. Smiling upward he says, "No need to call the police, we're already here!"

"Did someone break in?" the neighbor says.

"Tried to but, we scared him off!" says Loki with a wave.

"Uh … okay … " says the man. "You having a Halloween Party at the precinct?"

Loki leans on a leg and stares upward, his mouth open, unsure of what to make of that question.

"Yes," says Brett quickly as he helps his brother get up.

"Go back inside," says Bryant, grimacing in pain. "We'll handle this and give you the rundown when we're done."

"This is my building!" the man says.

"Don't want to disturb any evidence," says Brett quickly.

Loki raises an eyebrow. They must really want to keep his presence here under wraps.

"Okay," says the neighbor uncertainly, but he goes back inside.

Loki sees lights along the block come on and hears doors and windows opening. Feeling safe enough in the police officer uniform, he turns back to Brett and Bryant and says, "No, the only thing worse than an unconscious partner is a partner who fakes her orgasms." Shuddering involuntarily, Loki says, "It's like the sound of cockatrice nails on steel. Can't stand it." He shudders again. "The worse sort of lie and I *hate* being lied to."

"You're … drunk … " Bryant says, eyes widening.

Loki shrugs. "What makes you think so?"

"Besides the monologue?" says Brett.

"You're blue," says Bryant.

Backing up, Loki looks down at his hands. They are still blue. "Basilisk dung," Loki whispers.

He looks longingly toward Amy's door. Her bed is warm and soft, but the two agents are still glaring at him suspiciously. He can't try his luck. Turning, he's about to leave when a thought occurs to him. Skin going hot, he says, "If you thought Miss Lewis was in such danger, why did it take you so long to come to her rescue?"

Brett and Bryant glance at each other, looking slightly abashed.

Loki sneers at them. "You *both* deserve broken arms," but he doesn't feel like administering that justice just now. Shaking his head he wills the blue to vanish from his skin. He starts to walk away, but Brett calls out, "Steve said you wouldn't hurt her."

Loki turns back to him. Brett stands, arm locked with his brother's, gaze locked on Loki.

"We were defying his orders when we came in," Brett says.

"We had a bit of an argument first," says Bryant.

Loki lifts an eyebrow, suddenly feeling something like affection—toward Steve for understanding, or the two small scrappy mortals who would risk their careers defying orders, he can't tell. Either way, he blames the sentiment on the alcohol.

He's suddenly very hungry. And he'd like another drink.

Without looking back, he walks down the street toward a familiar watering hole on Taylor Street, not worried if he is being followed.

The establishment is nearly empty and just about to close when he arrives. Wet from his short trip in the rain, he slides up to the bar and orders the usual. Turning around he surveys his surroundings. A curvy brunette he's noticed several times before catches his eye from a booth and smiles.

His eyebrows go up. Taking that as an invitation, she walks across the floor in his direction. She's wearing a burgundy wrap dress with a deep v-neck that does nothing to hide her very generous breasts. Despite the hardness around her eyes, she has a tiny perky nose, and perfectly shaped bow lips that give her a young appearance. She's just his type. He smirks. How interesting.

Steve is in his new, non-magically sealed office—he stopped watching the clock around 2 a.m.. Rain from the freak storm has moved into Chicago. It has been beating on his window for hours now. Sometimes it lessens to a drizzle, but it doesn't let up.

Leaning back in his chair, he crosses his hands over his stomach. He is glaring up at Brett and Bryant. They're wet and shivering, Bryant's arm is in a cast. They both look abashed, and very nervous. Good.

"We depend on Loki's trust right now and you've gone a long way to destroying that trust," Steve says, his tone clipped. He rocks back in his chair and says nothing for a few minutes, just letting them squirm.

Bryant coughs. Brett clears his throat.

Glaring at them Steve says, "There's no 'I' in the word 'team,' Gentlemen." It's a cliche, but effective.

Both men shuffle their feet.

From the front of the office comes the sound of voices. Steve sits up in his chair. Director Jameson strolls in Steve's door like he owns the place, two men in black he's brought up from DC right behind him. Smiling down at Steve, Jameson bobs his head. "I did it, Agent Rogers."

Steve's breath comes out of him in a rush, and his jaw drops. Outside the office, he hears other agents who are part of Jameson's D.C. posse shouting. "Guantanamo has been notified! They're prepping the room. They'll be ready for us."

Steve half stands from his chair.

Outside in the hallway someone else shouts, "The plane with the Promethean containment cell is on its way!"

"What?" Steve says, turning to Jameson.

Dipping his chin, smile turning to a smirk, Jameson says, "I've just caught Loki—and I'm going to keep him. And get some real answers."

Continued in *Chaos*, Part III of *I Bring the Fire*

Author's Note

Thank you for taking a chance on this self-published novel and seeing it to the end.

Because I self-publish, I depend on my readers to help me get the word out. If you enjoyed this story, please let people know on Facebook, Twitter, in your blogs, and when you talk books with your friends and family.

Want to know about upcoming releases and get sneak peeks and exclusive content?

Follow me on Tumblr: ibringthefireodin.tumblr.com

Facebook: www.facebook.com/CGockelWrites

Or email me: cgockel.publishing@gmail.com

Thank you again!